Forty-
Turkish Fairy Tales

Collected and Translated by
Dr. Ignácz Kúnos

with illustrations by
Willy Pogany

Originally published by
GEORGE G. HARRAP & Co. London
[1913]
* * * * * * *

Resurrected by
ABELA PUBLISHING, London
[2010]

Ignacz Kúnos

Forty-Four Turkish Fairy Tales

Typographical arrangement of this edition
© Abela Publishing 2010

Abela Publishing,
London
United Kingdom
2010

ISBN-13: 978-1-907256-37-0

email: Books@AbelaPublishing.com

www.AbelaPublishing.com/FortyFourTales

Acknowledgements

Abela Publishing acknowledges the work that

Dr. Ignácz Kúnos did in compiling

Forty-Four Turkish Fairy Tales

in a time well before any electronic media was in use.

* * * * * * *

A percentage of the net profit from the sale of this book

will be donated to charities for educational purposes.

* * * * * * *

YESTERDAYS BOOKS for TOMORROWS EDUCATIONS

Publisher's Note

It is important to note that this book was compiled during the latter half of the 1800's and early 1900's – well over a century ago. As such some of the language and terminology is dated and in some cases archaic. Some terminology, especially when describing or referring to other races, is not what we would use in the 21st century. But for the sake of authenticity and in order to stay true to the original work, these have been left *in situ*.

The publisher asks the reader to not be offended but to accept that this was how people spoke, wrote and behaved a century ago.

John Halsted
Abela Publishing

Preface

The stories comprising this collection have been culled with my own hands in the many-hued garden of Turkish folklore. They have not been gathered from books, for Turkey is not a literary land, and no books of the kind exist; but, an attentive listener to "the storytellers" who form a peculiar feature of the social life of the Ottomans, I have jotted them down from time to time, and now present them, a choice bouquet, to the English reading public. The stories are such as may be heard daily in the purlieus of Stamboul, in the small rickety houses of that essentially Turkish quarter of Constantinople where around the tandir the native women relate them to their children and friends.

These tales are by no means identical with, nor do they even resemble, those others that have been assimilated by the European consciousness from Indian sources and the "Arabian Nights." All real Turkish fairy tales are quite independent of those; rather are they related to the Western type so far as their contents and structure are concerned. Indeed, they may only be placed in the category of Oriental tales in that they are permeated with the cult of Islam and that their characters are Moslems. The kaftan encircling their bodies, the turban on their heads, and the slippers on their feet, all proclaim their Eastern origin. Their heroic deeds, their struggles and triumphs, are mostly such as may be found in the folklore of any European people. It is but natural that pagan superstition, inseparable from the ignorant, should

vii

be always cropping up in these stories. Like all real folklore they are not for children, though it is the children who are most strongly attracted by them, and after the children the women. They are mostly woven from the webs of fancy in that delectable realm, Fairyland; since it is there that everything wonderful happens, the dramatis person being as a rule supernatural beings.

Nearly all Turkish stories belong to the category of fairy tales. These marvellous scenes are enacted in that imaginary country wherein Padishahs have multifarious relations with the rulers of the fairy world. The Shahzadas, their sons, or the Sultanas, their daughters, are either the only children of their parents, or else they appear as three or seven brothers or sisters, whose careers are associated with miraculous events from birth onward. Their kismet, or fate, is controlled by all-powerful dervishes or peri-magicians. Throughout their lives, peris, to the number of three, seven, or forty, are their beneficent helpers; while dews, or imps, are the obstructors of their happiness. Besides the dews, there are also ejderha, or dragons, with three, seven, or more heads, to be encountered, and peris in the form of doves to come to the rescue in the nick of time. Each of these supernatural races has its separate realm abounding with spells and enchantments. To obtain these latter, and to engage the assistance of the peris, the princes of the fairy tales set out on long and perilous journeys, during which we find them helped by good spirits (ins) and attacked by evil ones (jins). These spirits appear sometimes as animals, at others as flowers, trees, or the elements of nature, such as wind and fire, rewarding the good and punishing the evil.

The fairyland of the Turks is approached by a threefold road; in most cases the realm can be reached only on the back of a Pegasus, or by the aid of the peris. One must either ascend to the seventh sphere above the earth by the help of the anka-bird, or descend to the seventh sphere below the earth by the help of a dew. A multitude of serais and kiosks are at the disposal of the heroes of the tales; thousands of birds of gayest plumage warble their tuneful lays, and in the flower-gardens the most wonderful odours intoxicate the senses.

Turkish fairy tales are as crystal, reflecting the sun's rays in a thousand dazzling colours; clear as a cloudless sky; and transparent like the dew upon a budding rose. In short, Turkish fairy tales are not the stories of the Thousand and One Nights, but of the Thousand and One Days.

I. K.

Contents

Ignace Kúnos

The Creation

ALLAH, the most gracious God, whose dwelling, place is the seventh heaven, completed the work of creation. Seven planes has the heaven and seven planes also the earth--the abode of evil spirits. In the heavenly ways reside the peris, or good spirits; in the earthly darkness the dews, or evil spirits. The light of heaven is in conflict with the darkness of earth--the peris with the dews. The peris soar to heaven, high above the earth; but the dews sink down into the darkness under the earth. Mountains bar the road to heaven, and only the good spirits can reach the Copper Range, whence the way is open to the Silver Mountains and the Hills of Gold. Evil spirits are blinded by the ineffable radiance of heaven. Their dwelling place is the depths of the earth, the entrance to which is at the spring of waters. There tarry the white and the black sheep, into whose wool the evil spirits penetrate, and are so conveyed to their realm on the seventh plane. On the white sheep they return to the earth's surface. Peris and dews are powerful, and both were witnesses of the creation of earth's original

inhabitant, the First Man.

Allah created the First Man, and appointed him the earth for his dwelling-place. And when the First Mortal appeared upon the earth and the peris rejoiced over Allah's wonderful work, the Father of Evil beheld it, and envy overcame his soul. Straightway he conceived a plan whereby to bring to nought that beneficent work.

He would implant the deadly seed of sin in this favoured creature of the Almighty; and soon the First Man, all unsuspecting, received on his pure body the damnable spittle of the Evil One, who struck him therewith in the region of the stomach. But Allah, the all-merciful, the overcomer of all things, hastened to tear out the contaminated flesh, and flung it to the ground. Thus originated the human navel. The piece of flesh, unclean by reason of the Evil One's spittle having defiled it, obtained new life from the dust, and thus, almost simultaneously with man, was the dog created--half from the human body and half from the Devil's spittle.

Thus it is that no Mahometan will harm a dog, though he refuses to tolerate him in his house. The animal's faithfulness is its human inheritance, its wildness and savagery are from the Evil One. In the Orient the dog does not increase, for while the Moslem is its protector, he is at the same time its implacable enemy.

The Brother and Sister

Once Upon a Time there was an old Padishah who had a son and a daughter. In due time he died and his son reigned in his stead, and it was not long before the young man dissipated the whole fortune bequeathed by his father.

One day he said to his sister, "My dear, we have spent all our fortune. If it should become known that we have no money we should have to leave this neigh-bourhood, as we could had better go away quietly now, before it is too late." So they gathered their belongings together, and left the palace secretly in the night. They journeyed they knew not whither until they reached a great plain of apparently limitless dimensions. Almost overcome by the heat of the day and ready to succumb to fatigue they presently espied a pool. "Sister," said the brother to the maid, "I can make no further step with. out a drink of water." "But brother," she answered, "who knows whether it is water or not? As we have endured so long, surely we can hold out a little longer, when perhaps we shall find water."

3

But the brother objected. "No, I go no further; I must drink if I am to live." There upon the sister fetched a draught, which the young man drank greedily; and scarcely had he done so than he was transformed into a stag.

The maid lamented bitterly. What should she do now? What was done was done, and they resumed their journey. They wandered on over the great plain until they came to a large spring by a tall tree; here they decided to rest. "Sister," said the stag, "climb the tree; I will go and endeavour to find food." The maid accordingly climbed the tree, and the stag went foraging in the vicinity. Soon he caught a hare, which the sister prepared for their meal. In this way the two lived from day to day until several weeks had passed by.

Now it chanced that the Padishah's horses were accustomed to be watered from the spring by the tree. In the evening slaves brought them, and while they were quenching their thirst in a trough, the animals saw the reflection of the maid on the clear surface of the water, and timidly drew back. The slaves thinking that the water was perhaps not clean, emptied the trough and refilled it. Still the horses shrank back and refused to drink, and at length the slaves related this unaccountable incident to the Padishah.

"Perhaps the water is muddy," suggested the potentate. "Oh no," answered the slaves, "for we have emptied the trough and refilled it with fresh water." "Go back," said the Padishah, "and look around; probably there is something in the neighbourhood that frightens them." So they went

4

again, and drawing near they caught sight of the maid in the top of the tree. Immediately they went back to their master with the news of their discovery. The Padishah, deeply interested, hurried to the spot, and, looking up into the tree, saw a maiden beautiful as the full moon, whom to see was to desire. "Are you a spirit or a fairy?" called out the Padishah to her. "Neither spirit nor fairy, but a child born of man," answered the maid.

In vain the Padishah besought her to come down; she had not sufficient courage to do so and the Padishah, aroused to anger, gave orders to fell the tree. The slaves took hatchets and hacked and split the tree on every side, and it was almost ready to fall when night came down upon them and they were compelled to postpone their task. They had hardly disappeared when the stag came out of the forest, and seeing the state of the tree, he questioned his sister as to what had transpired.

"You did well," said the stag when he had heard the story. "Do not come down under any circumstances." Then going to the tree, the stag licked it, and lo! the trunk became thicker than it was before.

Next morning the stag went into the forest again, and when the Padishah's people came, great was their surprise to see that not only was the tree whole but that it was even thicker than before. Nevertheless they resumed their work, and had about half completed their task when night once more suspended the operations. To be brief, when the slaves had gone home the stag came again and licked the tree, with the same result as before, only that the trunk was thicker than ever.

Scarcely had the stag gone away next morning than the Padishah came again with his woodcutters, and seeing that the tree was whole and sound he decided to seek other means to accomplish his purpose. He went therefore to an old woman who followed the calling of a witch and relate the story, promising her much treasure if she would entice the maiden down from the tree.

The witch willingly undertook the task, and carrying to the spring an iron tripod, a kettle, and other things, she placed the tripod on the ground with

She poured the water beside the vessel.

the kettle on the top of it, but bottom upward. Then drawing water from the spring, pretending to be blind, she poured the water not in the vessel but outside it. The maiden seeing this and believing the woman to be really blind, called to her from the tree:

"Mother, you have set the kettle upside down and the water is falling on the ground."

The Padishah gave orders to fell the tree

"Oh my dear," began the old creature, "where are you? I cannot see you. I have brought dirty clothes to wash. For the   love of Allah, come and place the kettle aright, so that I can get on with my washing." But fortunately the maiden remembered the stag's warning and remained where she was.

Next day the witch came again, stumbled under the tree, lit a fire, and brought forth meal. Instead of the meal, however, she began to place ashes in the sieve. "Poor blind woman!" called the maiden from the tree, "You are not putting meal but ashes into your sieve." "I am blind, my dear," said the witch fretfully, "I cannot see; come down and help me." Once again, however, her ruse was unsuccessful and the maiden could not be induced to disregard her brother's warning.

On the third day the witch came once more to the tree, this time bringing a lamb to slaughter. But as she took up the knife she attempted to press the handle instead of the blade into the animal's throat. The maiden, unable to endure the torture of the poor creature, forgot everything else and came down to put it out of its misery. She soon repented of her rashness, for hardly had she set foot upon the ground than the Padishah, who was hidden behind the tree, pounced upon her and carried her off to his palace.

The maiden found such favour in the eyes of the Padishah that he desired ardently to marry her at once, but she refused to consent until her brother, the stag, was brought to her. Slaves were therefore dispatched to find the stag and they soon brought him to the palace. This done, the

8

twain never left each other's side; they slept together and arose together. When the marriage was celebrated, the stag still would not quit his sister, and when at night they retired, he struck her lightly with his forefeet saying "This is the brother-in-law's bone; this is the sister's bone."

Time comes and goes, story time more quickly, and with lovers the most quickly of all. Ours would have lived altogether happily but for a black slave-woman in the palace who was overcome with jealousy because the Padishah had chosen the maiden from the tree instead of herself. This woman awaited an opportunity for revenge which was not long in coming. In the vicinity of the palace was a beautiful garden, in the midst of which was a large pond. Here the Sultan's wife was accustomed to come for pastime; in her hand a golden drinking-cup, on her feet silver shoes. One day as she stood by the pond the slave darted from her hiding-place and plunged her mistress head first into the water, to be swallowed by a large fish which swam in the pond.

The black woman returned to the palace as though nothing had happened, and donning her mistress's robes she put herself in her place. When night came the Padishah inquired of his supposed wife what had happened that her face was so changed. "I have been walking in the garden and have become sunburnt," she answered. The Padishah, nothing doubting, drew her to his side and spoke words of consolation; but the stag came in, and recognising the deception, stroked the pair gently with his forefeet saying; " This is the brother-in-law's bone; this is the sister's bone."

9

The slave was now fearful lest she might be exposed by the stag, so she set herself to contrive a means to get rid of him.

Next day she feigned illness, and by money and fine words persuaded the physicians to tell the Padishah that his consort was dangerously ill and only by eating a stag's heart could she hope for recovery. The Padishah went to his supposed wife and asked her whether it would not grieve her if her brother, the stag, were slaughtered. "What am I to do?" sighed she; "if I die evil will befall him. It is better he should be killed; then I shall not die, and he will be delivered from his animal form." The Padishah thereupon gave orders to sharpen the knife and heat water in the boiler.

The poor stag perceived the hurrying to and fro, and understood full well its dire significance. He fled to the pond in the garden and called three times to his sister:

> "The knife is being sharpened,
> The water in the boiler is heated;
> My sister, hasten and help!"

Thrice he was answered from the interior of the fish:

> "Here am I in the fish's stomach,
> In my hand a golden drinking-cup,
> On my feet silver shoes,
> In my lap a little Padishah!"

For a son had been born to the Sultan's wife even while she lay in the fish's stomach.

The Padishah, with some followers intent on the capture of the stag, came up in time to overhear the conversation at the pond. To draw out the water was the work of a few minutes; the fish was seized, its belly slit, and behold! there lay the Sultan's true consort, a golden drinking-cup in her hand, silver shoes on her feet, and her little son in her arms. Transported with joy the monarch returned to the palace and related the occurrence to his suite.

Meanwhile the stag, by chance licking up some of the blood of the fish, was changed again into human form. He rejoined his sister, and judge of the additional happiness which she felt at seeing her beloved brother again in his natural shape.

The Padishah now commanded the Arabian slave-woman to be brought before him, and demanded of her whether she preferred forty swords or forty horses. She answered: "Swords to cut the throats of my enemies; for myself forty horses, that I may ride." Thereupon was the vile woman bound to the tails of forty horses, which setting off at a gallop tore her to pieces.

The Padishah recovers his wife

Then the Padishah and his consort celebrated their marriage a second time. The Stag-Prince also found a wife among the ladies of the court; and for forty days and forty nights there were rare festivities in honour of the double wedding. As they ate, drank, and accomplished their object; let us also eat, drink, and accomplish that which we have set out to do.

Ignace Kúnos

Fear

Once a very long time ago there was a woman who had a son. Sitting, both together one evening, the mother said to her son: "Go, my child, and shut the door, for I have fear." "What is fear?" the boy asked his mother. "When one is afraid" was the answer.

"What then can this thing fear be?" pondered the son: "I will go and find it." So he set out, and came to a mountain where he saw forty robbers who lighted a fire and then seated themselves around it. The youth went up and greeted them, where on one of the robbers addressed him:

"No bird dares to fly here, no caravan passes this place: how then dost thou dare to venture?"

"I am seeking fear; show it to me."

"Fear is here, where we are," said the robber.
"Where?" inquired the youth.

Then the robber commanded: "Take this kettle, this flour, fat, and sugar; go into that cemetery yonder and make helwa therewith."

"It is well," replied the youth, and went.

In the cemetery he lit a fire and began to make the helwa. As he was doing so a hand reached out of the grave, and a voice said:

A hand reached out of the grave

"Do I get nothing?" Striking the hand with the spoon, he answered mockingly:

"Naturally I should feed the dead before the living."

15

The hand vanished, and having finished cooking the helwa the youth went back to the robbers.

"Hast found it?" they asked him.

"No," replied he. "All I saw was a hand which appeared and demanded helwa; but I struck it with the spoon and saw no more of it."

The robbers were astonished. Then another of them remarked: "Not far from here is a lonely building; there you can, no doubt, find fear."

He went to the house, and entering, saw on a raised plat. form a swing in which was a child weeping; in the room a girl was running hither and thither. The maiden approached him and said: "Let me get upon your shoulders; the child is crying and I must quieten it." He consented, and the girl mounted. While thus occupied with the child, she began gradually to press the youth's neck with her feet until he was in danger of strangulation. Presently, with a jerk that threw him down, the girl jumped from his shoulders and disappeared. As she went a bracelet fell from her arm to the floor.

Picking it up, the youth left the house. As he passed along the road, a Jew, seeing the bracelet, accosted him. "That is mine," he said.

"No, it is mine," was the rejoinder.

"Oh, no, it is my property," retorted the Jew.

"Then let us go to the Cadi," said the youth. "If he awards it to thee, it shall be thine; if, however, he awards it to me, it remains in my possession."

So accordingly they went, and the Cadi said: "The bracelet shall be his who proves his case." Neither, however, was able to do this, and finally the judge ordered that the bracelet should be impounded till one of the claimants should produce its fellow, when it would be given up to him. The Jew and the youth then parted.

"That is mine" he said

On reaching the coast, the boy saw a ship tossing to and fro out at sea, and heard fearful cries proceeding from it. He called out from the shore: "Have you found fear?" and was answered with the cry, "Oh, woe, we are sinking!"

17

Quickly divesting him self of his clothes, he sprang into the water and swam toward the vessel. Those on board said: "Someone is casting our ship to and fro, we are afraid." The youth, binding a rope round his body, dived to the bottom of the sea. There he discovered that the Daughter of the Sea (Deniz Kyzy) was shaking the vessel. He fell upon her, flogged her soundly, and drove her away. Then, appearing at the surface, he asked: "Is this fear?" Without awaiting an answer he swam back to the shore, dressed himself, and went his way.

Now as he walked (along he saw a garden, in front of which was a fountain. He resolved to enter the garden and rest a little. Three pigeons disported themselves around the fountain. They dived down into the water, and as they came up again and shook themselves each was transformed into a maiden. They then laid a table, with drinking glasses. When the first carried a glass to her lips the others inquired: "To whose health drinkest thou?" She answered: "To that of the youth who, in making helwa, was not dismayed when a hand was stretched out to him from a grave." As the second maiden drank, the others again asked: "To whose health drinkest thou?" And the answer was: "To the youth on whose shoulders I stood, and who showed no fear though I nearly strangled him," Hereupon the third took up her glass. "Of whom art thou thinking?" questioned the others. "In the sea, as I tossed a ship to and fro," the maiden replied, "a youth came and flogged me so soundly that I nearly died. I drink his health."

Hardly had the speaker finished when the youth himself appeared and said: "I am that youth." All three maidens hastened to embrace him, and he proceeded: "At the Cadi's I have a bracelet that fell from the arm of one of you. A Jew would have deprived me of it but I refused to give it up. I am now seeking its fellow."

The maidens took him to a cave where a number of stately halls that opened before him overwhelmed him with astonishment. Each was filled with gold and costly objects. The maidens here gave him the second bracelet, with which he went directly to the Cadi and received the first, returning without loss of time to the cave. "You part from us no more," said the maidens. "That would be very nice," replied the youth, "but until I have found fear I can have no rest" Saying this he tore himself away, though they begged him earnestly to remain.

Presently he arrived at a spot where there was an immense crowd of people. "What is the matter?" the youth inquired, and was informed that the Shah of the country was no more. A pigeon was to be set free, and he on whose head the bird should alight would be declared heir to the throne. The youth stood among the curious sightseers. The pigeon was loosed, wheeled about in the air, and eventually descended on the youth's head. He was at once hailed as Shah; but as he was unwilling to accept the dignity a second pigeon was sent up. This also rested on the youth's head. The same thing happened a third time. "Thou art our Shah!" shouted the people. "But I am seeking fear; I will not be your Shah," replied he, resisting the efforts of the crowd to carry him off to the palace. His words were repeated to the widow of the late ruler, who said: "Let him accept the dignity for tonight at least; tomorrow I will show him fear." The youth consented, though he received the not very comforting intelligence that whoever was Shah one day was on the following morning a corpse. Passing through the palace, he came to a room in which he observed that his coffin was being made and water heated. Nevertheless, he lay down calmly to sleep in this chamber; but when the slaves departed he arose, took up the coffin, set it against the wall, lit a fire round it and reduced it to ashes. This done, he lay down again and slept soundly.

When morning broke, slaves entered to carry away the new Shah's corpse; but they rejoiced at beholding him in perfect health, and hurried to the Sultana with the glad tidings. She thereupon called the cook and commanded: "When you lay the supper tonight, put a live sparrow in the soup-dish."

Evening came. The young Shah and the Sultana sat down to supper, and as the dish was brought in the Sultana said:

"Lift the lid of the dish."

"No," answered the youth; "I do not wish for soup."

"But please lift it," repeated the Sultana persuasively. Now as the youth stretched out his hand and lifted the lid, a bird flew out. The incident was so unexpected that it gave him a momentary shock of fear. "Seest thou! " cried the Sultana. "That is fear."

"Is it so?" asked the youth. "Thou wast indeed afraid," replied the Sultana.

Then the marriage feast was ordered, and it lasted forty days and forty nights. The young Shah had his mother brought to his palace and they lived happily ever after.

A bird flew out

He observed that his coffin was being made

The

Three Orange Peris

In olden time, when there was abundance of all things, we ate and drank the whole day long, yet went hungry to bed. At this time there lived a Padishah whose days were joyless, for he had no son.

Sorrowfully he set out with his lala, and as they wandered, drinking coffee and smoking tobacco, they came to a wide valley. They sat down to rest, and suddenly the valley resounded with the cracking of whips, and a white. bearded dervish, clad in green, with yellow shoes, appeared before them. The Padishah and his companion trembled with

fright, but when the dervish approached and saluted them with "Selâmin alejküm!" they took courage and returned the greeting: "Ve alejküm selâm!"

"Whither bound, Padishah?" inquired the dervish.

"If thou knowest that I am the Padishah thou canst also tell me the remedy for my grief," answered he.

Taking an apple from his breast and presenting it to the Padishah, the dervish said: "Give one half to the Sultana and eat the other yourself," and immediately disappeared. The Padishah accordingly went home, gave half of the apple to his consort and ate the other half himself, and

23

before long a Shahzada, or Crown Prince, was born in the palace. The Padishah was beside himself with joy. He gave money to the poor, set slaves free, and prepared a feast for everybody.

The Prince grew and attained his fourteenth year. One day he accosted his father with the request: "My Padishah and father, have built for me a small marble palace, with two fountains, from one of which shall flow oil and from the other honey."

The Padishah loved his only son so much that he ordered the palace to be built with the two fountains, in accordance with the boy's desire. Now as the Prince sat in his palace looking on the two fountains which yielded oil and honey, an old woman appeared with a jug in her hand, intending to fill it at the fountain. The Prince took up a stone and cast it at the old woman's jug and broke it to pieces. Without a word the woman withdrew. Next day she came again, and just as she was about to fill her jug the Prince once more threw a stone and broke the vessel. Without a word the old woman went away. On the third day she reappeared, and for the third time her jug was shattered by the Prince. Said the old woman: "I pray Allah thou mayst be smitten with love for the three Orange Peris." She then went away, and was seen no more.

From that moment the Prince was seized as with a devouring fire. He pined and faded, and the Padishah, observing his son's condition, called in physicians and hodjas, but no one could cure the Prince's malady. "Oh, Shah," said the son to his father one day, "my dear father, these people can do me no good; their efforts are in vain. I love the three Orange Fairies, and shall have no peace till I find them."

"Oh, my child," lamented the Padishah, "thou art my only one. If thou forsake me, then can I have no joy."

But as the Prince continued to get worse, the Padishah thought it better to withhold no longer his permission for the boy's setting out; he might perhaps find the three fairies and return home.

Laden with costly treasures the Prince set forth. Over hill and down dale, ever onward he pursued his way. On a boundless plain he found himself suddenly confronted with the gigantic Dew-mother. Standing astride upon two hills, one foot on each, she crunched resin in her jaws, and the sound could be heard two miles away. Her breathing raised storms, and her arms were nine yards long.

"How do you do, mother?" the youth said to her, putting his arm round her waist.

25

"Hadst thou not called me 'mother' I would have swallowed thee," returned the woman. Then she asked him whence he came and whither he would go.

"Oh, dear mother," sighed the boy, "such misfortune is mine that it were better you did not ask and I did not answer."

"But tell me," demanded the woman.

"Oh, dear mother," he sighed again, "I am in love with the three Orange Fairies. Can you not show me the way to them?"

"Silence!" commanded the woman; "it is forbidden to utter that word. I and my sons guard ourselves against them but I know not where they dwell. I have forty sons, who go up and down in the earth; perhaps they may know."

When evening came, before the return of the Dew-sons, the woman picked up the Prince and struck him gently, whereupon he was transformed into a water-jug.

She was only just in time, for suddenly the forty Dew-fellows appeared and cried: "We smell the flesh of man, mother!"

"But," returned the mother, "what should a man be doing here? You had better sit down to your supper."

So the Dew-fellows sat down to their meal, during the course of which the mother inquired: "If you had a mortal brother, what would you do with him?"

"What should we do with him?" they all answered in chorus. "We should love him as a brother."

On receiving this assurance the Dew-mother struck the water-jug and the Prince appeared. "Here is your brother," she said, presenting him to her forty sons. The Dews welcomed the youth with joy, called him their brother, gave him a place beside them, and demanded of their mother why she had not produced him before the meal. "My children," she replied, "he could not have eaten the food you are accustomed to; mortals eat fowl, beef, mutton and such."

Immediately one of the Dews got up, fetched a sheep, and set it before the youth.

"You simpleton!" scolded the woman; "it must first be cooked."

So the imp took the sheep away, and returned with it roasted, setting it once more before the Prince. Having eaten till he was satisfied, the Prince put the rest aside. Noticing this, the imps inquired why he did not eat it all, and their mother informed them that the children of men did not eat so much as Dew-fellows.

"Let us see how mutton tastes," said one of the imps, and in a couple of mouthfuls the whole sheep was gone.

29

Next morning the woman said to her sons: "your brother has great grief." "What is it?" they asked; "we may be able to help him." "He is in love with the three Orange Fairies," proceeded the mother. "We know not the dwelling-place of the Orange Fairies; we never go in their neighbourhood; but perhaps our aunt knows." "Take the youth to her," ordered the woman; "greet her on my behalf, tell her this is my son, and that I wish her, if possible, to help him." The Dews accordingly conducted the Prince to their aunt, and told her all.

This old witch had sixty sons, and not knowing herself where the Orange Fairies lived, she awaited the return of her progeny. As she was uncertain how her sons would receive the visitor, she struck him gently and turned him into a vessel. "We smell the flesh of man!" the Dews shouted as they ran into the room. "No doubt you have been eating human flesh," answered their mother. "Now come to your supper." The sons sat down to eat eagerly. Then the woman struck the vessel, and the sixty Dews, on beholding the little mortal, received him heartily, offered him a seat, and set food before him.

"My sons," said the imps' mother on the following day, "this child is in love with the three Orange Fairies; can you not take him to them?" "It is certain we cannot," they answered, "but perhaps our other aunt knows the way." "Then take him to her," said the woman; "greet her on my behalf, tell her the boy is my son and will be hers; she may be able to help him."

The imps accordingly conducted the youth to their aunt and related all. "Oh, my children," she answered, "I can do nothing, but when my eighty sons return this evening I will inquire of them."

The sixty Dews took leave of the Prince, and toward evening the Dew mother gave him a knock and turned him into a broom, which she put behind the door. Hardly had she done this than the eighty Dews came home, and began muttering about the smell of human flesh. During supper their mother asked them what they would do if they had a mortal brother. As they all swore a solemn oath to do him no harm, she took the broom, struck it lightly, and the Prince appeared.

The imps received him cordially, inquired after his health, and set food before him. Then the woman asked them whether they knew where the three Orange Fairies lived, as their new brother was in love with them. With a cry of joy the youngest Dew-son sprang up and said that he knew. "Then," rejoined the mother, "take the youth there that he may accomplish his desire."

Next morning the imp and the Prince set out on their journey. As they proceeded the young Dew said: "Brother, we shall soon reach a large garden, in which there is a pond, where the three oranges will be found.

When I cry, 'Shut your eyes--open your eyes!' do so, and seize whatever presents itself."

Proceeding a little farther, they came to the garden, and as the Dew caught sight of the pond he cried to the Prince: "Shut your eyes--open your eyes!" The Prince saw the three oranges on the smooth surface of the pond, seized one and put it in his pocket. Again the Dew cried: "Shut your eyes--open your eyes!" Obeying, the Prince seized the second orange, and likewise the third. "Now," said the Dew, "take care not to open the oranges at any spot where there is no water, or you will repent it." Promising to follow his advice, the Prince parted from the Dew, the one going to the right, the other to the left.

As the Prince travelled up hill and down dale he remembered the oranges and took one out of his pocket with the intention of opening it. Hardly had he inserted his knife in the peel than a lovely maiden, beautiful as the full moon, sprang out, crying: "Water! give me water!" and as there was no water near, she vanished immediately. The Prince deeply regretted what he had done, but it could not be helped now.

Some hours elapsed, he had walked many miles, and again he thought of the oranges. He took out the second, slit it, and behold! out sprang a maiden lovelier than the first. She also demanded water, and, seeing none, likewise vanished.

"I must take better care of the third," thought the Prince as he tramped wearily onward. On reaching a spring he drank of it, and resolved to open his third orange. He did so, and a maiden more lovely than either of the others appeared. As she also asked for water, the Prince led her

'The smashed the jug'

to the spring, gave her to drink, and she remained with him.

The Prince was anxious that the maiden should enter his father's city with befitting state. So he persuaded her to hide in a tree near the spring, while he went to fetch a coach and gorgeous raiment. When he had gone away a black slave-woman came to the spring for water. Seeing therein the reflection of the maiden from the tree above, and thinking it was her own image, she soliloquised: "I am much more beautiful than my mistress. Why should I carry water for her? Rather should she carry it for me," and she threw down her jug so violently that it broke in pieces. She returned to the house, and when her mistress asked where the jug was, the negress turned upon her scornfully " I am more beautiful than you; henceforth you must fetch me water." The mistress, holding up the mirror, answered "Are you out of your wits? Look in the glass," and the negress, looking, saw that she was really black. Without another word she again took a jug and went to the spring to fill it. Arrived there, she saw a second time the reflection of the maiden in the tree and mistook it for her own.

"I am after all more beautiful than my mistress," she cried aloud. Throwing down her jug, she once more went to the house. Again the mistress asked why she had brought no water. "I am more beautiful than you; you must fetch me water," was the retort. "You are mad, girl," returned the mistress, again holding the mirror up before the swarthy face of the slave, who, realising that she was indeed a negress, took a third jug and went yet a third time to the spring. The reflection of the maiden again appeared in the water, and the negress was just about to

The negress looked up

dash her jug to pieces when the maid called to her from the tree: "Break not your jug; what you behold in the water is my reflection, not your own."

The negress looked up, and seeing in the tree a being so wondrously beautiful lovelier than anyone she had ever seen before--she addressed her in words of honeyed flattery:
"Oh, most charming of all maidens, surely you must be tired from sitting up there so long. Come down and lay your weary head in my lap."

The bait was taken, and as the maiden's head lay in her lap, the negress took a hair pin and thrust it into her skull. But at the very moment the murderous intention was accomplished the maiden was transformed into an orange coloured bird and flew away, leaving the negress by the tree.

Shortly afterwards the Prince returned in a magnificent coach, and clad in gold brocade. Glancing at the tree and seeing the swarthy features of the negress, he asked what had happened. "Leave me here and go away," answered the negress. "The sun has quite spoilt my complexion." What could the poor Prince do? He put the supposed maiden in the coach and took her to his father's palace.

The courtiers awaited the arrival of the fairy bride with eager curiosity; when they saw the negress they were at a loss to imagine what the Prince could find attractive about her. "She is not a negress," explained the Prince; "only as she was in the sun so long she has become somewhat sunburnt; she will soon become white again." With these words he led her to her apartments.

Near the Prince's palace was a large garden. Here one day the Orange Bird flew in, and, alighting on a tree, called to the gardener.

"What wilt thou of me?" asked the gardener.

"How is the Prince?" inquired the bird.

"Quite well," was the answer.

"And how is his black wife?" was the next inquiry.

"Oh, she is quite well, but keeps to her apartments," replied the gardener.

At this the bird flew off. Next day it came again, and repeated the questions of the previous day. On the third day also it did the same; and it came to pass that every tree on which the bird had sat withered away. Shortly afterward, as the Prince was walking in the garden, seeing so many withered trees he spoke to the gardener. "Why do you not take proper care of these trees?" he asked; "they are all withered! " Hereupon the gardener related the incident of the bird and its questions, and observed that though he had done his utmost for the trees it was all in vain. The Prince commanded him to smear the trees with birdlime, and when the bird was caught to bring it himself to the palace. So the bird was caught and taken to the Prince, who put it in a cage.

As soon as the negress saw the bird she knew it was really the beautiful maiden. She now pretended to be dangerously ill, sent for the chief physicians, and, bribing them, got them to report to the Prince that only by eating a certain kind of bird could she possibly recover.

When the Prince heard that his wife was very ill he called the physicians before him and asked what was to be done. They told him that the Princess could only be cured if a certain kind of bird were given her to eat. "1 have lately caught such a bird," said the Prince, and he commanded that the captive should be killed and served up to his wife.

But by chance one of the bird's beautiful feathers fell to the floor, and lodged, without anyone observing it, between two planks.

Time passed, and the Prince was still waiting for his wife to turn white. In the palace was an old woman who taught reading and writing to the inmates. One day, being about to ascend the stairs, she espied a bright object. She picked it up, and saw that it was a bird's feather with spots on it that sparkled like diamonds. She took the feather to her own room and stuck it in a crevice in the wall.

One day while she was in attendance at the palace the feather fell from its position, and ere it could reach the floor, behold! it was trans formed into a lovely maiden, of dazzling beauty. The maiden swept the floor, cooked the dinner, and put everything in order, after which she resumed the form of a feather and went back to her place on the wall. When the old governess arrived home she was astonished. She looked everywhere, but could find no clue to the riddle.

Next morning while she was in the palace the feather again assumed human form and acted as on the day before. On the third day the old woman, determined to solve the mystery, instead of leaving her apartments locked the door as though she intended to go to the palace as usual, but hid herself. Soon she saw a maiden in the room, who, after putting everything in proper order, set about the cooking. When all was ready the dame ran in and caught the mysterious maiden and demanded an explanation. The latter related her adventures, telling how

37

the negress had twice taken her life, and how she had come there in the form of a feather.

"Grieve not, my daughter," said the old dame, consoling her, "I will soon put the matter right.' She lost no time in going to the Prince, whom she invited to supper the same evening.

After supper coffee was brought in, and as the maiden set down the cups the Prince chanced to look into her face, and immediately swooned away.

When he had been brought to consciousness again he asked who the maiden was. "My servant," answered the old woman. "Whence have you obtained her?" demanded the Prince. "Will you not sell her to me?" "How can I sell you what already belongs to you?" returned the dame. Taking the maiden by the hand, she led her to the Prince, exhorting him thenceforth to guard his Orange Fairy with more care.

The Prince took his true bride home in triumph to his palace, ordered the negress to instant execution, and celebrated his new wedding feast for forty days and forty nights. This happy end attained, we will once more stretch ourselves on our divan.

The Rose Beauty

In olden times, when the camel was a horse-dealer, the mouse a barber, the cuckoo a tailor, the tortoise a baker, and the ass still a servant, there was a miller who had a black cat. Besides this miller, there was a Padishah who had three daughters, aged respectively forty, thirty, and twenty years. The eldest went to the youngest and made her write a letter to her father in these terms:

"Dear father, one of my sisters is forty, the other thirty, and they have not yet married. Take notice that I will not wait so long before I get a husband."

The Padishah on reading the letter sent for his daughters and thus addressed them: "Here are a bow and arrow for each of you; go and shoot, and wherever your arrows fall, there you will find your future husbands."

Taking the weapons from their father, the three maidens went forth. The eldest shot first, and her

39

arrow fell in the palace of the Vezir's son; she was accordingly united to him. The second daughter's arrow fell in the palace of the son of the Sheikh-ul-Islam, and him she got for a husband. When the youngest shot, however, her arrow fell into the hut of a wood-cutter. "That doesn't count," cried everybody; and she shot again. The second time the arrow fell in the same spot; and a third attempt met no better success.

The Shah was wrathful with his daughter on account of her letter, and exclaimed: "you foolish creature, that serves you right. Your elder sisters have waited patiently and are rewarded. You, the youngest, have dared to write me that impertinent letter: you are justly punished. Take your woodcutter and be off with you." So the poor girl left her father's palace to be the wife of the woodcutter.

In the course of time a beautiful girl-baby was born to them. The wood-cutter's wife bitterly lamented the fact that her child must have so poor a home, but even while she wept three wonderful fairies stepped through the wall of the hut into the dismal room where the child lay. Standing by her cot, each in turn stretched out a hand over the sleeping infant.

Said the first fairy: "Rose-Beauty shall she be called; and instead of tears, pearls shall she shed."

Said the second fairy: "When she smiles, roses shall blossom." Said the third: "Wherever her foot falls shall grass spring up!" Then the three disappeared as they had come.

40

Years passed away. The child grew and attained her twelfth year, developing such loveliness as none had ever seen before. To gaze once upon her was to be filled with love for her. When she smiled roses blossomed; when she wept pearls fell from her eyes, and grass grew wherever her feet trod. The fame of her beauty spread far and wide.

The mother of a certain Prince heard of Rose-Beauty and resolved that this maiden and no other should become her son's bride. She called her son to her and told him that in the town was a maiden who smiled roses, wept pearls, and under whose feet grass grew; he must see her.

The fairies had already shown the maid to the Prince in a dream, and thus kindled in him the fire of love; but before his mother he was shy and refused to seek the object of his passion. The Sultana therefore insisted, and finally ordered a lady of the palace to accompany him on his quest. They entered the hut, explained the purpose of their visit, and in the name of Allah demanded the maiden for the Shahzada. The poor people were overcome with joy at their good fortune; they promised their daughter, and commenced preparations for her departure.

Now this palace-dame had a daughter, who somewhat resembled the Rose-Beauty, and she was displeased that the Prince should marry a poor girl instead of her own daughter. Accordingly she concocted a scheme to deceive the people and bring about the Prince's marriage to her own child. On the wedding-day she gave the woodcutter's daughter salt food to eat, and took a jug of water and a large basket and put them in the bridal coach wherein the

Rose-Beauty, herself, and her daughter were about to set out for the palace.

On the way the maiden, complaining of thirst, asked for a drink of water. The palace-dame answered: "I shall give you no water unless you give me an eye in exchange." Nearly dying of thirst, the maiden took out one of her eyes and gave it to the cruel woman for a drink of water.

As they proceeded the torments of thirst again overcame the poor maiden, and again she asked for water. "I will give you drink, but only in exchange for your other eye," answered the woman. So great was her agony that the victim yielded her other eye. No sooner had the woman got it in her possession than she took the now sightless Rose-Beauty, bound her in the basket, and had her carried to the top of a mountain.

The woman now hastened to the palace and presented her daughter, clad in a gorgeous wedding garment, to the Prince, saying: "Here is your bride," The marriage was accordingly celebrated with great festivity; but when the Prince came to lift his wife's veil he saw that she was not the one revealed to him in his dream. As, however, she resembled the dream-bride somewhat, he held his peace.

The Prince knew that the maiden of his dream wept pearls, smiled roses, and that the grass grew under her feet; from this one, however, came neither pearls, roses, nor grass, He suspected more than ever that he had been deceived, but "I will soon find out" he thought to himself, and spoke no word on the subject to anyone.

Meanwhile the poor Rose-Beauty on the mountaintop wept and moaned, pearls rolling down her cheeks from her sightless eye-sockets until the basket in which she lay bound was filled to overflowing. A scavenger at work on the road heard the sounds of grief and cried out in fear: "Who is that, a spirit or a fairy?" The maiden The maiden answered: "Neither a spirit nor a fairy, but a human being like yourself."

The scavenger, reassured, approached the basket, opened it, and saw the blind girl and the pearls she had shed, He took her home to his miserable hovel, and being alone in the world, adopted her as his own child. But the maiden constantly bemoaned the loss of her eyes, and as she was always weeping the man now had nothing else to do but gather the pearls she shed and go out and sell them. Time rolled on. In the

Who is that? cried the scavenger

palace was merriment, in the scavenger's hovel grief and pain. One day as the Rose-Beauty was sitting at the door, she smiled at some pleasant recollection, and forthwith a rose appeared. Said the maiden to the scavenger: "Father, here is a rose; take it to the Prince's palace and say thou hast a rose of a rare kind to sell. When the palace dame appears, say it cannot be sold for money, but for a human eye." The man took the rose, went to the palace and cried aloud: "A rose for sale; the only one of its kind in the world."

Indeed, it was not the season for roses. The palace-dame, hearing the scavenger's cry, resolved to buy the rose for her daughter, thinking that when the Prince saw the flower in his wife's possession his suspicions would be set at rest. Calling the poor man aside, she inquired the price of the rose. "Money cannot buy it," replied the scavenger, "but I will part with it for a human eye." Hereupon the woman produced one of the Rose-Beauty's eyes and gave it in exchange for the rose. Carrying the flower immediately to her daughter, she fixed it in her hair, and when the Prince saw her he began to fancy that she might after all be the maiden the fairies had showed him in his dream, though he was by no means sure. He consoled himself with the thought that soon the matter would be cleared up.

The old man took the eye and gave it to the Rose-Beauty. Praising Allah, she fixed it in its place, and had the joy of being able to see quite well once more. In her newfound happiness the maiden smiled so much that ere long there were quite a number of roses. One of these she

44

gave to the scavenger that he might go with it to the palace and secure her remaining eye. Scarcely had he arrived at the palace than the woman saw him with the rose and thought to herself: "All is coming right; the Prince is already beginning to love my daughter. I will buy this other rose, and as his love strengthens he will soon forget the woodcutter's child." She called the scavenger and demanded the rose, which the man said could only be sold on the same terms as the first. The woman willingly gave him the other eye and hastened with the flower to her daughter, while the old man went home with his prize.

The Rose-Beauty, now in possession of both her eyes, was even lovelier than before. As now she smilingly took her walks abroad roses and grass transformed the barren hillside into a veritable Eden. One day while the maiden was walking in the neighbourhood, the palace-dame saw her and was dismayed. What would be her daughter's fate if the truth became known? She inquired for the scavenger's dwelling, hastened to him, and frightened the old man out of his wits by accusing him of harbouring a witch. In his fright he asked the woman what he should do. "Ask her about her talisman," she advised; "then I can soon settle the matter." So when the girl came in the first thing her foster-father did was to ask her how it was that, being human, she could work such magic.

Suspecting no harm, she in. formed him that at her birth the fairies gave her a talisman whereby she could bring forth pearls, roses, and grass as long as the talisman lived.

"A Rose for sale"

"What is your talisman?" inquired the old man. "A young stag that lives on the mountain; when it dies I must die too," answered the maiden.

Now in the stag's heart was a red coral, that escaped observation; and when the Prince's wife was eating it fell to the floor and rolled under the stairs.

Next day the palace-dame came secretly to the scavenger, and learned from him what the talisman was. With this precious know ledge she hastened joyfully home, imparted the information to her daughter, and advised her to ask the Prince for the stag. Without delay the young wife complained to her lord of indisposition, saying she must have the heart

Rose-Beauty with her child in her arms

of a certain mountain stag to eat. The Prince sent out his hunters, who ere long returned with the animal, slaughtered it and took out its heart, which was cooked for the pretended invalid.

At that same instant the Rose-Beauty also died. The scavenger buried her, and mourned for her long and sincerely.

A year later there was born to the Prince a daughter who wept pearls, smiled roses, and under whose tiny feet grass grew. When the Prince saw that his child was a Rose-Beauty, he easily persuaded himself that his wife was really the right one. But one night in a dream the Rose-Beauty appeared to him and said: "Oh, Prince, my own bridegroom, my soul is under the palace-stairs, my body in the cemetery, thy daughter is my daughter, my talisman the little coral."

As soon as the Prince awoke he went to the stairs and searched for and found the coral. He carried it to his room and laid it on the table. When his little daughter came in she took up the coral, and hardly had her fingers touched it than both vanished. The three fairies conveyed the child to her mother, the Rose-Beauty, who, as the coral fell into her mouth, awakened to a new life.

The Prince, in his restless state, went to the cemetery. Behold! there he found the Rose-Beauty of his dreams with his child in her arms. They cordially embraced, and as mother and daughter wept for joy pearls streamed from the eyes of both; when they smiled roses blossomed, and grass sprang up wherever their feet touched.

The palace-dame and her daughter were severely punished and the old scavenger was invited to live with the Rose-Beauty and the Prince at their palace. The reunited lovers had a magnificent wedding-feast and their happiness lasted for ever.

Ignacz Kúnos

The Silent Princess

There was once a Padishah who had a son, and the little Prince had a golden ball with which he was never tired of playing. One day as he sat in his kiosk, playing as usual with his favourite toy, an old woman came to draw water from the spring which bubbled up in front of the mansion.

The Shahzada, merely for a jest, threw his ball at the old woman's jug and broke it. Without a word she fetched another jug and came again to the spring. For the second time the Prince threw his ball at the jug and broke it. The old woman was now angry, yet, fearing the Padishah, she dared not say a word, but went away and bought a third jug on credit, as she had no money. Returning a third time to the spring, she was in the very act of drawing water when again the young Prince's ball struck her jug and shattered it to pieces. Her anger could no longer be suppressed, and, turning toward the Shahzada, she cried:

"I will say only this, my Prince: may you fall in love with the Silent Princess," With these words she went her way.

The Prince ere long found himself brooding on the old dame's words and wondering what they could mean. The more he dwelt upon them the more they took possession of his mind, until his health began to suffer; he grew thin and pale, he had no appetite, and in a few days he was so ill that he had to remain in bed. The Padishah could not understand his son's malady; physicians and hodjas were summoned, but none could do any good.

One day the Padishah asked his son whether he could throw any light on the strange complaint from which he was suffering. Then the boy described how three times in succession he had broken an old woman's jug, and related what she had said to him, finally expressing his conviction that neither physicians nor hodjas could effect his cure. He asked his father's permission to set out in quest of the Silent Princess, for he felt that only in this way could he be freed from his affliction. The Padishah saw that the boy would not live long unless his mysterious disease were cured; so, after considerable hesitation, he gave his permission and appointed his lala to accompany the young Prince on his journey.

Toward evening they set out and as they took no care of their appearance, in six months they looked more like wild savages than a noble prince and his lala.

They had quite forgotten rest and sleep; the thought of eating and drinking never occurred to them. At last they arrived at the summit of a mountain. Here they noticed that the rocks and earth glistened like the sun.

An old man approached them

Looking round, they saw that an old man approached them. The travellers inquired the name of that region. The old man informed them that they stood on the mountain of the Silent Princess. The Princess herself wore a sevenfold veil, but that fact notwithstanding, the glitter they observed around them was caused by the extraordinary brilliance of her countenance. The travellers now inquired where the Princess resided. The old man answered that if they proceeded straight on for six months longer they would reach her serai. Hitherto many men had lost their lives in vain attempts to elicit a word from the Princess. This news, however, did not dismay the Prince, who with his lala again set off on the journey.

After long wanderings they found themselves at the summit of another mountain, which they noticed was blood-red on every side. Going forward, they presently entered a village. Here the Prince said to his lala "I am very tired; let us rest a while in this place and at the same time make some inquiries." Accordingly they entered a coffeehouse, and when it became known in the village that travellers from a distant land were in their midst the inhabitants came up one after the other to offer their greetings. The Prince inquired of them why the mountain was blood-red. He was informed that three months' journey distant lived the Silent Princess, whose red lips reflected their hue on the mountain before them; she wore seven veils, spoke not a word, and it was said that many men had sacrificed their lives on her account. On hearing this the youth was impatient to put his fate to the test; he and his lala accordingly set out to continue their journey.

After many days they saw another great mountain in the distance, and concluded it must be the dwelling-place of the object of their quest. In due time they arrived at the foot of the mountain and began the ascent. Above them towered a proud castle, the residence of the Silent Princess; and as they approached near enough to see, they observed that it was built entirely of human skulls, The Prince remarked to his lala, " These are the heads of those who have perished in the attempt to make the Princess speak. Either we attain our object, or our skulls will be used for a similar purpose."

53

Before attempting to enter the castle they took up their lodgings in a hân for a few days. All this time they heard nothing but weeping and lamentation: "Oh my brother!" "Oh my son!" Inquiring the cause of the general grief, the travellers were answered: "Why do you ask? It appears you also are come to die. This town belongs to the father of the Silent Princess. Whoever wishes to attempt to make her speak must first go to the Padishah, who, if he permits it, will send an escort with the hero to the Princess." When the youth heard this he said to his lala: "We are nearly at the end of our journey. We will rest a few days longer and then see what fate has in store for us," They continued their sojourn at the hân, and took daily walks about the tscharschi. While thus occupied one day the Prince saw a man with a nightingale in a cage.

The bird caught his fancy so much that he resolved to buy it. The lala remonstrated, reminding the youth that they had a more weighty affair on hand. The Prince, however, refused to listen, and finally purchased the bird for a thousand piasters, took it to his lodging, and hung up the cage in his room.

Once when the Prince was alone and wondering by what means he could make the Princess speak, somewhat saddened by the gloomy reflection that failure meant death, he was startled to hear the nightingale thus address him: "Why so gloomy, my prince? What troubles you?"

The man had a nightingale in a cage

The Prince trembled, not being sure whether it was the bird or a spirit that spoke to him. Growing calmer, he thought that perhaps it was the manifestation of Allah's grace, and accordingly told the nightingale the story of his love for the Silent Princess, and that he was at his wits' end to think how he should get into her presence. The bird replied: "There is nothing to worry about. It is as easy as can be. Go this evening to the serai, and take me with you. The Sultana wears seven veils; no one has ever seen her face, and she sees no one. Put me in my cage under the lamp-stand, and ask the Sultana how she is. She will vouchsafe no answer, however. Then say that as she will not condescend to speak you will converse with the lamp-stand. So begin to speak, and I will reply."

The Prince followed this counsel and went direct to the Padishah's palace. When the Shah was informed that the newcomer wished to go to his daughter, he received the Prince and endeavoured to dissuade him from his

55

intention. He represented that thousands already had tried in vain to make the Princess speak. He had vowed, however, to give her in marriage to the one who could succeed in eliciting a word from her; on the other hand, he who tried and failed forfeited his head. As the Prince might see for himself, his daughter's castle was built entirely of human skulls.

The hardy youth could not be moved from his purpose; he cast himself at the feet of the Padishah and vowed either to accomplish his object or perish in the attempt. Thus there was no more to be said: the Padishah ordered the Prince to be taken into the presence of his daughter.

It was evening when the youth found himself in the Princess's apartment, He put down his cage under the lamp-stand, bowed himself low before the Princess, inquired after her health, and spoke also on matters of less importance. No answer came. Then said the Prince to the Princess: "It is getting rather late, and you have not yet favoured me with a single word. I will now address the lamp-stand. Even though it has no soul it may have more feeling than you." At these words he turned to the lamp-stand and asked: "How are you?" And the answer came directly: "Quite well; though it is many years since anyone spoke to me. Allah sent you to me this day, and I feel as glad as if the whole world were mine. May I entertain you with a story?"

The Prince nodding assent, the voice proceeded: "Once there was a Shah who had a daughter, whom three Princes desired to marry. The father said to the wooers:

56

'Whichever of you excels the others in enterprise shall have my daughter.' The young men accordingly set off together, and coming to a spring they resolved to take different directions, in order to avoid any collision with each other's pursuits. They agreed, however, to leave their rings under a stone, at the spring, each to take his own up again when he returned to the spot, thus furnishing an intimation to him who returned last of all that the others had already reached home.

"The first learnt how to go a six months' journey in an hour, the second how to make himself invisible, the third how to bring the dead to life again. All three arrived back simultaneously at the spring. He who could make himself invisible said the Padishah's daughter was very ill and would die in two hours; the other said he would prepare a medicine that would restore her to life again; the third volunteered to deliver the medicine. Quicker than lightning he was at the palace, in the chamber where the Princess lay dead. Hardly had the medicine touched her lips than she sat up as well as ever she had been. Meanwhile both the others came in and the Shah commanded all three to relate their experiences.

The nightingale paused for a few moments and then resumed: "Oh my Shahzada, which of the three Princes thinkest thou best deserved the maiden?" The Prince answered: "In my opinion, he who prepared the medicine." The nightingale contended for him who acquainted the others of the Princess's condition, and so they hotly disputed the matter. The Silent Princess thought to herself: "They are quite forgetting him who could go a six months' journey in an hour." As the dispute continued she could endure it no longer, and, lifting her sevenfold veil, she cried: "You fools! I would give the maiden to him who brought the medicine. But for him she would have remained dead."

The Padishah was immediately informed that his daughter had at length broken her silence. But the Princess protested that as she had been the victim of a ruse the youth should not be considered to have succeeded in his task until he had induced her to speak three times. Now said the Shah to the Prince: "If you can make her speak twice more she shall belong to you."

The youth left the monarch's presence, went to his lodgings, and began to ponder the matter. While deep in thought, the nightingale said: "The Sultana is angry at having broken her silence, and has smashed the lamp stand, so tonight put me on the other stand by the wall."

Accordingly, when evening was come the Prince repaired with his nightingale to the serai. Entering the Princess's apartment, he put the birdcage on the stand by the wall, and addressed the Sultana. As she disdained to answer, he turned to the stand and said: "The Princess refuses to speak; therefore I will converse with you. How are you?" "Quite well, thank you," came the answer at once. "I am glad the Sultana would not speak, otherwise you would not have spoken to me. As it is, I will tell you a story, if you will listen." "With great pleasure," returned the Prince. "Let me hear it."

58

"I will now address the lamp-stand"

So the nightingale commenced: "In a certain town there once lived a woman with whom three men were in love-- Baldji-Oglu the Honey. maker's Son, Jagdji-Oglu the Tallowmaker's Son, and Tiredji-Oglu the Tanner's Son. Each used to visit the woman in such wise that neither knew of the others' visits. While brushing her hair one day, the woman discovered a grey strand, and said to herself, 'Alas! I am growing old. The time will soon come when my friends will become tired of me. I must make up my mind to get married.' Next day she invited the three lovers to visit her, at different hours. The first arrival was Jagdji, who found the woman in tears. Asking the cause of her grief, he was answered: 'My father is dead, and I have buried him in the garden; but his spirit appears to torment me. If you love me wrap yourself in the winding-sheet and go and lie for three hours in the grave; then my father's spirit will haunt me no more.' Saying this, the woman led him to the open grave which she had made, and as Jagdji would have drowned himself for her sake he cheerfully donned the winding-sheet and lay down in it.

"In the meantime came Baldji, who inquired of the woman why she wept. She repeated the story of her father's death and burial, and giving him a large stone, told him to go to the grave, and when the ghost appeared, to hit him with it. No sooner had Baldji taken his leave and gone to the grave than Tiredji came in. He also sympathised with the woman and inquired what was the trouble. 'How can I help but weep,' said the woman, 'when my father is dead and buried in the garden. One of his enemies is a sorcerer; he is now lying in wait to carry off the body; as you may see he has already opened the grave with that intention. If you can bring me the corpse out of the grave all will be well; if not, I am lost.' The words were scarcely uttered before Tiredji had gone to the grave to take up Jagdji and bring him into her presence. But Baldji, thinking there were two ghosts instead of one, endeavoured to hit both with the stone. Meanwhile, Jagdji, believing the ghost had struck him, sprang out of the grave and dropped the winding-sheet. Then the three men recognised each other and explanations were demanded.

"Now, my Prince," said the nightingale, "which of the three most deserved the woman? I think Tiredji." But the Prince was for Baldji, who had put himself to so much trouble; and so they commenced to argue as before, taking care to avoid mentioning Jagdji. The Princess, who had been listening attentively to the narrative, was disappointed that the deserts of Jagdji were not taken into consideration, and she delivered her opinion with some warmth.

The news that the Silent Princess had again spoken was carried to the Padishah in his palace. Yet once more must she be compelled to speak. As the youth was sitting in his room the nightingale informed him that the Princess was so furious for having been tricked into speaking again that she had broken the wall-stand to pieces. Next evening, therefore, he must put the birdcage behind the door.

The third and final interview found the Princess no more amiable than usual; and as she refused to open her mouth the Prince tried his conversational powers on the door.

The door (or rather the bird behind it) related the following story:

There once were a carpenter, a tailor, and a softa travelling together. Coming to a certain town, they hired a common dwelling and opened business. One night when the others were asleep the carpenter got up, drank coffee, lit his chibouque, and formed an image of a charming maiden out of the small pieces of wood lying about the room. Having finished, he lay down again and fell asleep. Shortly afterwards the tailor woke up, and, seeing the image, made suitable clothing for it, put it on, and went to sleep again. About dawn the softa awoke, and, seeing the image of the lovely girl, prayed to Allah to grant it life. The softa's prayer was heard, and the image was transformed into an incomparably beautiful living maiden, who opened her eyes as one waking from a dream. When the others rose all three men set to disputing as to the possession of the lovely creature. Now to which, in justice, should she belong? In my opinion, to the carpenter." Thus the nightingale broke off.

The Prince thought the maiden should belong to the tailor, and as on the previous occasions a lively debate ensued. The Princess's ire was aroused at the softa's claim being neglected, and she exclaimed: "you fools! the softa should have her. She owed her life to him; she therefore belonged to him and to no one else."

Hardly had she finished speaking than the news was carried to the Padishah. The Prince had now rightfully won the Princess--silent no longer. The whole town put on a festive appearance and began preparations for the wedding. The Prince, however, wished his marriage to take place in his father's palace; and great was the rejoicing when he arrived home with his bride. Forty days and forty nights were the festivities kept up; and the old woman whose jugs had been broken was installed in the palace as dady, a post she filled happily to the end of her days.

Ignácz Kúnos

Kara Mŭstafa
The Hero

There was once a woman who had a husband who was so timid that he never dared to go out alone. On one occasion the woman was invited to a party, and as she was about to set out her husband implored her to make haste back, as he would be forced to remain in the house until her return. She promised to do so; and had hardly been with her friends half an hour when she got up to take leave. "Why must you go home so soon?" asked her hosts. She answered that her husband was at home waiting for her. "Why does he wait?" they asked.

"He dare not go out without me," was the reply. "That is strange," observed the women, and prevailed upon her to remain a little longer. They advised her that next time she went out with her husband after dark, she should slip away from him, and leave him alone in the darkness. By that means he would be cured.

The woman followed this advice, and on the first opportunity that offered, she left her husband alone in the darkness. The man cried out in his terror until at last he fell asleep where he waited. At daybreak he awoke, and went angrily into the house.

Among his possessions was a rusty old knife bequeathed him by his father. He took it up and while cleaning it uttered a resolution not to live with his wife any more. He accordingly set out and came to a place where honey had been spilt, on which a swarm of flies were regaling themselves. Drawing his knife across the sticky mass, he found that he had killed sixty of the flies. He drew it across a second time and counted seventy victims. Immediately he went to a cutler and ordered him to engrave on the knife: "At a single stroke Kara Mustafa, the great hero, has killed sixty, and at the second stroke seventy." The inscription finished, the knife was returned to its owner, who went his way.

Presently he came to a wilderness, and when night fell he lay down and slept, sticking his knife into the earth. Now in this locality dwelt forty Dews, one of whom took an early walk every morning. The Dew saw the sleeping man and the knife, and as he read the inscription upon the latter he was seized with terror. Seeing that Mustafa was now waking up, the Dew, with a view to appeasing this redoubtable person, begged him to join his brothers' company. "Who are you?" asked the hero. "We are Dews to the number of forty, and if you will deign to join us we

65

shall be forty one." "I am willing," said Mustafa; "go and tell the others."

The Dew was seized with terror

Hearing this the Dew hastened to his fellows and said: "My brothers, a hero desires to join us. His immense strength may be gathered from the inscription on his knife: 'At a single stroke Kara Mustafa, the great hero, has killed sixty, and at the second stroke seventy.' Let us put everything in order, for he will be here directly."

But the Dews hastened to meet Mustafa, who when he saw them felt his courage sink. However, he managed to address them. "God greet you, comrades!" he exclaimed. The Dews modestly returned his greeting and offered him a place among them. By and by he inquired: "Is there among you any fellow like me?" The Dews assured him that there was not. Thus satisfied, Mustafa proceeded: "Because, if so, let him step forth and try his strength with me." "Where shall his equal be found?" exclaimed the Dews, as they walked home.

The Dews were obliged to carry their water from a long distance, and this duty was performed in turn by each of their number. Being of gigantic stature and strength, they were of course able to carry a quantity impossible for a mere mortal. On the following day one of the Dews accosted Mustafa: "It is your turn to fetch the water, and we are sorry to say the well is far away." Being afraid of the hero, the Dews naturally addressed him somewhat apologetically. Mustafa reflected, and then asked for a rope. It was given him, and he proceeded with it to the well. The Dews, full of curiosity to know what he intended to do with the rope, looked on from a distance, and saw him attach it to the stonework of the well. Astonished, they ran up and shouted to him to know what he was about. "Oh," he answered, "I am only going to put the well on my back and bring it home, so that none of us need go so far for water again!" They begged him for Allah's sake to desist, and he promised to do so on the understanding that they would not trouble him again with the duty of water-carrying.

A few days afterwards it was Mustafa's turn to fetch wood from the forest. Again he asked for the rope, and went.

The Dews hid themselves and watched him. On the edge of the forest they saw him drive a peg into the ground and fix the rope, which he then drew round the trees. By chance the wind rose and shook the trees to and fro. "What are you doing, Mustafa?" shouted one of the Dews. "Oh, I am only going to take home the forest all at once instead of piecemeal, to save trouble." "Don't shake the trees! " cried all the Dews. "You will destroy the whole forest. We would rather fetch the wood ourselves."

The Dews were now more afraid of Mustafa than ever, and they called a council to deliberate on the best means of getting rid of their formidable associate. It was eventually decided to pour boiling water upon him during the night while he slept, and thus kill him. Fortunately for himself, however, he overheard the conversation, and prepared accordingly. When evening came he went to bed as usual. The Dews heated the water and poured it through the roof of his dwelling. But Mustafa had laid a bolster in the place where he should have been; on the bolster he had placed his fez, and he had drawn up the bedcover. Then he betook himself to a corner of the room, where he lay down and slept soundly out of harm's way. When morning broke the Dews came in the belief that he was dead, and knocked at the door. "Who's there?" came a voice from the inside. The astonished and affrighted Dews called to him to get up, as it was already nearly midday. "It was very hot last night," he observed; "I lay bathed in perspiration." The astonishment of the Dews that boiling water had no further effect upon him than to make him perspire may be imagined.

The Dews next resolved to drop forty iron balls upon Mustafa while he slept: those would surely kill him. This plan also our hero overheard. When bedtime came he entered his room and arranged the bolster as before, putting his fez upon it and drawing up the cover, after which he retired to his corner to await developments. The Dews mounted the roof, and lifting some of the tiles, looked down upon what appeared to be their sleeping companion. "Look, there is his chest; there is his head," they whispered, and thud came the balls one after the other.

Next morning the Dews went to Mustafa's house and knocked at the door. This time no answer came, and they began to congratulate themselves that the hero would trouble them no more. But as a measure of precaution they knocked again and also uttered loud shouts. Then they found their rejoicing had been premature, for Mustafa's voice was heard: "I couldn't sleep last night for the mice gambolling over me; let me rest a little longer." The Dews were now nearly crazy. What manner of man was this, who thought heavy iron balls were mice?

A Few days afterwards the Dews said to Mustafa: "In the adjoining country we have a Dew-brother: will you fight a duel with him?" Mustafa inquired whether the Dew were a strong fellow. "Very," was the reply. "Then he may come." In saying this, however, our hero was ready to die of fright. When the gigantic Dew appeared on the scene, he proposed to preface the duel by a wrestling bout. This being agreed to, they repaired to the field. The Dew caught Mustafa by the throat and held him

69

in such a mighty grasp that his eyes started from their sockets. "What are you staring at?" demanded the Dew, as he relaxed his grip on Mustafa's neck. "I was looking to see how high I should have to throw you so that all your limbs would be broken by your fall," answered our hero in well-simulated contempt. Hearing this, all the Dews fell upon their knees before him and begged him to spare their brother. Mustafa accordingly graciously pardoned his adversary; and the Dews further entreated him to accept a large number of gold-pieces and go home. Secretly rejoicing, he accepted the proffered money and expressed his willingness to go. Taking a cordial farewell of them all, he set out in the company of a Dew, who had been deputed to act as his escort.

When he arrived in sight of his home Mustafa saw his wife looking out of the window; and as her gaze rested upon him she cried, "Here comes my coward of a husband with a Dew!" Mustafa made a sign to her, behind the Dew's back, to say nothing, and then began to run toward the house. "Where are you going in such a hurry?" demanded the Dew. "Into the house to get a bow and arrow to shoot you," was the answer of the flying hero. On hearing this the Dew made off back again to rejoin his brothers.

Mustafa had hardly had time to rest in his home when news was brought of a fierce bear that was playing havoc in the district.

The inhabitants went to the vali and begged him to order the hero to slay the depredator. "He has already encountered forty Dews," they said. "It is a pity that the bear should kill so many poor people."

The vali sent for Mustafa and informed him that it was unseemly that the people should be terrorized by a bear while the province held such a valorous man as himself.

Then spake Mustafa: "Show me the place where the bear is, and let forty horse-men go with me." His request was granted. Mustafa went into the stable took a handful of small pebbles, and flung them among the horses. The creatures all with the exception of one began to rear. This Mustafa himself took. When the horsemen saw what he did, they remarked to the vali that the man was mad and they were not disposed to help him to hunt the bear. The vali advised them: "As soon as you hear the bear, go away and leave him to it, to do what he will."

So the cavalcade set out, and when presently they came to the bear's hiding-place the mounted escort left our hero in the lurch and rode back. Mustafa spurred his steed, but the animal would not move, and the bear came at him with ungainly strides.

Seeing a tree close at hand, our hero sprang on to the back of his horse, clutched at the overhanging branches, and pulled himself up.

"What are you staring at?" demanded the Dew.

The bear came underneath the tree and was preparing to ascend when Mustafa, letting go his hold, alighted on its back, and boxed bruin's ears so severely that he set off in the direction the horsemen had taken. Catching sight of them, he yelled: "Kara Mustafa, the hero, is coming!" Whereon they all wheeled round, and, understanding the situation, dispatched the bear with their lances.

"Where are you going in such a hurry?"

After this the fame of Kara Mustafa spread far and wide. The vali conferred upon him various marks of honour, and he enjoyed the respect of his neighbours to his long life's end.

The Wizard Dervish

A Long Time Ago lived a Padishah who had no son.

As he was taking a walk with his lala one day, they came to a well, near which they stopped to wish. A dervish suddenly appeared and cried: "All hail, my Padishah!" upon which the latter made answer: "If you know that I am the Padishah, then can you tell me the cause of my sorrow." The dervish drew an apple from his breast and said: "Your sorrow is that you have no son. Take this apple; eat half yourself and give the other half to your wife; then in due time you shall have a son. He shall belong to you till his twentieth year afterwards he is mine." With these words he vanished.

The Padishah went home to his palace, and cut the apple, sharing it with his wife according to the instructions of the dervish. Sometime later, as the wizard had promised, a little prince came to the palace and the Padishah, in his great joy, ordered the happy event to be celebrated throughout his dominions.

When the boy was five years old a tutor was appointed to teach him reading and writing. In his thirteenth year he began to take walks and go on journeys, and soon after wards he took part in the hunting excursions also. When he was nearing his twentieth year his father began to think of finding him a wife. A suitable maiden being discovered,

75

the young couple were betrothed, but on the very day of the wedding, when all the guests had assembled in readiness for the ceremony, the dervish came and carried off the bridegroom to the foot of a mountain. With the words "Remain in peace" he went away. In great fear the young Prince looked around him, but saw nothing more alarming than three white doves flying towards the river on whose bank he was resting.

As they alighted, they were transformed into three beautiful maidens, who entered the water to bathe. Presently two of them came out, resumed their bird forms, and flew away. As the third maiden left the water, she caught sight of the young Prince. Much astonished at his presence, she inquired how he had come there.

"A dervish carried me hither," he answered, whereon the girl rejoined: "That dervish is my father. When he comes, he will take you by your hair, hang you on that tree, and flog you with a whip. 'Dost know? he will ask, and to this question you must answer, 'I know not.'" Having given this advice, the girl, transforming herself into a white dove, flew quickly away.

Presently the young Prince saw the dervish approaching with a whip in his hand. He hung the youth by his hair to a tree; flogged him soundly, and asked, "Dost know?" When the young Prince answered "I know not" the dervish went away. For three days in succession the youth was beaten black and blue; but when the dervish had satisfied himself that his victim under stood nothing at all, he set him free.

When the youth was out walking one day the dove came to him and said: "Take this bird and hide it. When my father asks which of the three maidens you desire, point to me; if, however, you do not recognise me, produce the bird and answer: 'I desire the maiden to whom this bird shall fly.'"

Saying this the dove flew away.

The next day the dervish brought with him the three maidens and asked the youth which of them pleased him best. The youth accordingly produced the bird and said that he desired her to whom the bird should fly. The bird was set free and alighted on the maiden who had instructed him. She was given in marriage to the youth, but without the consent of her mother, who was a witch.

While the youth and the maiden were walking together, they saw the mother coming after them. The maiden, giving the youth a knock, changed him into a large garden, and by another knock changed herself into a gardener. When the woman came up she inquired: "Gardener, did not a maiden and a youth pass this way?" The gardener answered: "My red turnips are not yet ripe-- they are still small." The witch retorted: "My dear Gardener, I do not ask about your turnips, but about a youth and a maiden." But the gardener only replied: "I have set no spinach, it will not be up for a month or two." Seeing she was not understood, the woman turned and went away. When the woman was no longer in sight, the gardener knocked the garden, which became a youth again, and knocked herself and became a maiden once more.

They now walked on. The woman turning back and seeing them together, hastened to overtake them. The maiden also turned round and saw her mother hurrying after them. Quickly she gave the youth a knock and turned him into an oven, knocked herself and became a baker. The mother came up and asked: "Baker, have not a youth and a maiden passed this way?" "The bread is not yet baked--I have just put it in; come again in half an hour, then you may have some," was the answer. At this the woman said: "I did not ask you for bread; I inquired whether a youth and a maiden had passed this way." The reply was as little to the point as before. "Wait a while; when the bread is ready we will eat" When the woman saw she was not understood she went away again. As soon as the coast was clear the baker knocked the oven, which became a youth, and knocked herself back into a maiden; then they pursued their way.

Looking back once more the woman again saw the youth and the maiden.

She now realised that the oven and the baker were the runaways in disguise, and hurried after them. Seeing that her mother was coming, the maiden again knocked the youth and changed him into a pond; herself she changed into a duck swimming upon the water. When the woman arrived at the pond she ran to and fro seeking a place whence she could reach the opposite side. At length, seeing she could go no further, she turned round and went home again. The danger over, the duck struck the pond and changed it into the youth; and transformed herself into a maiden as before; upon which they resumed their journey.

Wandering onward they came at length to the birthplace of the youth, where they entered an inn. Then said he to the maiden: "Remain here while I fetch a carriage to take you away." On the road he encountered the dervish, who seized him and transported him immediately to his father's palace, and set him down in the great hall where the wedding-guests were still waiting. The Prince looked round at them all, and rubbed his eyes, Had he been dreaming? "What can it all mean?" he said to himself.

Meanwhile, the maiden at the inn, seeing that the youth returned not, said to herself: "The faithless one has forsaken me." Then she transformed herself into a dove, and flew to the palace. Through an open window she entered the great hall, and alighted on the Prince's shoulder. "Faithless one!" she said reproachfully, "to leave me alone at the inn whilst you are making merry here!" Saying this, she flew back immediately to the inn.

When the youth realised that it was no dream, but fact, he took a carriage and returned without delay to the inn, put the maiden into the coach, and took her to the palace. By this time the first bride had grown tired of waiting for so eccentric a bridegroom and had gone home. So the Prince married the dervish's daughter, and the wedding festivities lasted forty days and forty nights.

Igntaci Kűnos

The Fish Peri

Here was once a fisherman of the name of Mahomet, who made a living by catching fish and selling them. One day, being seriously ill and having no hope of recovery, he requested that, after his death, his wife should never reveal to their son that their livelihood had been derived from the sale of fish.

The fisherman died; and time passed away until the son reached an age when he should begin to think about an occupation. He tried many things, but in none did he succeed. Soon afterwards his mother also died, and the boy found himself alone in the world and destitute, without food or money. One day he ascended to the lumber-room of the house, hoping to find there something he might be able to sell.

During his search he discovered his father's old fishing-net. The sight of it convinced the youth that his father had been a fisherman; so he took the net and went to the sea. A modest success attended his efforts, for he caught two fish, one of which he sold, purchasing bread and coal with the money. The remaining fish he cooked over the coal he had bought, and having eaten it, he resolved that he would follow the occupation of a fisherman.

It happened one day that he caught a fish so fine that it grieved him either to sell it or to eat it. So he took it home, dug a well, and put the fish therein. He went supperless to bed, and being hungry he got up early next morning to catch more fish.

When he came home in the evening we may imagine his astonishment at finding that his house had been swept and put in order during his absence. Thinking, however, that he owed it to his neighbours' kindness, he prayed for them and called down Allah's blessing upon them.

Next morning he rose as usual, cheered himself with a sight of the fish in the well, and went to his daily work. On returning in the evening he found that again everything in the house had been made beautifully clean and tidy. After amusing himself for some time by watching the fish, he went to a coffeehouse where he tried to think who it could be that had put his house in order. His reflective mood was noticed by one of his companions, who asked what he was thinking about. When the youth had told the story his companion inquired where the key was kept, and who remained at home during the fisherman's absence. The youth informed him that he carried the key with him, and that there was no living creature about except the fish. The companion then advised him to remain at home next day and watch in secret.

The youth accordingly went home, and next morning instead of going out, merely made a pretence of doing so. He opened the door and closed it again, then hid himself in the house. All at once he saw the fish jump out of the well and shake itself, when behold! it became a beautiful maiden. The youth quickly seized the fish's skin, which it had shed, and cast it into the fire. "You should not have done that," said the maiden reprovingly, "but as it cannot now be helped, it does not matter."

Being thus set free, the maiden consented to become the youth's wife, and preparations were made for the wedding. All who saw the maiden were bewildered by her beauty and said she was worthy to become the bride of a Padishah. This news reaching the ears of the Padishah, he ordered her to be he saw her he fell in love determined to marry her.

Therefore he sent for the youth, and said to him: "If in forty days you can build me a palace of gold and diamonds in the middle of the sea, I will not deprive you of the girl; but if you fail, I shall take her away." The youth went home very sadly and wept. "Why do you weep?" asked the maiden. He told her what the Padishah had commanded,

Some plates of food fel out of the coffee-mill

but she said cheerfully: "Do not weep; we shall manage it. Go to the spot where you caught me as a fish and cast in a stone. An Arab will appear and utter the words 'your command?' Tell him the lady sends her compliments and requests a cushion. He will give you one take it, and cast it into the sea where the Padishah wishes his palace built. Then return home."

The youth followed all these instructions, and next day, when they looked toward the place where the cushion had been thrown into the sea, they saw a palace even more beautiful than that the Padishah had described. Rejoicing, they hastened to tell the monarch that his palace was an accomplished fact.

Now the Padishah demanded a bridge of crystal. Again the youth went home and wept. When the maiden heard the cause of his new grief she said: "Go to the Arab as before, and ask him for a bolster. When you get it, cast it in the sea before the palace." The youth did as he was counselled, and looking round, he saw a beautiful bridge of crystal. He went directly to the Padishah and told him that the task was fulfilled.

As a third test, the Padishah now demanded that the youth should prepare such a feast that everyone in the land might eat thereof and yet something should remain over. The young fisherman went home, and while he was absorbed in thought the maiden inquired what was the matter. On hearing of the new command she advised: "Go to the Arab and ask him for the coffee-mill, but take care not to turn it on the way." The youth obtained the coffee-

mill from the Arab without any difficulty. In bringing it
home he began quite unconsciously to turn it, and seven
or eight plates of food fell out. Picking them up, he
proceeded homewards.

On the appointed day everyone in the land, in accordance
with the Padishah's invitation, repaired to the fisherman's
house to take part in the feast.

Out of the egg sprang a great mule.

Each guest ate as much as he wanted, and yet in the end a
considerable portion of food remained over.

Still obdurate, the Padishah ordered the youth to produce
a mule from an egg. The youth described to the maiden
his latest task, and she told him to fetch three eggs from
the Arab and bring them home without breaking them. He
ob tamed the eggs, but on his way back dropped one and
broke it. Out of the egg sprang a great mule, which after

84

running to and fro finally plunged into the sea and was seen no more.

The youth arrived home safely with the two remaining eggs. "Where is the third?" asked the maiden. "It is broken," replied the youth.

"You ought to have been more careful," said the maiden, "but as it is done it can't be helped." The youth carried the eggs to the Padishah, and asked permission to mount upon a bench. This being granted, he stood on the bench and threw up the egg. Instantly a mule sprang forth and fell upon the Padishah, who sought in vain to flee. The youth rescued the monarch from his danger, and the mule then ran away and plunged into the sea.

In despair at his inability to find an impossible task for the youth, the Padishah now demanded an infant not more than a day old, who could both speak and walk. Still undaunted,, the maiden counselled the youth to go to the Arab with her compliments, and inform him that she wished to see his baby nephew. The youth accordingly summoned the Arab, and delivered the message. The Arab answered: "He is but an hour old: his mother may not wish to spare him. However, wait a bit, and I will do my best."

To be brief, the Arab went away and soon reappeared with a newly born infant. No sooner did it see the fisherman than it ran up to him and exclaimed: "We are going to Auntie's, are we not?" The youth took the child home, and immediately it saw the maiden, with the word

85

"Auntie!" it embraced her. On this the youth took the child to the Padishah.

When the child was brought into the presence of the monarch, it stepped up to him, struck him on the face, and thus addressed him: "How is it possible to build a palace of gold and diamonds in forty days? To rear a crystal bridge also in the same time? For one man to feed all the people in the land? For a mule to be produced from an egg?"
At every sentence the child struck him a fresh blow, until finally the Padishah cried to the youth that he might keep the maiden himself if only he would deliver him from the terrible infant. The youth then carried the child home.
He wedded the maiden, and the rejoicings lasted forty days and forty nights.

The child struck him on the face.

Three apples fell from the sky: one belongs to me, another to Husni, the third to the storyteller. Which belongs to me?

The Horse-Dew
and the Witch

Once a Padishah had three daughters. Before setting out on a journey he called his daughters before him and instructed them to feed his favourite horse personally, and not to entrust that duty to any other, as he would allow no stranger near it. The Padishah went away, and the eldest daughter carried food to the stable: the horse, however, would not permit her to approach him. The second daughter made the attempt, with no better result. Then the youngest went to the horse, who was perfectly quiet, and willingly received the food and drink from her hands.

The two eldest sisters were glad thus to be relieved of an irksome and disagreeable duty.

When the Padishah returned home his first inquiry was as to whether his horse had been properly attended to during his absence. "He would not allow us even to go near him," answered the two elder daughters, "but our youngest sister has fed him."

87

On hearing this the monarch said that she should be wife to the horse, his other daughters being given in marriage to the Vezir and Sheik-ul-Islam respectively, The triple wedding festivities lasted forty days, and the youngest then went to her stable, while her sisters were taken to their splendid palaces,

Only in the daytime, however, had the youngest sister a horse for a husband and a stable for a dwelling. By night the stable was transformed into a rose garden and the horse into a handsome youth. Thus they lived in the utmost felicity, no one except themselves knowing their secret.

He unhorsed his brother-in-law

It came to pass that the Padishah arranged a tournament in the court yard of the palace, and the bravest of all the knights who took part therein were the husbands of the monarch's eldest daughters, "Look!" said they to their sister of the stable, "our husbands are like lions: see how beautifully they throw their lances. Where is your horse-husband?" At this the horse shook himself, changed into human form, mounted a steed, and begging his wife not to reveal his identity, he plunged into the fray. He overcame all the combatants, unhorsed his brothers-in-law, then vanished as completely as though he had never been there.

Next day the tournament was continued, and the elder sisters treated the youngest with scorn and contempt; but again the unknown hero appeared, struck down all his opponents, and vanished as before.

On the third day the horse-knight said to his wife: "If at any time I am in danger, or you are in need of help, burn these three hairs, and wherever you may be, I will come to you." Then he hastened to the tournament and fought again with his brothers-in-law. His prowess evoked universal admiration even his sisters-in-law could not withhold their tribute of praise; but in ill-natured raillery they said to their youngest sister: "See how these knights understand the tournament; they are not like your horse-husband."

The poor woman could no longer forbear to answer that the beautiful and valiant knight was her husband; but even as she turned to point him out, he vanished. This reminded her that he had warned her never to divulge the secret. Overcome with remorse, she awaited eagerly his return to the stable, but in vain; neither horse nor man came--neither roses nor garden were to be hers that night.

"Woe is me!" she groaned, "I have betrayed my husband; I have broken my promise; thus am I punished!" She did not close her eyes all night, but wept until morning. When it was daylight she went to her father the Padishah, and with tears told him what had happened, vowing that she would go in search of her husband even if she journeyed to the ends of the earth. In vain her father attempted to dissuade her. He reminded her that her husband was a Dew and consequently she would never find him; but all his arguments failed to shake her resolution.

Grief stricken she set out on her quest, and walked so long that at last she sank exhausted at the foot of a mountain. Here, remembering the three hairs, she burned one of them, and the next instant her husband enfolded her in his arms. Both were almost speechless with joy.

"Did I not counsel you never to betray our secret to anyone?" gently chided the youth. "If my mother sees us now she will separate us immediately. This mountain is our abode; my mother will be here directly, and woe to us if she catch sight of us."

The poor girl was terrified at these words, grieving bitterly that no sooner had she found her husband than she must lose him again. The Dew-son pitied her, gave her a light blow and changed her into an apple, which he put upon a shelf. Shrieking loudly, the witch flew down from the mountain, crying that she could smell human flesh and that human flesh she must have. In vain her son denied it--she refused to believe him.

"If you will swear on the egg to do it no harm, I will show you what I have hidden," said the youth. The witch accordingly promised, where on the youth gave the apple a light blow and the beautiful maiden appeared. "Behold my wife!" said he. The old woman said nothing, but set her daughter-in-law some simple tasks, and went back to her work.

For a few days the husband and wife were allowed to live in peace, but the old witch was only waiting till her son went away from home to wreak her vengeance on his wife. At last she found an opportunity. "Sweep and don't sweep," she commanded the maiden, and went away. The poor girl was perplexed to know what she must "sweep" and what "not sweep." Recollecting the hairs, she took one and burnt it. Instantly her husband appeared, and she told him her difficulty. He explained that she must "sweep" the room and "not sweep" the courtyard.

The maiden acted accordingly. Towards evening the witch came in and asked whether the work was done. "I have swept and not swept," answered the daughter-in-law. "You deceitful thing!" scolded the old woman, "you have not thought that out for yourself; my son has certainly taught you."

Next day the old witch came again and gave the maiden three bowls, which she ordered her to fill with her tears. The maid wept and wept continually, but failed to fill even one of the vessels. In her difficulty she burnt the third hair, whereupon her husband appeared and advised her to fill the bowls with water and add a quantity of salt thereto.

This the maiden did, and when the old woman came home in the evening, she was shown the three vessels duly filled. "You cunning creature!" stormed the witch, "that is not your own work; but you and my son shall not cheat me again."

The witch scolded her again.

On the following day she ordered her daughter-in-law to make a pancake. But though the maiden sought everywhere, not a single ingredient for the purpose could she find. This time she could expect no help, for her husband was away, and the three magic hairs had all been burned. The youth, however, suspecting his mother's wicked intentions, returned home unexpectedly to his wife, and seeing her in such grief he suggested that they should flee. "My mother will not rest until she has wrought your ruin," he said. "Let us escape before she returns." So they went together out into the wide world.

In the evening the witch came home, and saw that both her daughter-in-law and son were missing. "The wretches have abandoned me!" she shrieked, and calling her witch-sister to her, she sent her to follow the fugitives and bring them back. The second witch got into a bowl, made a whip out of snakes, and was off like a lightning-flash. But the Dew-son, seeing his aunt behind them in the distance, gave the maiden a light blow and changed her into a swimming-bath. He transformed himself into a bath attendant, and stood before the door. The witch came up, alighted from the bowl, and inquired of him whether he had seen a youth and a maiden. "I am just warming the bath," answered the youth; "there is no one in; if you do not believe me, go in and see for yourself." The woman, perceiving she could do nothing with him, re-entered the bowl, went back to her sister, and reported the failure of her errand.

The witch asked her whether she had met anyone on the way. "Oh yes," answered she, "I spoke to the attendant at the door of a swimming bath, but he was either deaf or stupid, for I could get nothing out of him." "you were even more stupid," scolded the witch, "not to recognize that the bath and the attendant were my daughter-in-law and son." Now she called another sister and sent her after the fugitives.

The Dew-son looking back, saw his other aunt coming towards them in a bowl. He knocked his wife gently and she became a spring; he himself stood beside and drew water. The witch came up and asked whether he had seen anything of a youth and a maiden. "This spring has excellent drinking-water," the fellow answered with an air of simplicity. The woman, thinking he was too stupid to understand her questions, hurried back to her sister with the intelligence that she could see nothing of the missing couple. The witch inquired whether she had seen anyone on the way. "Only an imbecile drawing water from a spring," was the answer. "That imbecile was my son," exclaimed the witch in a great rage, "and the spring was his wife. I see I shall have to go myself." So she stepped into the bowl, made a whip out of snakes, and set off.

Looking back the youth now saw that his mother herself was coming. Striking the maid gently he turned her into a tree, and himself into a snake coiled round it. The witch knew them, and would have torn the tree to pieces if she could have done so without harming her son. So she said to the snake, "My son, at least show me the little finger of the maid and then I will leave you in peace."

The son saw that the only way to get rid of his mother was to do as she asked. He therefore allowed one of the maid's fingers to become visible this his mother immediately devoured, and then vanished.

At another gentle blow from her husband the maid again resumed her human form; and the two went home to her father, the Padishah. His talisman having been destroyed, the youth became a mortal, and as he was no longer a Dew, his witch-mother had no more power over him. The Padishah rejoiced in the return of his lost children, their marriage was again celebrated with great pomp, and after the old monarch's decease they reigned in his stead.

Ignacz Kúnos

The Simpleton

At the time when Allah had many servants and mankind much sorrow, there was a poor woman who had three sons and a daughter. The youngest son was somewhat simple and lay all day by the fireside.

One day the two elder sons went into the fields to work, and before leaving requested their mother to cook them something to eat and send it to them by their sister. In the neighbourhood a Dew with three heads had erected his dwelling, and the brothers instructed their sister which way to take in order to avoid him.

When the dinner was ready the maiden set out to take it to her brothers, but she mistook her way and strayed into the path leading to the Dew's house. She had walked but a few steps when the wife of the three-headed Dew stood before her and asked her how she came there. She chatted

96

with the trembling girl until she had enticed her into the house, promising to hide her from her husband.

But the Dew with the three heads was there waiting for the maiden. As she entered the woman said that she would soon have a meal ready. "I will knead the dough," she said, "but you, my daughter, must make the fire." Scarcely had the girl begun to build up the fire than the Dew stole in, opened his mouth, and swallowed her just as she was.

In the meantime the men were expecting their dinner; they waited and waited, but neither girl nor dinner were forthcoming. Evening fell, and when the two brothers, arriving home, learnt that their sister had set out in the fore noon, they suspected what had befallen her. She must have strayed into the Dew's locality. The eldest brother, after a little reflection, resolved to go to the Dew and demand the girl.

O my stomach! O my stomach! cried the youth.

Walking along, smoking his chibouque and smelling the flowers, he came to a baking-oven by the roadside. By the oven stood a grey-bearded man, who asked him where he was going. The brother told him of the misfortune which he feared had overtaken his sister, and added that he was seeking the Dew with the three heads, in order to kill him.

"You cannot kill the Dew," rejoined the old man, "until you have eaten of the bread baking in this oven." The youth thought that would be no great feat. Taking a loaf out of the oven, he bit it, then commenced to run until he had left man, oven, and bread far behind.

Stopping to take breath, he saw a man carrying a vessel filled with wine. To this man the brother spoke of his business with the Dew, "You can do nothing to the Dew," said the man, "until you have drunk some of this wine." The youth accordingly attempted to drink, but crying, "Oh, my stomach! Oh, my stomach!" he ran from the spot and never paused until he reached two bridges. One bridge was of wood, the other of iron; on the opposite side thereof stood two apple-trees, one bearing sour, the other sweet apples.

The Dew with the three faces was waiting on the road to see which bridge the youth would choose, the wooden or the iron one; which apples he would eat, the sweet or the sour. Fearing the wooden bridge might break down, the youth crossed by the iron one; as the sour apples were not ripe, he plucked the sweet ones. The Dew had now learnt enough. He sent his wife to meet the youth, and she enticed him into the house. Very shortly he found himself in the Dew's stomach beside his sister.

Now the second son set out in quest of his brother and sister. He also could not eat the bread, and the wine gave him stomach-ache. He also crossed over the iron bridge, ate the sweet apples, and arrived eventually in the Dew's stomach.

We will now turn our attention to the youngest son. The mother observing the simpleton get up from the fireside, begged him not to forsake her in her old age. The others had done so, but he at least should remain with her. But the youth would not listen. "No," said he, "till my sister and my brothers are rescued, and the Dew killed, I cannot rest."

Rising from his corner, he shook the ashes from him, and at that moment such a storm arose that all the farmhands ran home, leaving their ploughshares in the fields. The simpleton collected all these shares together and took them to a blacksmith, requesting him to make of them a spear which, when thrown into the air, should fall on his finger without breaking. When the smith had made the spear, the youth threw it up in the air, and as it fell back on his little finger, it broke in fragments.

Again the simpleton shook the ashes from him and another storm arose which sent all the field labourers hurrying home. Again he collected the ploughshares and took them to the smith. The second spear was made, but this also was shattered at the trial.

For the third time the youth raised a storm, after which he collected all the remaining ploughshares and had them made into a spear. This time it did not break when it fell back on his finger. "That will do," said the simpleton, and went his way.

Before long he arrived at the baking-oven. The baker greeted him, and learning that he was on his way to kill the Dew, informed him that he could accomplish his purpose only after eating the bread, and drinking wine out of the vessel that he would find farther on. The simpleton accepted his task, ate up all the bread, drank all the wine, and as he journeyed further he came to the wooden and iron bridges, with the apple-trees beside them.

The Dew was watching anxiously, and his courage sank when he saw the youth's actions. "Any child of man can go over the iron bridge," thought the simpleton to himself, and so he chose the wooden one. "There is also no art in eating sweet apples," he said, and chose those that were sour. "With this fellow we must deal in a different manner," called the affrighted Dew to his wife. "Get ready my spear; we must fight it out"

The simpleton had already seen the Dew afar off; he walked directly up to him and greeted him civilly. "If thou hadst not greeted me," said the Dew, "I should have swallowed thee." "And for my part," retorted the youth, "I should have killed thee with a spear-thrust hadst thou not returned my greeting."

100

"If thou art so valiant," said the Dew with the three heads, "have at thee with the spear!"

The Dew, taking his spear in hand, threw it with all his might at the youth, who caught it on his little finger, where it was shattered to pieces. "Now it is my turn," said the simpleton. He threw his spear with such force that, as it struck the Dew, the latter's spirit departed through his nose. "Strike once more, if thou art a good fellow," gasped the Dew; but as the youth answered "Never! " the Dew breathed his last. Now the youth sought the Dew's wife. When they opened the body of the wizard, the two brothers and their sister came out. With the simpleton they now wended their way homeward.

While in the stomach of the Dew the brothers and sister had become very thirsty; coming to a well they requested their younger brother's help in procuring water to drink. All took off their girdles, fastened them together, and let the eldest down the well. He was scarcely half, way down when he began to bellow with fear: "Oh, draw me up, I am burning!"

He was pulled up immediately, and the second brother next essayed the task, but the same thing happened also with him.

"Now it is my turn," said the simpleton, "but mind you do not draw me up however much I may beg you to do so." So they let him down, and though they heard his cries of fear they took no heed, but lowered him to the bottom of the well. Here he found a room, and entering, he beheld three maidens, beautiful as the full moon. They were very much alarmed at sight of the youth, and implored him with tears to leave the Dew's cave, but he would not listen.

To be brief he killed the Dew and delivered the three maidens, whom the wizard had robbed from their father, the Sultan, seven years before.

The simpleton intended to give the two eldest in marriage to his brothers and wed the youngest himself.

Having filled his jug with water he led the maidens to where the rope still hung. The eldest was the first to be drawn up, and the eldest brother took her under his care, as his youngest brother requested; then ascended the second, who was to be protected by the second brother; lastly, the third maiden was helped up. She advised the youth to ascend first and allow her to follow him. "Thy brothers will be angry that thou hast chosen the most beautiful maiden for thyself," she said, "and from envy they will not draw thee out of the well."

"Then will I find my own way out," answered the youth. Seeing that she could not persuade him, she took a box and gave it to him, saying: "When thou art in danger, open this box. If thou strikest the flint it contains, an Arab will appear and execute all thy commands.

If thy brothers should abandon thee here in the well, go to the Dew's palace and stand by the pond there. Two sheep come daily, a black one and a white one; if thou shouldst seize the skin of the white one, thou wouldst be conveyed to the surface of the earth; but if thou shouldst seize that of the black sheep, thou wouldst go down into the underground regions."

On this she was drawn up to the top of the well. Hardly had the brothers set eyes on her than they both fell in love with her, and as she had foretold, they left the simpleton down the well.

What was he to do now? He went back to the palace, stood by the pond, and awaited the coming of the sheep. Presently a white and a black sheep sprang in. The youth seized the black one instead of the white, and in a trice found himself in the underground country. "I will take a stroll about this territory," he thought to himself, and began to walk on.

He walked day and night, up hill and down dale, till, unable to go farther, he stopped to rest by a tall tree. His eyes beheld a long snake creeping up the tree. The creature would have swallowed a nest of young birds if the youth had not rescued them just in time.

Grasping his spear firmly in his hand, he severed the snake in two, Then he stretched himself out under the tree, where, overcome by fatigue and the great heat, he fell sound asleep.

Meanwhile came the little birds' mother, who was the emerald anka, queen of the Peris. Seeing the sleeping youth, she mistook him for the enemy that year by year killed her children, and would have torn him to pieces had not the little birds cried to her to do him no harm. They told her how he had killed their enemy the snake, and looking round, the anka saw the severed body of the reptile.

She flicked the flies from the sleeper, and spread her wings to shield him from the sun, so that when he awoke he saw the bird's wings over him like a tent.

He seized the black one

The anka told him she wished to reward him for his generous deed, and inquired what he would like. "Transport me to the surface of the earth," was his answer.

"I will take you up," said the emerald-bird, "if you have forty hundredweight of mutton and forty bottles of water. Put them on my back and then get up yourself. When I say 'Gik!' feed me, and when I say 'Gak!' give me drink."

The Dew's spirit departed through his nose.

The youth thought of the box. He opened it, took out the flint and struck it. "What is thy command, my sultan?" exclaimed the Arab of the monstrous lips, who instantly appeared. "Forty hundredweight of mutton and forty bottles of water." In a few minutes the meat and the water were on the bird's back; the youth also mounted, and when the anka cried "Gik!" he gave her meat and when she cried "Gak!" he gave her drink. She flew from one plane of the earth to the other, and ere long reached the surface, where the youth alighted. The bird promised to wait until he returned.

The youth now took out the box and commanded the Arab to bring him news of the three sisters. In a short time the Arab brought the maidens themselves. They all mounted on the bird's back, loaded her with meat and water, and flew away to the native land of the three maidens,

"Gik!" cried the anka, and they gave her meat; "Gak!" and they gave her water. But as there were now four human beings to be fed also, there was not sufficient meat to last throughout the journey and there was no more wherewith to supply the bird. When the anka cried "Gik!" the youth took his sword, cut a piece from his leg and stuck it in the bird's beak. The anka, perceiving it was the flesh of a mortal, ate it not, but held it fast in her beak. When they reached the land of the three sisters, she told him that it was impossible for her to go farther.

The Anka flew away to the land of the three maidens.

His leg was so painful that the youth could not walk a step. "Go," said he to the bird, "I will rest here a little."

"Oh, you foolish youth!" answered the emerald-bird, and taking the flesh from her beak she pressed it into its place. Instantly the leg was healed.

Great was the astonishment in the town at the homecoming of the Sultan's daughters. The old Padishah could scarce believe his eyes. He embraced and kissed them, heard their story, and gave his kingdom as well as his youngest daughter to the simpleton.

The youth invited his mother and sister to the wedding, and his sister was given in marriage to the son of the Vezir. The rejoicings lasted forty days and forty nights, but happiness until the end of their days.

Ignacz Kúnos

The Majic Turban the Majic Whip and the Majic Carpet

There were once two brothers, whose parents were dead. With his share of the inheritance the elder opened a shop, but the younger squandered his portion in foolish pleasures. A day came when the latter had no more money, so he went to his brother and begged a few paras.

When he had spent those, he went again to his brother and obtained more money. This practice he continued until eventually the elder realized that in order to save the remnant of his fortune, he must sell his business and emigrate to Egypt. The younger, however, got wind of his brother's intention, and before the ship sailed, he stole on board without being observed and hid himself. The elder brother, fearing that if he discovered his intention the younger would follow him, avoided showing him, self on deck. Hardly had the ship set sail than both appeared on the deck, and the elder saw that his plan had failed, and that his younger brother would still be as a burden hanging round his neck. The elder brother was angry, but anger was of no avail; the ship bore them both to Egypt.

110

After they had disembarked,
the elder said to the younger:
"Remain here while I
procure mules to carry
us farther."

Accordingly the younger
sat down on the shore to
await the other's return—
but in vain. "I will seek him,"
he said to himself, and set
out after his brother.

He took short steps and
long strides and travelled
in this wise for six months,
when looking backward one
day he saw that nevertheless he had accomplished only a
short distance. Then he took longer strides and went for
half a year forward, gathering violets, and in this way he
came to the foot of a mountain. Here, seeing three fellows
quarrelling, he went up and asked them the cause of their
difference.

"We are the children of one father," said the eldest; "he
died not long ago and left behind him a turban, a whip,
and a praying-carpet. Whoever sets the turban on his head
becomes invisible. Whoever sits on the carpet and cracks
the whip, flies away like a bird. Who shall have the
turban, who the whip, and who the carpet? This is the
matter about which we are continually wrangling."

"All three things should belong to one of us," they all cried.

"I am the eldest--they ought to belong to me." "No, to me, the second son." "Oh no, to me, the youngest." With words and sticks they belaboured each other so mercilessly that the prodigal had much difficulty in separating them.

"Not so," said he, "I will make an arrow out of a piece of wood and shoot it. You will all run after it, and whichever of you brings it back to me becomes the possessor of the three things."

The arrow sped its way, and the three brothers ran after it. While this was happening, however, our prodigal was thinking: "I have only to put on the turban, sit on the carpet, crack the whip, and in a twinkling I shall be where my brother is." To think was to act, and before he was aware of moving he found himself at the entrance to a large city.

As soon as he had arrived in the town he was informed by one of the Padishah's entourage that the Sultan's daughter disappeared every night. Whoever could discover what became of her would be given the maiden in marriage and half of the kingdom besides. "I will solve the mystery," said the prodigal; "take me to the Padishah; if I fail, here is my head!" He was accordingly taken to the palace, and at night posted at the door of the Princess's sleeping-chamber, to await with one eye open whatever should happen.

She pricked the soles of his feet with a pin

The Princess waited until she thought he would be asleep and then peeped cautiously round the door. He appeared to be in a sound sleep, but, to make assurance doubly sure, she pricked the soles of his feet with a pin, and as he did not stir, she took up the candle in her hand and went out stealthily by a side-door.

Putting the turban on his head, the young man rose and followed her. As he came outside he saw before him an Arab, on whose head rested a golden basin, and in this bowl sat the Princess. The prodigal immediately sprang into the basin, nearly upsetting it as he did so. The Arab, astonished, asked the maiden what she was doing, for he had nearly dropped her. "I have not moved a finger," answered the maiden; "I am sitting in the basin exactly as you put me."

When the Arab took a few steps he perceived that the basin was unusually heavy. (The young man was, of course, rendered invisible through wearing the magic turban.)

"What has happened to you, lady?" asked the Arab; "today you are so heavy that you nearly crush me."

"Nothing, dear lala," replied the Princess. "I am neither heavier nor lighter."

Shaking his head dubiously, the Arab set out and ere long they came to a splendid garden, the trees of which were composed of silver set with diamonds. The prodigal broke off a branch and put it in his

The Arab perceived that the basin was unusually heavy

pocket, where, at the trees began to sigh: "A mortal has injured us! A mortal has injured us!" The Arab and the Princess were bewildered and knew not what to think.

However, they journeyed farther and ere long came to another garden, the trees of which were of gold and precious stones. Here also the young man broke off a branch, whereupon all the trees commenced to groan so loudly that the heavens were shaken. "A mortal has

114

injured us!" they complained. The Arab was dumb with amazement.

Now they reached a bridge, crossing which they arrived at a palace, where a multitude of slaves awaited the Princess. Folding their arms over their breasts, they bowed themselves to the earth. The Sultan's daughter alighted from the basin, stepping on to the Arab's body and thence to the earth. As slaves brought her a pair of slippers studded with jewels, the prodigal seized one and put it in his pocket. The other the Princess put on and then looked about for the missing one, but it had entirely disappeared.

Angry, she entered the palace, and the young man followed her the turban on his head and the whip and carpet in his hands. The maiden entered an apartment in which she found the Dew whose lips swept heaven and earth. He asked her where she had been so long. She told him about the young man who had been set to watch her, but the Dew consoled her and assured her that there was no need for her to be anxious.

The slave dropped the cup

They both sat down, and sherbet in diamond-studded cups was brought by a slave. As the Sultan's daughter reached out her hand to take one, the young man struck the slave's arm, whereon he dropped the cup, and it fell broken to the floor. The young man picked up a fragment and put it in his pocket.

"Did I not tell you," cried the Sultan's daughter, "that nothing goes right today? I will not take any sherbet; I will not take anything. I will go home again." The Dew calmed her, and ordered other food to be brought by a different slave. The table was laid, and many dishes were set thereon; but while they ate, the young man, who was hungry, also helped himself The Dew and his visitor nearly swooned with fright when they realized that there was a third--and invisible--guest.

The Dew was now quite perturbed, especially as so much of the confectionery and so many of the cups disappeared. He himself advised the Sultan's daughter to return home earlier than usual that day, and he was about to kiss the Princess in farewell, when the invisible youth tore them apart.

BOTH grew pale and summoned the lala. The maiden, sitting in the bowl, ordered the slave to take her home. The prodigal quickly seized a sword from the wall and severed the Dew's head from his body. As the head fell to the ground, heaven and earth trembled, and groans and wailing arose. "Woe to us! a mortal has killed our king!" Even the prodigal was terrified, knowing not where he was. He quickly spread his carpet, sat thereon, and cracked his whip. When the Sultan's daughter arrived back, behold! the young man was already outside the door of her chamber, apparently fast asleep and snoring loudly.

"Interfering pig!" grumbled the Princess in a fury, "thou hast caused me enough unhappiness today." So saying, she again pricked the soles of his feet with a pin, and as he gave no sign she concluded that he was still asleep.

Next morning the prodigal was sent for, and asked whether he had solved the mystery of the Princess's nocturnal disappearances. If he had not, his head would be cut off. "Oh yes, I know all," he answered, "but I shall not tell you; take me to the Padishah." Brought before the ruler, he promised to tell him all if he would assemble together the inhabitants of the city. "Thus I can easily find my brother," he thought to himself. Accordingly all the inhabitants were collected in the marketplace, where the Padishah and his daughter sat on a dais. Near at hand stood the prodigal, who related the account of his adventure from beginning to end. "Do not believe it, father; it is not true!" frequently interrupted the Princess.

Here the youth took from his pocket the jewelled branch, the golden slipper, the costly plate; and just as he was describing the death of the Dew-King he caught sight of his brother in the crowd. He said no more and heard no more, but sprang down to join his brother, who at once began to run. The prodigal ran after him, and at length caught him.

When they both returned the younger begged the Padishah to give the Princess and half the kingdom to his brother. For himself, the magic turban, the magic carpet, and the magic whip were enough; with those he could

117

always procure a livelihood. His only desire was always to be near his brother.

The Sultan's daughter rejoiced when she heard of the death of the Dew-King, who had cast a spell over her. Now that this spell was broken she felt nothing but abhorrence for the monster, and in her joy at being free she was quite willing to become the wife of the prodigal's brother. Their wedding festivities lasted forty days and forty nights. I was there also, and when I asked for pilaf the cook gave me such a blow on my hand that it has been lame ever since.

The prodigal severed the Dew's head from his body

Ignacz Kúnos

Mahomet the Bald Head

When the camel was a messenger, when frogs could fly, and when I used to roam up hill and down dale, there lived two brothers together. Besides their mother and poverty they had a little live-stock which they had inherited from their father.

Now the younger brother, who was bald, conceived one day the idea of dividing their little property; so he went to his elder brother and said: "you see these two stalls; the one is quite new, the other almost worn out. Let us turn all the cows loose, and those that return to the new stall shall be mine, the others yours." "Oh, no, Mahomet," answered the other, "those that return to the old stall shall be yours." Mahomet agreed. The cows returned to the new stall except a miserable old blind one.

Mahomet uttered not a word of complaint or dissatisfaction, but daily drove his blind cow to pasture, returning regularly every evening.

One day as Mahomet was sitting by the road. side, the wind blowing violently through the trees made the branches bend and creak. Mahomet accosted the tree thus: "Eh, creaker, have you seen my brother?" The tree apparently not hearing, creaked all the louder. Mahomet repeated his question, and as again the tree did not reply the bald-head became furious, took his axe and proceeded to cut it down. But lo! an avalanche of gold-pieces fell out of the hollow trunk through the incisions he had made. Making use of what little sense he had, Mahomet went home and borrowed an ox from his elder brother, yoked it to a cart, procured sacks, which he filled with earth, and went therewith to the tree. Arrived at the spot, he emptied the sacks and refilled them with the gold. On his return home he amazed his brother with the sight of so much wealth.

The younger brother was again seized with a desire to divide--the elder, we may be sure, having no objection this time. He borrowed a measure from a neighbour, exciting that worthy man's curiosity as to what that stupid fellow Mahomet could have to measure. The neighbour smeared the inside of the measure with bird lime, and when the bald-head returned the article a gold-piece was found adhering to it. This neighbour related his discovery to another, that one to a third, and in a short time the whole village knew of Mahomet's luck.

The possession of so much gold occasioned the two brothers much perplexity. They did not know what to do with it. Eventually they took spades, dug a deep trench, buried the money, and hastened to leave their native place. After setting off, however, the elder bethought himself that he had not locked the house-door, and he dispatched the younger to see to it. On reaching home it occurred to Mahomet that he ought to secure his mother's silence; so he heated a boiler of water, put the old lady in, and kept her there until she uttered no further sound. He then took her out, supported her against the wall with a broom, put the door on his back and went with it to his brother in the forest.

He put the old lady in the boiling water

When the elder saw the door and understood what had happened to his mother he became very angry with the bald-head, who flattered himself that he had done something extremely clever in bringing away the door to prevent anyone opening it. The elder took the younger by the scruff of his neck and shook him violently. While reflecting what he should do further he saw three horsemen riding along the road. In their fright the brothers thought the cavaliers were pursuing them, and anxious to escape they climbed up a tree, carrying the door with them. As it was already dark they were not discovered. Mahomet reflected that they were lucky to have escaped with their lives, and in this grateful frame of mind he let the door fall on the head of one of the cavaliers who was just passing beneath.

The rider whom it struck put spurs to his horse and galloped quickly away with the cry: "Mercy on us! It is the end of the world!" A few days after this adventure the elder brother had had enough of the younger's vagaries, and secretly forsook him. What could Mahomet do now? He was alone in the world, He wandered on, weary and hungry, till at length he reached a village. He took up his position at the door of the djâmi and begged paras and food from the passersby.

A little man with a thin beard came out of the djâmi, and on seeing Mahomet asked him if he would like to become his servant. "Yes," answered Mahomet, "if you promise never to be angry with me whatever happens. If ever you become angry with me, I have the right to kill you; if, on the other hand, I ever become angry with you, you have the right to kill me." As it was very difficult to obtain a servant in this locality, the man agreed to this extraordinary condition.

The bald-head commenced his duties by slaughtering all his master's fowls and sheep. "Are you angry with me, master?" he asked. "No, of course not. Why should I be angry?" returned the affrighted man. Henceforth, however, Mahomet's duties consisted of sitting in the house doing nothing.

The master's wife was afraid that soon it might be her turn to follow the fowls and sheep, so in order to escape from the madman she persuaded her husband to go away with her secretly by night. But Mahomet, hearing of their intention, hid himself in the luggage, and when it was opened in another village he stepped out. Now the husband and wife took counsel together, and as a measure of safety resolved that all should sleep at night on the seashore; Mahomet should go with them, and they would seize the opportunity while he slept to cast him into the sea and drown him. Mahomet, however, had so much cunning that he threw in the woman instead, and she was drowned. "Are you angry with me, master?" he asked. "Why should I not be angry with thee, thou wretch!" cried the man. "Thou hast not only ruined me in fortune and brought me to beggary, but now thou hast bereft me of my wife!" Upon this the bald-head seized him, and, reminding him of the condition of his employment, cast him also into the sea after his wife.

Mahomet, once more alone in the world, tramped about, drank coffee, and smoked his pipe. One day he found a five-para piece, with which he bought leblebi. While eating them he accidentally dropped one, which fell into the well and was lost. Now Mahomet began to cry: "I want my leblebi! I want my leblebi!" and this loud bellowing brought to the surface an Arab with two such immense lips that one swept the sky and "What willst thou?" he dem

"I want my leblebi" said Mahomet

leblebi! I want my leblebi!" the bald-head continued to scream. The Arab disappeared in the well, and presently came up again holding in his hands a small table. Giving it to the bald-head, he said: "When thou art hungry say, 'Table, be laid!' and when thou art satisfied say, 'Table, enough!"

Mahomet took the table and went to the village. When hungry he had only to say, "Table, be laid!" and the most expensive dishes were set before him; the food was so delicious he hardly knew of what to partake first. In his conceit he thought, "I should like the villagers to see this," so he invited them all to supper. When they arrived and saw neither fire nor food, they concluded their host was jesting with them. But when the fellow brought in his little table and pronounced the words, "Table, be laid!" the feast was ready in a moment. All ate their fill, and went home envying their bald neighbour and devising various schemes to deprive him of his wonderful piece of furniture. Finally it was settled that one of their number should creep into Mahomet's house during his absence and steal the magic table.

Thus it came about that Mahomet felt the pangs of hunger once more, What should he do? He went to the well and began to cry: "I want my leblebi! I want my leblebi!" and the Arab appeared. "Where is the table?" "It has been stolen!" The Arab with the thick lips popped down into the well and reappeared with a hand-mill. Giving it to the bald-head, he said: "Turn to the right--gold; turn to the left--silver." So the fellow took the mill home, and turned so many times right and left that his floor was strewn with money. He was now a richer man than ever had been in the village before.

Somehow the villagers got wind of the precious mill, and one fine day it was missing. "I want my leblebi! I want my leblebi!" was again the cry at the well. The Arab came up and demanded: "Where are the table and the mill?" "Both have been stolen from me," lamented the bald-head. The Arab went down again and appeared with two sticks, which he gave to our hero, cautioning him strictly against saying other than the words, "Cudgels, come together!"

"Stop cudgels!" he exclaimed

Mahomet took the sticks and examined them. Desiring to put their efficacy to the test, he pronounced the words, "Cudgels, come together!" and immediately they flew out of his hands and commenced to beat him most mercilessly. "Stop, cudgels!" he exclaimed as soon as he had overcome his surprise, and they ceased belabouring him. Though sore from his chastisement, Mahomet was glad nevertheless, for he had already thought of the use to which he should apply his sticks.

Hastening home, he invited all the villagers to his house, though without divulging his reason for calling them thus together. They came eagerly, full of curiosity to see what other wonderful thing he had to show them. At the auspicious moment Mahomet introduced his couple of sticks, and at the words "Cudgels, come together!" fearful strokes descended on the heads and bodies of the guests. They began to cry out for mercy, but Mahomet declined to utter the formula by which the punishment ceased until all had promised to return him the table and the mill. The articles were brought back without loss of time and peace was restored.

The bald-head took his three magic gifts and went to his native village, where he rejoined his brother. Being now wise and wealthy, our hero, as well as his brother, married and lived a merry life. Henceforth there was no more prudent man in the village than Mahomet the Bald-head.

The Storm Fiend

Two cats made a spring, the frog flew with wings, aunt flea fell down, and the rocks fell on her. The cock was an imam, the cow a barber, the goslings danced; all this happened at the time when a Padishah was old.

This old Padishah had three sons and three daughters. One day he was taken ill, and in spite of all the hodjas and physicians that surrounded him his condition failed to improve. He sent for all his sons and spoke thus to them: "When I am dead that one of you shall be Padishah who keeps watch by my grave for three nights. As for my daughters, give them in marriage to the first who ask for them." He died and was buried with all the pomp and ceremony suitable to his high station.

In order that the kingdom might not remain long without a Padishah, the eldest son went to his father's grave, spread his carpet and prayed thereon till midnight, and then patiently waited for the dawn. But suddenly a fearful noise broke upon the darkness; the youth, appalled, took to his heels and ran home without stopping.

The next night the second son went to the tomb, and sat there till midnight; but as before a fearful noise arose, and he ran back home as fast as his legs could carry him.

He bound the old man

Now came the turn of the youngest. He took up his handschar, put it in his girdle, and went to the cemetery. About midnight arose such a tremendous noise that the heavens and the earth appeared to be shaken thereby. The youth proceeded in the direction of the sound, and came into the presence of an immense dragon. Drawing his handschar he plunged it into the dragon with all his might. The monster had hardly sufficient strength left to cry out:

"If thou art the right man stab me once more."

"Not I," answered the Prince. The dragon accordingly expired. The Prince wished to cut off his ears and his nose,

131

but he could not see in the darkness, and as he was groping about he noticed a light in the distance. He walked in the direction of the light, and as he approached it he saw an old man in a corner. This man had two balls of twine in his hand, a black one and a white one. The black he was winding up, and the white he allowed to roll on the ground.

"What art thou doing, father?" asked the Prince. " It is my occupation, my son; I wind up the night and set the day rolling."

The Prince rejoined: "My occupation is more difficult than thine, father." Saying this he bound the old man so that he could no longer let loose the day, and went on to seek a light. Presently he arrived at a castle under whose walls he found forty men holding a council.

"What are you about?" asked the Prince. " We want to get into the castle to rob it," was the answer, "but we know not how to accomplish it."

"I will help you," said the Prince, "if you will give me a light" The robbers promised quite willingly. He took nails, knocked them in the wall from the ground up to the roof, climbed up thereby, and called down that each man should come up singly. As they ascended one by one the youth at the top struck off their heads and threw their bodies into the courtyard until he had destroyed all the forty thieves. This done he entered the castle, in the courtyard whereof was a magnificent palace. Opening the door he saw a snake coiled round a column by the side of the staircase. He thrust it through with his sword, but quite forgot to with draw the weapon, so that it was left sticking in the creature's body. Mounting the stairs he entered a chamber, where he found a beautiful maiden asleep. Closing the door, he looked into another chamber and found another maiden more beautiful than the first. Closing this door also, he went to a third chamber, which was completely covered with metals; here a beautiful maiden was sleeping: one so charming that he fell a thousand times in love with her.

Here a beautiful maiden was sleeping

He now closed this door also, climbed the castle wall and descended the other side by means of the nails. Then he went straight to the old greybeard whom he had bound. "My son," cried the elderly man before the youth came up to him, "why have you been so long away? My ribs are aching from my long bondage." The youth set him free and the old man now let the white ball roll farther. The

133

youth returned to the dragon, cut off his ears and nose and put them in his pocket. He now returned home to the palace, where in the meantime his eldest brother had been made Padishah. Of his adventure he said nothing, but let things take their course.

"I want to marry your eldest sister," said the lion

Some time afterwards a lion came to the palace and appeared before the Padishah, who asked him what he wanted. "To marry your eldest sister," answered the lion, "I cannot give her to a beast," said the Padishah, and the lion would have been sent away if the youngest Prince had not observed:

"Our father laid it upon us that she was to be given to him who should first ask for her."

On this he took the maiden by the hand and delivered her to the lion, who went away with her.

Next day came a tiger and demanded the Padishah's second sister. The two elder brothers were unwilling to give her to him, but the youngest challenged them to fulfil their father's wish, and the maiden was accordingly given to the tiger.

On the third day a bird flew into the palace and requested the youngest Princess. The Padishah and his brother again would not consent, but the youngest insisted, and in the end the bird flew off with the maiden. The bird was the Padishah of the Peris, the emerald anka.

We will now return to the castle.

Here also dwelt a Padishah who had three daughters. Going out early in the morning he perceived that someone had been in the palace. He passed into the courtyard, and near the staircase espied the huge snake, cut in two by the sword. Proceeding farther he saw the forty corpses. "No enemy can have done this, but a friend," he mused; "he has delivered us from the robbers and the snake. This sword belongs to our good friend, but where is he?" He took counsel on the matter with his lala.

"We can only find out," said the Vezir, "if we prepare a great feast and invite everybody to partake of it. We must watch all our guests very closely, and whoever carries the sheath belonging to the sword is our friend." So the

135

Padishah gave orders for the feast to be prepared and everybody invited thereto.

The feasting lasted forty days and forty nights, and one day the lala said: "Everybody has come to the feast except the three Princes." Accordingly they were sent for, and when they came it was noticed that the youngest had the sheath belonging to the sword. Immediately the Padishah sent for him, and said:

"You have rendered me a valuable service; what may I give you in recompense?"

"Nothing less," answered the Prince, "than your youngest daughter."

"Woe is me! my son, would you had not asked for her!" sighed the Padishah; "my crown, my kingdom are yours, but ask not for this maiden!"

"If you will give me the maiden I will accept her," answered the Prince "otherwise I want nothing."

"My son," implored the Padishah, in great sorrow, "I will give you my eldest daughter, I will give my second daughter, but I dare not part from my youngest daughter. The Storm Fiend demanded her in marriage, and as I would not give her to him I have been compelled to secure her in a metal chamber, so that this Dew cannot get near her. This Storm Fiend is so powerful that no cannon can injure him; no eye can perceive him; like the wind he appears, and like the wind he disappears."

136

In vain the Padishah urged the youth to dismiss the youngest Princess from his mind, and thereby keep himself out of danger; the Prince would not listen. Seeing that his reasoning was useless and at length growing weary of the matter, the Padishah withdrew his objections and the marriage took place. The two brothers married the two other maidens and went back to their own country, while the youngest remained, in order to protect his wife from the evil machinations of the Dew.

Thus the Prince lived happily with his beautiful wife for some time. One day he said to her, "My dear one, it is long since I went from your side; I would like to go hunting for one brief hour."

"Oh woe! my king," answered she, "I know only too well that if once you leave me you will never see me again."

But at length she yielded. He took his weapons and went into the forest. The Storm Fiend now had the opportunity he had long awaited. He was afraid of the brave Prince and dared not take the Princess from his side; but no sooner had the Prince left the palace than the Storm Fiend entered and carried off the girl.

Shortly afterwards the Prince returned home and missed his wife. He hastened to the Padishah, but the Dew had stolen his wife and she was nowhere to be found. He wept and lamented bitterly, casting himself to the earth. Then he arose, mounted his steed, and went forth resolved to rescue his wife or die in the attempt.

137

He wandered without resting for days and weeks, his sore affliction spurring him ever onwards. At length he described a palace, but so faintly that he could scarcely be said to see it. This was the palace of his eldest sister. The Princess was looking out of the window and wondering at the sight of a human being in her locality, where no bird ever flew or caravan came. She recognised her brother, and when they met so great was their joy that they could not speak for kissing and embracing.

In the evening the Princess said to the Prince: "Soon my husband the lion will be here; although he treats me well, he is after all a beast and may do you harm." So she hid her brother.

When the lion came home the Princess and he sat together and con. versed, and she asked the lion what he would do if one of her brothers should come there. "If the eldest came," answered her husband, "I would kill him at a blow; if the second came, him also would I kill; but if the youngest came, I would take him in my arms and lull him to sleep." "That one has arrived," answered his wife. "Then bring him here quickly, that I may see him," cried the lion; and when the Prince stood before them, the lion knew not what to do for very joy. He inquired whence he came and whither he went. The youth now related what had happened to him and said he was going to find the Storm Fiend.

"I know him only by name," said the lion, "but I counsel you to have nothing to do with him, for you can do no good." But the Prince was restless; he would remain only

138

one night, and on the following morning he mounted his horse and set out. The lion accompanied him a short distance to put him on the right road, then they both went different ways.

The Prince travelled onward, until he came to another palace, which belonged to his second sister. She espied a man coming along the road, and no sooner recognised her brother than she ran out to meet him and led him into the palace. The hours sped happily until towards evening the Princess observed:

"My tiger-husband will soon be here; I will hide you so that no harm befall you." So she hid her brother.

In the evening the tiger came home and his wife asked him what he would do if by chance one of her brothers should come to see them.

"The two eldest I would kill," said the tiger, "but if the youngest came I would rock him to sleep on my knees." So the Princess fetched the Prince her brother, and the tiger manifested great joy at seeing him.

The youth related the story of his bereavement and asked the tiger if he knew the Storm Fiend. "By name

The Tiger manifested great joy

only," answered the tiger; and he also besought the youth to renounce so dangerous a quest. But at daybreak the Prince set forth again. The tiger put him on the right road, and they parted company.

Crossing a desert, he saw something looming dark in the distance. Wondering what it might be, he proceeded ahead and by and by perceived that it was a palace, the home of his youngest sister. The Princess glanced through the window, and uttered a joyful cry: "Oh, my brother!" His arrival gave great happiness; he rejoiced to have seen all three of his sisters, but he thought of his wife and his heart was heavy with grief.

Towards evening the Princess said to her brother: "My bird-husband will be here soon; I will hide you until I have ascertained how he is disposed to receive you." So she hid her brother.

With loud-flapping wings the anka flew in, and he had hardly rested before his wife asked him what he would do if one of her brothers should visit them.

"The two eldest," said the bird, " I should take in my beak, fly with them up to the sky and drop them to the earth; but the youngest I would take on my wings and let him go to sleep."

At this the Princess called in her brother.

"My dear child," exclaimed the bird, " how come you here? Had you no fear on the road?"

140

The youth told his grief and requested the anka to take him to the Storm Fiend.

"That is not so easily done," answered the bird; " but if you should encounter him, you would gain so little thereby that it were better to remain with us and relinquish your purpose."

"No," said the resolute Prince, "either I deliver my wife or I perish in the attempt."

Seeing he could not be turned from his purpose, the anka described the way to the palace of the Storm Fiend, "Just now he sleeps and you can take away your wife," he said; "but if he awakes and sees you, all is over. You cannot see him, for no eye can behold him, no sword can harm him, so beware."

Next day the youth set out and soon came in sight of an immense palace which had neither doors nor chimneys. This was the home of the Storm Fiend. His wife was sitting by the window, and on seeing him she sprang down crying: "Woe, my Sultan!" The Prince embraced her, and of his joy and her tears there was no end until the Princess remembered the cruel Dew. "He fell asleep three days ago," said she. "Let us hasten away from here before his forty days' sleep is ended." She also mounted a horse and they sped quickly away. They had not travelled far, however, before the fortieth day expired and the Storm Fiend awoke. He went to the Princess's chamber and called to her to open the door, that he might see her face

141

for an instant. Receiving no answer he suspected evil, and forcing open the door found the Princess was not there.

"So, Prince Mahomet, you have been here and carried off the Sultan's daughter! But wait a while, I'll soon catch you both!"

Saying these words he calmly sat down, drank coffee and smoked his pipe, then he got up and hurried after them.

Without stopping to rest the Prince and Princess galloped onward, but presently the latter felt the wind raised by the Dew and said: "Oh, my king, woe is me, the Storm Fiend is here!"

The invisible monster fell upon them, seized the youth, broke his arms and legs, and smashed his head and his bones, leaving not a single member whole.

"As you have killed him, allow me at least to collect his bones and put them in a sack," the Princess tearfully implored the fiend. " I may perhaps find someone to bury them." The Dew offering no objection, the Princess put the Prince's bones in a sack. Then she kissed his horse on the eyes, bound the sack on his back, and whispered in his ear: "My horse, take these bones to the right place."

The Dew carried the Princess back to his palace, but the power of her beauty was so great that the fiend was like a prisoner in her hands. She refused to allow the monster in her presence; he dared show himself only before the door of her chamber.

In the meantime the horse galloped away with the youth's bones, and stopped before the palace of the youngest sister, where he neighed so loudly that the Princess came out to see what was the matter. On seeing the sack and her brother's bones she began to weep bitterly and cast herself violently to the earth as though she would break her own bones. She could hardly contain herself until the return of her husband the anka.

With loud flapping of wings the bird-Padishah, the emerald anka, came home, and when he saw the poor Prince's broken bones he called his subjects--all the birds of the world--together and asked: "Which of you was ever in the Garden of Eden?" "An old owl was there once," was the answer, "but now he is so aged and infirm that he can scarcely move."

The anka dispatched a bird with orders to bring the owl. So the bird flew away and presently returned with the old owl on his back.

"Eh, father, were you ever in the Garden of Eden?" inquired the Padishah.

"Yes, my son," hooted the ancient one, "but it was a long, long time ago, before I was twelve years old. I have never been there since."

The bird returned with the old owl on its back

"As you have been there once," said the anka, "go there a second time and bring me a small phial of water." The owl protested that he could not go, the way was so very long and he had hardly any strength left; but his excuses were in vain. The Padishah set him on the back of a bird, and so they flew to the Garden of Eden, procured the water and returned to the nest.

The anka now took the youth's bones, put them all together in their proper places, and sprinkled them with the water of Paradise. The youth began to yawn as though he were just awaking from sleep. He looked around and asked the anka where he was and where his wife was. "Did I not tell you," said the anka, "that the Storm Fiend would catch you? He broke your bones, which we found in a sack. Now let him alone, or next time he will not even leave your bones in a sack."

But the Prince was unwilling to abandon his purpose, and once more set out to find his wife.

"If you must have her at any cost," advised the anka, "go first and ask your wife to find out what is the Dew's talisman. If you can discover that, the power of the Storm Fiend can be destroyed."

So the Prince, mounting his steed once more, hastened to the palace of the fiend, and as he was asleep the Prince was able to speak to his wife. In great joy the Princess promised to discover the Dew's talisman, saying that she would even use flattery if no other means served. The Prince hid himself in a neighbouring mountain to await the result.

When the Storm Fiend awoke from sleep at the end of forty days, he went to the Princess's apartment, and knocked at the door. "Get out of my sight!" cried the maiden from within. "you sleep for forty days, while I am left alone and wearied of my life."

The Dew was happy that she had even deigned to speak to him, and asked her joyfully what he could give her to drive away her melancholy. "What can you give me?" retorted the Princess. "you are only wind yourself! Perhaps, however, you have a talisman with which I might amuse myself?"

"Oh, lady," answered the Dew, " my talisman is in a far-off country, and it is very difficult to reach. If only there were another such man as your Mahomet, he might possibly succeed."

The Princess was now curious about the talisman, and flattered the Dew so much that at length he divulged his secret. He begged her to sit by his side a little. The maiden granted him this favour, and thereby got possession of the history of the Storm Fiend's talisman, "On the surface of the seventh sea," began the Dew, "there is a large island; on this island is an ox grazing; in the ox's stomach is a golden cage; in the cage is a white dove. That little white dove is my talisman." "But how can one get to this island?" asked the Sultan's daughter.

"In this way," said the Dew: "opposite the palace of the emerald anka is a high mountain; on the top of this mountain is a spring. From this spring forty sea-horses drink once a day. If anyone can be found clever enough to kick one of these horses while it is drinking, he can saddle and mount it, and it will take him wherever he wishes to go."

"Of what use is this talisman to me," asked the maiden, "if I cannot once get near it?" She drove the Dew out of her chamber and hastened to her husband with the news. The Prince quickly mounted his steed, went back to the palace of his youngest sister, and related the affair to the anka.

Early next day the anka called five birds. "Take the Prince to the spring on the mountain," he bade them, "and wait there till the magic sea-horses appear. While they are drinking catch one of them, strike it, saddle it, and put the Prince upon its back before it has time to take its head out of the water."

The anka's subjects picked up the Prince and carried him to the spring. As soon as the horses arrived the birds did exactly as the anka had ordered them. The Prince found himself on the back of the steed, whose first words were: "What is your command, my dear master?"

"On the surface of the seventh sea there is an island. I wish to go there," said Mahomet.

With "Shut your eyes!" the Prince flew through space; with "Open your eyes!" he found himself on the shore of the island.

Alighting from his horse and putting the bridle in his pocket, he went in search of the ox. Strolling about the island he met a Jew, who asked him how he had got there.

"I have been shipwrecked," answered the Prince; "the ship went down, and it was only with great difficulty that I managed to swim here." "As for me," said the Jew, "I am in the service of the Storm Fiend, who has an ox here, which I guard day and night. Would you like to be my servant? All you have to do is to fill this trough with water every day."

The Prince availed himself of the opportunity and was eager to get a glimpse of the ox. The Jew took him to the stall, and as soon as Mahomet was alone with the animal, he slit its stomach, took out the golden cage, and went with all speed to the shore. Pulling the bridle out of his pocket, he struck the waves therewith and his horse immediately appeared and carried him to the Storm Fiend's palace." The Prince lifted his wife up beside him and ordered: "To the emerald anka."

They arrived at the anka's palace just as the Dew awoke from his sleep. Seeing that the Princess was gone, he hastened after them. The Sultan's daughter felt the wind of the Dew, and knew that he had nearly over taken them. At this crisis the magic horse cried out to them to cut off the head of the dove which was in the cage. They had just enough time to do it; a moment more and it would have been too late! The wind suddenly ceased, for the fiend was now destroyed.

Full of joy they entered the palace of the anka, released the magic horse and left it to rest. Next day they went to the second sister, and on the third day to the third sister. The Prince now made the pleasing discovery that his lion brother-in-law was king of the lions and his tiger brother-in-law king of the tigers.

Finally they came to the Princess's own home. Their wedding was celebrated afresh for forty days and forty nights, after which they went to the Prince's kingdom. There he showed the dragon's ears and nose, and as he had fulfilled his father's wish he was elected Padishah. Afterwards Mahomet and his wife lived and reigned together in happiness until the end of their days.

They had just enough time to do it.

The Laughing Apple
and
the Weeping Apple

In olden time lived a Padishah who had three sons.

One day as the youngest was sitting in a kiosk, near which was a spring, there came an old woman to draw water. The boy threw a stone at her jug and broke it. Saying nothing the old woman went away, and presently returned with another jug. Again the youth threw a stone and shattered the jug. The woman went away as before, and returned a third time. The boy s[...] her jug and broke it as on the [...] Now spake the old woman:

"May you fall in love with the Laughing Apple and the Weeping Apple!" she said. With these words she disappeared.

A few days afterwards the words of the old woman began to take effect, and the King's son was actually in love with the Laughing Apple and the Weeping Apple. Day by day he grew paler and weaker. As soon as his father heard that he was ill, he sent for the hodjas and physicians, but such an in disposition was beyond their skill.

One day a physician told the Padishah that the youth was lovesick. Upon this the monarch went to his son and asked what ailed him. The youth answered that he was in love with the Laughing Apple and the Weeping Apple. "What is to be done?" asked the father. "Where are the two apples to be found?" Then said the youth: "With your permission I will go and seek them." The Padishah endeavoured to dissuade him, but the youth remained obstinate, determined at all costs to go in search of the apples. As his two elder brothers were willing to accompany him the father at length consented, and one day the party set out on their journey.

Up hill, down dale, and across the plains they wandered on, until one day they came to a spring where three roads met. Here was a notice set up for the information of travellers to the effect that whoever took the first road would return, whoever took the second road might return or not return; whoever took the third road would never return. The eldest of the brothers said he would take the first road, the middle brother elected to take the doubtful

152

road, while the youngest was willing to take the road which promised no return. Here they separated the youngest said: "How may we know which of us returns first? Let us take off our rings, put them under this stone, and as we return let each one take up his ring again." Thus they agreed, and set out on their several ways.

The eldest walked on and on until he reached a land where there was a swimming-bath, and he engaged himself as a servant. The middle brother also wandered on and on until he came to a land where there was a coffeehouse; he entered and became an attendant.

Now we will see how the youngest fared. After long journeying he arrived one day at a spring where he saw an old woman drawing water. He accosted her with the words: "Mother, could you give me shelter just for tonight?' She answered: "My son, I have only a small hut, so small that when I lie down my feet are outside;

He accosted the old woman

where then could I put you?" He showed the old woman a handful of gold, and begged her to find room for him somewhere. As soon as she caught sight of the gold-pieces she said: "Come, my son, I have a large house. For whom should I make room if not for you?" Accordingly they

153

went home together. As they sat at supper the youth asked: "Tell me, mother, where can I meet with the Laughing Apple and the Weeping Apple?"

Hardly had the question left his lips than the old woman struck him on the mouth crying: "Silence! their names are forbidden here!"

The youth offered her another handful of gold, on receiving which she said: "Get up in the morning and cross that mountain opposite; there you will meet a shepherd--the shepherd of the palace in which the Laughing Apple and the Weeping Apple are to be found. If you can win his favour you may gain admittance to the palace. But take care, and as soon as you have obtained possession of the apples make haste back to me."

So next morning he went across the mountain and there found the shepherd, who was minding his sheep. He greeted him courteously, and the man returned the salutation. While in conversation the youth asked the shepherd about the Laughing Apple and the Weeping Apple. Hardly were the words out of his mouth than the shepherd struck him so violently in the face that he nearly fell. "Why do you strike me, shepherd?" asked the youth. "What! You still ask questions? I'll soon silence you!" answered the shepherd, and again he struck him in the face. But the youth pleaded more earnestly than before, and gave the shepherd a handful of gold.

Being thus placated, the shepherd said to the youth: "I will now kill a sheep, so that I may make a leathern bottle of its

154

skin; slip you into the skin. When it is evening and I drive the sheep home to the palace, you can go in with the sheep. At night when everybody is asleep go up to the first floor and steal unobserved into the chamber on the right.

The shepherd struck him violently in the face

There lies the Sultan's daughter in bed, and the apples will be found on the shelf near her. If you can get them away, it is well; but if not, it is all over with you.

The shepherd accordingly killed a sheep, hid the youth in its skin and drove the sheep to the serai. The youth succeeded in entering without discovery.

155

When night came on and everybody was asleep, the youth stole forth from the skin of the sheep, and crept carefully and slowly to the first floor. Entering the chamber indicated by the shepherd, he saw therein a bed on which lay a lovely maiden, beautiful as the moon at the full.

She had black eyebrows, blue eyes, and golden hair; her equal surely did not exist in the world. So beautiful was she that the youth was beside himself with astonishment. While he gazed upon the maiden, one of the two apples on the shelf began to laugh, the other to weep bitterly. The youth shut the door quickly and ran back to the sheep. The noise made by the apples awakened the maiden. She got up, and seeing no one, looked about the room, scolded the apples for their stupidity, and lay down again.

After a while the maiden fell asleep once more, and the youth went upstairs, opened the door slowly and carefully, and entered. He took a few steps towards the apples, and again one began to laugh, the other to weep. The maiden woke up, but saw no one. "You naughty creatures!" she cried; "this is the second time you have waked me; if you do so again I shall cut you through." Then she lay down again. When she was asleep the youth came again, opened the door, went straight to the apples, and as he took them from the shelf they began to laugh and weep. But the youth ran off, and when the maiden awoke for the third time there was nothing to be seen. "You impudent creatures!" she cried; "have you gone mad that you have waked me up a third time?" She struck them both and lay down again.

A short time afterwards the youth came a fourth time to the apartment, went to the shelf and took down the apples, which now made no sound, being angry at the treatment they had received. Quickly he made his exit and returned to the sheep.

When morning dawned the shepherd led his flock to the mountain. Then the youth crept out of the sheepskin, gave the shepherd another handful of gold, and saying "It was Allah's will!" went back to the house of the old woman.

When she saw the youth she filled a large basin with water, then killed a fowl and let its blood flow into the vessel. This done she put a plank into the water and set the youth upon it.

We will now return to the serai. When the maiden awoke, she saw that the apples were no longer on the shelf. "Oh, what has become of my apples?" she exclaimed, searching everywhere, but without avail. "Woe is me! my apples have been stolen. Three times they woke me, but I did not understand. A thief has been here!"

The maiden wept continually and sighed: "Oh, my apples! Oh, my apples!" When it came to the ears of her father, the Padishah, he ordered the gates of the city to be closed immediately, and a thorough search was instituted, but nowhere could the apples be found. He sent for the astrologers, who,

157

The youth was beside himself with astonishment.

consulting the stars, announced that he who had stolen the apples was at that moment in a ship on a sea of blood. "Oh, Padishah!" they said, "he must be very far away, for we know not where there is such a sea of blood." The monarch realized that there was no chance of catching the thief, so the city gates were opened again.

The youth presented the old woman with a few more gold-pieces, and commending her to Allah, he set off again in search of further adventures. Some days later he found himself by the spring where he had parted from his brothers. Lifting the stone under which they had put their rings, he saw that neither of his brothers had yet returned. Replacing his own ring on his finger, he now set out along the road taken by his middle brother.

He wandered on and on, uphill, down dale, and across the plains, drinking water from the river, resting in the desert, listening to the song of the nightingales, till one day he came to a certain country. Entering a town he sought out a coffeehouse, and while drinking coffee and smoking his chibouque he recognized his middle brother serving coffee. His brother, however, knew him not. Calling him aside, he spoke to him, asking him so many questions that at length the elder recognized his brother. Then they both set off together and in due time arrived at the spring. The second ring was taken up and the pair now resolved to look for their eldest brother. They discovered him eventually, and made themselves known to him, and now all three returned to the spring.

On the way they asked the youngest whether he had secured the apples. "Of course," answered he, and brought them forth. They had hardly glanced at the two apples than they fell in love with them, and begged their brother to let them hold the apples in their hands. The youth com plied and gave them up. Being now in possession of the magic fruit, the two elder resolved to kill their youngest brother and divide the apples between them.

They went to a coffeehouse, where they sat down in the garden, and after ordering something to eat, asked the proprietor for a mat. In the garden was an open well; this they covered with the mat, and their youngest brother (not knowing of the well) sat on the mat and fell down to the bottom. The others, affecting not to notice his disappearance, ate, drank, and smoked, and eventually rose up and went away. When they arrived home their father asked what had become of his youngest son. The brothers answered that they had found the Laughing Apple and the Weeping Apple, but their youngest brother had taken the way from which there was no returning, and consequently they had seen him no more. The father shed tears, but hoped that if his son were still living he would find his way home before long.

Now, when the youth fell down the well, which was dry, he was not killed, but merely stunned. He soon returned to consciousness, and shouted several times in the hope of being heard. The coffeehouse keeper happened to be taking a walk in the garden. Hearing the cry he sent down a man to bring up the youth. Thanking his rescuer cordially the youth went his way, but not to his father's

160

house; instead, he offered himself as apprentice to a tinsmith.

One day the Padishah whose daughter's apples had been stolen ordered a rosary of a thousand beads to be made, and this he sent by the hands of his servants into all countries. The magic power of this rosary was such that he who had stolen the apples would, on telling the beads, relate a full account of the incident.

At length the rosary reached the land where the three brothers lived. When the youth heard of it he informed his master, the tinsmith, that he would tell the beads. Word was sent to the Padishah's servants, who brought him the rosary and requested him to begin. The youth said he was willing to do so, but only in the presence of the Padishah of that land.

He was brought before the Padishah, to whom the affair was explained. The monarch consented to be a witness, and the rosary was handed to the youth, who began his task. He related a complete account of his adventures in search of the apples, and when he came to the part about his brothers casting him down the well, the rosary was finished. Now the Padishah, recognising his son, fell on his neck and kissed him, weeping for joy.

The strangers begged the Padishah to allow his youngest son to return with them, and consent was given; not, however, until the two wicked brothers had been severely punished. They started on their long journey and after many days came to the home of the apples. There the

161

youth was taken before the Padishah, who as soon as he saw him felt his heart go out to the young Prince. The monarch ordered him to tell the beads before him.

Once more the youth related his adventure with the apples. When the story was ended the Padishah offered him his daughter in marriage, so that both the youth and the maiden might rejoice in the possession of the apples they both loved. Very willingly the young Prince consented; and with festivities lasting forty days and forty nights the lovers were united.

As they attained happiness, we will now seek our divan.

The Crow Peri

There was once a man who had a son. The man spent the whole day in the wood, catching birds which he sold. One day the father died and the boy was left alone in the world. He did not know what his father's occupation had been, until one day among some things his parent had left he came across a bird trap. Taking it up he went to the forest and set it in a tree. Soon a crow flew by, alighted on the tree and was caught. The boy climbed up and was about to seize the bird, when it begged him to set it free in exchange for a much more beautiful and more valuable bird. It pleaded so earnestly that at length the boy liberated it.

He set the trap again and sat down at the foot of the tree to wait. Very soon another bird flew to the tree and was caught in the trap. The boy was astonished at its beauty;

never in his life had he seen such a lovely bird. Regarding it from all sides, he caressed it, and was about to carry it home when the crow flew near him and said: "Take this bird to the Padishah; he will buy it." So the boy put the bird in a cage and transported it to the palace. On seeing the beautiful little creature the Padishah was so pleased that he gave the boy more gold than he knew what to do with. The bird was placed in a golden cage and the

The Crow begged him to set him free

Padishah amused himself with it day and night.

The Padishah had a lala who was envious of the boy's fortune and racked his brains to think of a plan for depriving him of it. One day he went to the Padishah and said: "How beautiful this bird would look in an ivory kiosk!" "But, lala," answered the Padishah, "where could I get sufficient ivory?" "He who brought you the bird can also procure you the ivory," said the crafty lala.

The Padishah sent for the bird catcher and commanded him to procure enough ivory to build a kiosk for the bird. " But, Padishah," protested the youth, "wherever can I get so much ivory?" "That is your affair," answered the King. "I

164

will give you forty days in which to collect it: if it is not here by that time, I will have your head off."

In deep trouble the youth left the monarch's presence. While he was absorbed in thought the crow appeared and asked the cause of his grief. The bird-catcher told the crow what misfortune the little bird had caused him. "Sorrow not," returned the crow, "but go to the Padishah and ask him for forty wagons of wine."

The youth went to the palace and obtained the wine. As he was coming away with it the crow flew up and said: "Near the forest are forty drinking-troughs. All the elephants come there to drink; go and pour the wine into the troughs, and then when all the elephants are lying stupefied on the ground, cut off their tusks and take them to the King."

The youth acted according to the crow's instructions, and took the forty wagons loaded with ivory back to the palace. The King was so delighted with the quantity of tusks that he rewarded the bird-catcher lavishly. The kiosk was soon built and the bird put in. The beautiful creature hopped about joyously in its new home, but it did not sing. "If its master were here," suggested the wily lala," it would have the desire to sing." "Who knows who was its owner and where he can be found?" answered the King sadly. "He who brought you the ivory can surely discover the owner of the bird," said the lala.

So the Padishah called the youth and ordered him to find out the former owner of the bird. "How should I know who was its owner?" said the bird-catcher, "I caught it in the wood." "That is your affair," returned the King. "If you do not find him, you shall be put to death. I will give you forty days to seek him."

The youth went home and wept most bitterly; but the crow appeared and inquired why he sorrowed. The poor youth told his story. "That trifle is not worth so many tears," replied the crow. "Go immediately to the King and request a large ship, large enough to accommodate forty maidens, with a garden and also a very beautiful bath on board." The bird-catcher went to the Padishah and told him what was required for the voyage. The ship was built according to his wish. The youth went aboard, and while he was considering whether he should sail to the right or to the left, the crow once more appeared. "Sail always to the right," he instructed, "and stop not until you come to a high mountain. At the foot of this mountain dwell the forty peris. When they see your ship they will all desire to inspect it. However you must let only the queen come on board, for she is the owner of the little bird. While you are showing her the ship, set sail and stop not again until you have arrived home."

So the youth sailed away in his ship, bore always to the right and stayed not until he reached the mountain. There on the seashore the forty peris were taking a walk, and as soon as they spied the ship they wished to inspect it. The Queen begged the bird-catcher to let them see the interior of the vessel, as they had never seen a ship before. The Queen only, however, was permitted to come aboard, and a canoe was sent to the shore to fetch her. The fairy was delighted with the beautiful ship. She walked the deck, promenaded in the garden, and seeing the bath exclaimed: "As I am here I will also bathe."

So she went into the bath, and while she was therein the ship set sail. By the time the Peri had finished her bath the ship was already far out at sea. Hurrying on deck she saw they were almost out of sight of land, and she broke into loud cries of despair. What would happen to her? Where were they taking her? The youth, endeavouring to console her, told her that she was going to good people and to a royal palace.

Soon they reached the town whence the ship had set out, and the Padishah was told of the vessel's safe arrival. The fairy was conducted to the palace, and when she passed the bird's kiosk it began to sing so ravishingly that every one hearing it was enraptured. The fairy was now more at her ease, and she was completely reassured at meeting the Padishah, who admired her so much that he was unable to take his eyes off her. The marriage of the Padishah to the fairy took place soon afterwards, and the King was now the happiest man in the world. But the lala was bursting with rage.

One day the Queen was taken very ill. The medicine that would cure her illness was at home in her fairy palace, and the lala promptly advised that the bird-catcher should be sent to fetch it. Accordingly he embarked, but when about

The Queen is trapped

to set sail the crow appeared and inquired whither he was bound. The youth replied that the Queen was ill, and that he was going to her fairy palace to fetch the medicine. "You will find the palace on the other side of the mountain," said the crow. "Two lions guard the door. Take this feather with you, and if you stroke their maws with it, they will do you no harm."

The youth accepted the feather and set sail. Casting anchor before the mountain, he soon saw the palace. He went up to the entrance where stood the two lions, and when he stroked their maws with the feather they withdrew. The fairies, seeing the young man, suspected that their Queen was ill, so they gave him the medicine and he returned home again without delay. As he entered the Pen's apartment with the medicine, the crow alighted on his shoulder and thus they both stood before the patient. The Queen had already nearly expired, but the moment she took the medicine she revived. Opening her eyes, and seeing the bird-catcher with the crow upon his shoulder, she addressed the latter and said:

"You hateful bird, have you then no pity for this poor young man that you have caused him so much suffering?"

Then the Queen told her husband that this crow had once been her fairy-servant, whom she had changed into a crow as a punishment for her negligence.

"But now," said she, addressing the bird, "I pardon you, seeing that you still love me."

169

He stroked their jaws with the feather

On this the crow shook itself, and behold a lovely maiden stood before the bird-catcher! in accordance with the Queen's wish the King gave the crow-peri in marriage to the bird-catcher. The false lala was dismissed from his post and the young bird-catcher was made Vezir. Thus they all lived happily ever after.

The Forty Princess

and

The Seven-Headed Dragon

There was once a Padishah who had forty sons, and they spent the whole day in the forest, hunting and snaring birds.

When the youngest had completed his fourteenth year their father thought it was time they were getting married, so he called them together and spoke to them about the matter, "We are willing to marry," said the forty brothers, "but only if we can meet with forty sisters all having the same father and mother." The Padishah therefore sought throughout his dominions for such a family, but in vain: the greatest number of sisters in all the land was thirty-nine. "The fortieth will have to take another," said the Padishah to his sons. But they refused to agree to that, and begged their father to allow them to travel in foreign countries to seek the desired brides. What was the Padishah to do? As he could not dissuade them, he grudgingly granted their request. Before they set out,

171

however, the Padishah said to them: "There are three things which you must bear well in mind. When you reach

a large spring, do not spend the night anywhere near it. Farther on is a hân; do not spend the night there, either. Beyond the hân is a great plain; do not linger there a moment." The sons, promising to remember their father's advice, mounted their steeds and rode away.

Smoking and talking, they wended their forward course, and as evening drew on they came to the spring.

"Now we take not a single step farther," observed the eldest. "We are fatigued and it is night. Besides, what have forty men to fear?"

So they alighted, ate their supper, and lay down to rest. The youngest, the fourteen-year-old brother, kept watch, however. Towards midnight he heard a rustling sound. Cautiously he drew his weapon, and as the sound came nearer he saw a seven-headed dragon. Both beast and youth rushed to attack one another. Three times the dragon wrestled with the youth, but could obtain no advantage over him.

"Now it is my turn," cried the Prince, and with these words he struck the dragon such a powerful blow that six heads fell from his body.

"Strike once more," gasped the dragon. "Not I," returned the youth. The dragon sank to the earth, and behold! one of his heads began to roll, and it rolled and rolled till it reached a well. "Let him who has taken my life, take also my treasure," said the head as it fell down the well.

The youth now took a rope, bound one end to a rock, and with it let himself down the well. At the bottom he found

One of his heads began to roll.

an iron gate. Opening it and entering, he saw a palace even more beautiful than that of his father. In the palace were forty apartments, and in each apartment sat a maiden at an embroidery table, near which immense treasures were piled up.

"Are you a man or a jin?" asked the terror-stricken maidens. "I am a human being," answered the Prince. "I killed the seven-headed dragon and came to this place by following one of his rolling heads." Now the forty maidens rejoiced. They all embraced him and begged him to remain with them. Incidentally they informed him that they were forty sisters whom the dragon had stolen. He had killed their parents, and now they had not a single friend or relation in the wide world.

174

"We are forty brothers," said the Prince, "and seek forty maidens." Then he told them he must ascend to his brothers, but that soon he would come again to fetch them away. He came up from the well and went to the spring, where he lay down and fell asleep.

Early next morning when the forty brothers awoke, they began to laugh at their father's attempt to frighten them about the spring. They set off again and continued their way until evening, when behold! the hân their father had mentioned stood before them. "We go no farther tonight " said the elder Princes. The youngest, however, expressed the opinion that it might be well to follow their father's advice, but the others would not listen to him. They ate their supper, said their prayers, and lay down, but the youngest kept watch as before.

Towards midnight he again heard a noise. With his drawn sword in hand, the young Prince found himself confronting another seven-headed dragon, larger and more frightful than the one he had slain the day before. The dragon straightway attacked the youth, but without effect; then the youth fell on the dragon so furiously that six of his seven heads fell. The monster begged for another blow as a coup de grâce, but the Prince declined. As on the previous occasion one of the heads rolled into a well. The youth followed it and discovered a larger palace and greater treasures. Noting the place, he returned to his brothers, lay down, and fell asleep so soundly after the fatigues of his combat that his brothers had to rouse him next morning.

Mounting their horses again they pursued their journey up hill and down dale until by sunset they had reached a great plain. They ate and drank, and were just going to lie down when suddenly an awful shriek was heard and the mountains seemed to quake. Terror seized every one as they caught sight of a gigantic seven-headed dragon, spitting fire and roaring: "Who has killed my two brothers? Bring him to me that I may slay him!"

The youngest saw plainly that all his brothers were paralysed with fear and unable to do anything. He delivered to them the keys of both wells, telling them to take home the forty maidens and the treasure. He promised that when he had killed the dragon he would follow them. The thirty-nine sprang on their horses and rode away.

Now we will return to the youngest.

The conflict between the Prince and the dragon was a stern one, and they fought a long time without either overcoming the other. When the dragon realized that the struggle was in vain he said to the Prince: "If you will go to the land of Chinimatchin and bring me the Padishah's daughter, I will spare your life." The Prince consented to the condition, for he was too exhausted to continue the combat any longer.

She called him to the window.

Champalak--as the dragon was called--gave the Prince a bridle and instructed him as follows: "Every day a magic horse, Ajgyr, grazes here: Catch him, put this bridle on him, and command him to take you to the land of Chinimatchin."

So the youth took the bridle and waited for the magic horse. The golden-hued steed came flying through the air, and no sooner was the bridle laid upon him than he said: "Command me, little Sultan! Shut your eyes--open your eyes!" and behold there was the youngest Prince in the far-off land of Chinimatchin! He alighted from the horse, took off the bridle, and walked into the city.

Entering an old woman's hut, he asked whether she could find him lodgings. "Willingly," answered the old woman. She offered him a seat, and prepared some coffee. While he was drinking he made inquiries as to the condition of the country.

"A seven-headed dragon," said the old woman, "has fallen violently in love with our Sultan's daughter. For years there has been war on her account and we cannot get rid of the monster." "And the Sultan's daughter?" questioned

177

the Prince. "She inhabits a kiosk in the Padishah's garden," answered the old woman, "and away from it she dares not stir a step."

Next day the Prince went to the Padishah's garden and asked the gardener to take him into his service. He begged so earnestly that at length the man took pity upon him. "you have no other duty but to water the flowers," said the gardener. The Sultan's daughter saw the young man, and she called him to the window, asking him how he came to be in that land. The young man told her that his father was a Padishah, and then he described his fight with Champalak, and how he had promised to bring him the Sultan's daughter. "But fear not," continued the Prince, "my love is much greater than that of the dragon, and if you will come with me, I know how to destroy him."

The maiden had herself fallen in love with the handsome Prince, and moreover wished to escape from her constant imprisonment. Her trust in the Prince was so great that one night they left the kiosk together in secret and repaired to Champalak's plain. On the way they discussed what the maiden might do to discover the dragon's talisman, for through that talisman the Prince meant to destroy the monster.

We may imagine Champalak's joy when he saw the Sultan's daughter before him. "What happiness that you have come! What happiness that you have come!" he repeated again and again, as he caressed the Princess, who was weeping all the time. Days and weeks elapsed, but the

Princess never dried her tears. "If you would at least tell me
what your talisman is," she said one day to the dragon, "perhaps my days would not be quite so wearisome."

"My darling," replied the dragon, "it is guarded in a place impossible of access. In a certain country there is a large palace and whoever gets into it never gets out again." This was all the Prince needed to know. He took his bridle, threw it in the sea, and the golden-hued steed appeared.

"What happiness that you have come said the dragon

"What is your command, little Sultan?"

"To the palace of the dragon's talisman!"

"Shut your eyes--open your eyes!" and there he was at the palace. As the Prince dismounted, the magic horse said to him:"Fasten my bridle to the iron rings at the palace gate. When I neigh once, knock the rings together and the gate will open. The gate is a lion's jaw, and if you can cut it asunder with a single blow of your sword, you are safe. Otherwise your last hour has come."

179

Accordingly the Prince fastened the magic horse to the rings, and when it neighed the gate opened.

The Magic Horse flew after the dove

The Prince struck the gaping jaws of the lion a stout blow and split the creature asunder. This done he cut open its stomach, and took therefrom a cage containing three doves, so beautiful that their equals had never been seen before. Taking one in his hand he stroked its plumage, caressed it, and p-r-rr! it suddenly flew away. If the magic horse had not quickly flown after it, caught it, and wrung its neck, the Prince would never have met his ladylove again.

Now he remounted his magic horse. "Shut your eyes-- open your eyes!" and he found himself once more at Champalak's palace. At the gate the youth killed the other two doves, and as he went in the dragon fell an inert mass to the floor. Seeing the dead doves in the Prince's hand he implored him to let him stroke them once more before he died.

The youth, seized with pity, was about to offer the birds to the dragon when the Sultan's daughter ran in and tore them away. Upon this the dragon perished miserably. "Fortunate it was for you," said the magic horse, "that you did not give him the birds; new life for him was in their touch." As there was no further use for it, the bridle now disappeared, and with it the magic horse.

The Prince and the Sultan's daughter gathered together all the Dragon's treasures and bore them to the land of Chinimatchin.

The Padishah had become quite ill through worrying about the disappearance of his daughter. Search had been made for her throughout the length and breadth of his dominions, but as she could not be found the Padishah had come to the conclusion that she had fallen into the power of the dragon. When the Princess appeared again safe and sound, he gladly gave her in marriage to the Prince, and the wedding was celebrated with great rejoicings. After the honeymoon they set out, with a brilliant retinue of soldiers, for the palace of the Prince's father. The Prince was thought to have died long ago, and his claim to be indeed the Prince would hardly have been accepted, had he not related the story of the three dragons and the forty sisters. His thirty-nine brothers married thirty-nine of the sisters, the fortieth becoming the wife of the Princess of Chinimatchin's brother, and henceforth they all lived in the greatest happiness.

Kamer-taj
The Moon-Horse

There was once a Padishah who one day found a little insect.

The Padishah called his lala and they both examined the tiny creature. What could it be? What could it feed on? Every day an animal was killed for its sustenance, and by thus living it grew and grew until it was as big as a cat. Then they killed it and skinned it, hanging up the skin on the palace gate. The Padishah now issued a proclamation that whoever could guess correctly to what animal the skin belonged should receive the Sultan's daughter in marriage.

A great crowd collected and examined the skin from all sides, but no one was found wise enough to answer the question. The story of the skin spread far and wide until it

183

reached the ears of a Dew. "That is exceedingly fortunate for me," thought he to himself, "I have had nothing to eat for three days; now I shall be able to satisfy myself with the Princess." So he went to the Padishah, told him the name of the creature, and immediately demanded the maiden.

"Woe is me" groaned the Padishah, "how can I give this Dew my only daughter?" He offered him, in ransom for her, as many slaves as he liked, but all in vain! The Dew insisted on having the Sultan's daughter. Therefore the Padishah called the maiden and told her to prepare for the journey, as her kismet was the Dew. All weeping and wailing were fruitless. The maiden put on her clothes, while the Dew waited for her outside the palace.

The Padishah had a horse that drank attar of roses and ate grapes; Kamer-taj, or Moon-horse, was its name. This was the creature on which the Sultan's daughter was to accompany the Dew to his abode. A cavalcade escorted her a portion of the way and then, turning, rode back. Now the maiden offered up a prayer to Allah to deliver her from the fiend.

Suddenly the Moon-horse began to speak: "Lady, fear not! shut both your eyes and hold my mane firmly." Hardly had she shut her eyes when she felt the horse rise with her, and when she opened her eyes again she found herself in the garden of a lovely palace on an island in the midst of the sea.

184

The Dew was very angry at the disappearance of the maid. "Still, never mind!" he said, "I will soon find her," and went his way home alone.

"Lady, fear not!" said the Moonhorse.

Not far from the island a Prince sat in a canoe with his lala. The Prince, seeing on the calm surface of the water the reflection of the golden-hued steed, said to his lala that perhaps someone had arrived at his palace. They rode to the island, got out of the canoe, and entered the garden. Here the youth saw the beautiful Princess, who, however much she essayed to veil her face, could not succeed in hiding from him her loveliness.

"Oh, Peri!" said the Prince, "fear me not; I am not an enemy!" "I am only a Sultan's daughter, a child of man and no Peri," announced the Princess, and told the Prince how she had been delivered from the Dew. The Prince assured her that she could not have come to a better place. His

185

father also was a Padishah; with her permission he would take her to him, and by the grace of Allah he would make her his wife. So they went to the Padishah, the Prince told him of the maiden's adventure, and in the end they were married, merriment and feasting lasting forty days and forty nights.

For a time they lived in undisturbed bliss, but war broke out with a neighbouring kingdom and, in accordance with the custom of that period, the Padishah also must set out for the campaign. Hearing of this the Prince went to his father and asked permission to go to the war. The Padishah was unwilling to consent, saying: "you are young, also you have a wife whom you must not forsake." But the son begged so assiduously that in the end the Padishah agreed to stay at home and let Prince go in his stead.

The Dew discovered that the Prince would be on the battlefield, and he also made the further discovery that during his absence a son and a daughter had been born to him.

At that time Tartars were employed as messengers and carried letters between the Padishah at home and the Prince at the seat of war. One of these messengers was intercepted by the Dew and invited into a coffee house. There the Dew entertained him so long that night came on. The messenger now wished to be off, but was persuaded that it would be better to remain till morning.

The Prince sees the reflection.

At midnight, while he was asleep, the Dew searched his letter-bag and found a letter from the Padishah to the Prince informing the latter that a baby son and daughter had come to the palace during his absence. Tearing up this letter, the Dew wrote another to the effect that a couple of dogs had been born. "Shall we destroy them or keep them till your return?" wrote the Dew in the false letter. This missive he placed in the original envelope, and in the morning the Tartar arose, took his sack of letters, and went into the Prince's camp.

The Dew searched his letter bag

When the Prince had read his father's letter he wrote the following answer: "Shah and father, do not destroy the young dogs, but keep them until I return." This was given to the Tartar, who set out on his return journey.

He was again met by the Dew, who enticed him into a coffeehouse and detained him till next morning. During the night the Dew abstracted the letter and wrote another, which said: "Shah and father, take my wife and her two children and throw them down a precipice, and bind the Moon-horse with a fifty-ton chain."

188

In the evening of the day following the Tartar delivered the letter to the Padishah. When the Princess saw the Tartar she hastened joyfully to the monarch that he might show her her husband's letter. The Padishah, having read it, was astonished and dared not show it to the Princess, so he denied that any letter had arrived. The woman answered: "I have indeed seen the letter with my own eyes; perchance some misfortune has happened to him and you are keeping it from me." Then catching a glimpse of the letter she put forth her hand quickly and took it. Having read it the poor woman wept bitterly. The monarch did his best to comfort her, but she refused to remain longer in the palace. Taking her children she left the city and went forth into the wide world.

Days and weeks passed away and she was without food to appease her hunger or bed on which to rest her tired body, until worn out with fatigue she could go no step farther. "Let not my children die of hunger!" she prayed. Behold! instantly water gushed forth from the earth and flour fell from the skies, and making bread with these she fed her children.

In the meantime the Dew heard of the woman's fate and set out immediately to destroy the children. The Princess saw the Dew coming and in her terrible agony she cried: "Hasten, my Kamer-taj, or I die!" In the far-off land the magic horse heard this cry for help; he strained at his fifty-ton fetters but could not break them. The nearer the Dew came the more the poor Princess's anguish increased. Clasping her children to her breast, she sent up another despairing cry to the Moon-horse. The fettered steed strained still more at his chain, but it was of no avail. The Dew was now quite close upon her, and for the last time the poor mother shrieked with all her remaining strength. Kamer-taj, hearing it, put forth all the force he could muster, broke his chain, and appeared before the Princess. "Fear not, lady!" he said, "shut your eyes and grasp my mane," and immediately they were on the other side of the ocean. Thus the Dew went away hungry once more.

The Moon-horse took the Princess to his own country. He felt that his last hour had now come, and told his beloved mistress that he must die. She implored him not to leave her alone with her children. If he did, who would protect them from the evil designs of the Dew? "Fear not," the horse comforted her, "no evil will befall you here. When I am dead, off my head and set it in the earth. Slit up my stomach, and having done this, lay yourself and your children within it." Saying these words the magic horse breathed his last.

The Princess now cut off his head and stuck it in the ground, then opened his stomach and laid herself and her children in it. Here they fell fast asleep. When she awoke she saw that she was in a beautiful palace; one finer than either her father's or her husband's. She was lying in a lovely bed, and hardly had she risen when slaves appeared with water: one bathed her, others clothed her. The twins lay in a golden cradle, and nurses stood around them, soothing them with sweet songs. At dinnertime, gold and silver dishes appeared laden with delicious food. It was like a dream; but days and weeks passed away, weeks passed into months, and the months into a year, and still the dream--if dream it was--did not come to an end.

Meanwhile the war was over and the Prince hastened home. Seeing nothing of his wife he asked his father what had become of her and her children. The Padishah was astonished at this strange question. The letters were produced, and the Tartar messenger was sent for. Being closely questioned he related the account of his meeting with the Dew on both occasions. They now realized that the Dew had tampered with the messenger and the correspondence. There was no more thought of peace for the Prince until he had discovered his wife. With that intention he set out in the company of his lala.

They wandered on and on unceasingly. Six months had passed already, yet they-continued their way-over hill and down dale, never stopping to rest. One day they reached the foot of a mountain, whence they could see the palace of the Moon-horse. The Prince was entirely exhausted and said to his lala: "Go to that palace and beg a crust of bread and a little water, that we may-continue our journey.

The two children on their wooden horses greeted them

When he reached the palace gate, the lala was met by two little children, who invited him in to rest. Entering, he found the floor of the apartment so beautiful that he hardly dared set his foot upon it. But the children pulled him to the divan and made him sit down while food and drink were set before him. The lala excused himself, saying that outside waited his tired son, to whom he wished to take the refreshment.

"Father Dervish," said the children, "eat first yourself, then you can take food to your son." So the lala ate, drank coffee, and smoked, and while he was preparing to return to the Prince, the children went to tell their mother about their guest.

Looking out of the window, the Princess recognised the Prince her husband. She took food with her own hands, and putting it in golden vessels sent it out by the lala. On receiving it the Prince was struck with the richness of the service. He lifted the cover of one of the dishes, set it on the ground, and it rolled back to the palace of its own accord. The same happened with the other dishes, and when the last had disappeared, a slave came to invite the stranger to take coffee in the palace.

While this was happening the Princess gave each of her children a wooden horse, and sent them to the gate to receive the guests. "When the dervish comes with his son," said their mother, "take them to such and such an apartment." The dervish and his son came up, the two children on their wooden horses greeted them with a salaam and escorted them to their apartments. Again the

Princess took dishes of food and said to the children: "Take these to our guests and press them to eat. If they say they have already had sufficient and ask you to partake of the food, answer that you also are satisfied, but perhaps your horses are hungry, and put them to the table. They will then probably ask, how can wooden horses eat? And you must reply" (here she whispered something into the children's ears).

The children did as their mother had commanded them. The food was so delicious that the guests tried to eat a second time, but becoming satisfied very soon, they asked: "Will you not eat also, children?" "We cannot eat," answered the children, "but perhaps our horses are hungry," so saying they drew them up to the table. "Children," remonstrated the Prince, "wooden horses cannot eat." "That you seem to know," answered the children, "but apparently you do not know that it is impossible for little dogs to become human children such as we are." The Prince sprang up with a cry of joy, kissed and embraced both his children. His wife entering at the moment, he humbly begged her pardon for the suffering she had experienced. They related to each other all that had befallen them during the time of their separation, and their joy knew no bounds. Now the Princess and her children prepared to accompany the Prince back to his own kingdom. After they had gone some distance, they turned to take a farewell look at the palace, and lo! the windswept over the place as though no building had ever been there.

The Dew was lurking on the wayside, but the Prince caught him and killed him, and after that they arrived home without further adventure. Soon afterwards the old Padishah died, and the Prince became chief of the land.

Three apples have fallen from the sky. One belongs to the storyteller, the second to the listener, the third to me.

The Bird of Sorrow

In very remote times there lived a Padishah whose daughter was so much attached to her governess that she scarcely ever left her side.

One day, seeing the latter deep in thought, the Princess asked: "Of what are you thinking?" "I have sorrow," answered the governess. "What is sorrow?" questioned the Padishah's daughter; "let me also have it." "It is well," said the woman, and went to the tscharschi, where she bought a Bird of Sorrow in a cage. She presented it to the maiden, who was so delighted that she amused herself day and night with the creature.

Some time afterwards the Sultan's daughter, attended by her slaves, paid a visit to the Zoo.

195

She took with her the bird in its cage, which she hung upon the branch of a tree. Suddenly the bird commenced to speak. "Set me free a little while, Sultana," it pleaded, "that I may play with the other birds. I will come back again." The Princess accordingly set her favourite at liberty.

A few hours later, while the Princess was sauntering idly about the park, the bird returned, seized its mistress and flew off with her to the top of a high mountain. "Behold! this is sorrow," said the bird; "I will prepare more of it for you!" Saying this he flew away. The Princess, now hungry and thirsty, wandered about until she met a herdsman, with whom she exchanged raiment, so that she might disguise herself as a man for her better protection. After long wandering she came to a village where, finding a coffeehouse, she entered, and besought the proprietor to engage her as his assistant. The former, regarding her as a young man in need of employment, accordingly engaged her, and towards evening went home, leaving her in charge of the house. Having closed the shop, the girl lay down to sleep. At midnight, how. ever, the Bird of Sorrow appeared, broke all the cups and saucers and nargiles in the place, woke the maiden from her sleep, and thus addressed her: "Behold! this is sorrow; I will prepare more of it for you!" Having thus spoken he flew away as before. All night long the poor girl lay thinking what she should say to her master on the morrow. When morning came the proprietor returned, and seeing the woeful damage done, beat his assistant severely and drove her away.

Her eyes filled with bitter tears, she set out once more, and ere many hours arrived at a tailor's shop. As preparations were being made for the great religious feast of Bairam, the tailor was busy in executing orders for the serai. He was therefore in need of an extra hand, and took the youth, as he supposed the girl to be, into his service. After a day or two the tailor went away, leaving the maiden alone in the house. When evening came she closed the shop and retired to rest. At midnight came the bird again, and tore to shreds all the clothes on the premises, and waking up the girl, said: "Behold! this is sorrow;

The Master beat her soundly

I will prepare still more of it for you!" and flew off again. Next morning brought the master, who seeing the clothing all torn up, called his assistant to account. As the girl answered nothing, the master beat her soundly and sent her away.

Weeping bitterly she once more set forth, and by and by came to a fringe-maker's, where she was taken in. Being again left alone, she fell asleep. The Bird of Sorrow reappeared, tore up the fringes, woke the girl, made his customary speech, and flew away as on previous occasions.

197

When the master returned next morning and saw the mischief, he beat his assistant more cruelly than ever, and dismissed her. Overwhelmed with grief, the unhappy maiden again took her lonely way. Feeling sure that the Bird of Sorrow would give her no peace, she went into a mountain pass, where she lived in seclusion for many days, suffering the pangs of hunger and thirst, and in constant fear of the wild beasts that haunted the region. Her nights were spent in the leafy branches of a tree.

One day the son of a Padishah, when out hunting, espied the girl in the tree. Mistaking her for a bird, he shot an arrow at her, but it merely struck one of the branches. On approaching the tree to reclaim his arrow, the Shahzada observed that what he had supposed to be a bird appeared to be a man. "Are you an in or a jin?" he called out. "Neither in nor jin," was the response, "but a human creature like yourself." Where upon the Prince permitted her to descend from the tree, and took the seeming herdsman to the palace. Here, after bathing, she resumed the garments of a maiden. Then the royal youth saw that she was beautiful as the moon at the full, and straightway fell violently in love with her. Without delay he besought his father, the Padishah, to consent to his wedding with her. The Sultan commanded the maiden to be brought into his presence, and as he gazed upon her wonderful beauty, her loveliness and grace won his heart. The betrothal took place forthwith; and after a period of festivity lasting forty days and forty nights the marriage was celebrated. In due time a little daughter was born to the princely pair, a child gentle and fair to look upon, and giving early promise of becoming as lovely as its mother.

One midnight came the bird, stole the babe, and besmeared the mother's lips with blood. Then it woke the Princess, and said: "Behold, I am taking away your child; and still more sorrow will I prepare for you!" So saying the bird flew off. In the morning the Prince missed his little

daughter, and observed that his wife's lips were blood-stained. Going quickly to his father, the Padishah, he related the ominous occurrence.

"From the mountain - did you bring the woman," said the Padishah; "she is forsooth a daughter of the mountain and eats human flesh; there. fore I counsel

The bird stole the baby

you to send her away!" But the devoted Prince pleaded for his young wife and prevailed over his father.

Sometime later another daughter was born to them, which also the bird stole away under similar circumstances. This time the Padishah commanded that the mother should be put to death, though yielding at length to the earnest entreaties of his son he grudgingly consented to pardon her.

Time passed away, and eventually a son was born. The Prince, fearing that if this child also should disappear his beloved wife would surely be put to death, determined to lie awake at night and keep watch and ward over his loved ones. Tired nature, however, insisted on her toll and the Prince slept.

Meanwhile the bird returned, stole the babe, besmeared the Princess's lips with blood as before, and flew away. When the poor mother awoke and discovered her terrible loss, she wept bitterly; and when the Prince also awoke and found the child missing and his wife's mouth and nose dripping with blood, he hastened to his father with the awful intelligence. The Padishah, in a violent rage, again condemned the woman to death. The executioners were summoned; they bound her hands behind her and led her forth to execution. But so smitten were they with her ravishing beauty, and so stricken with pity for her sore affliction, that they said to her:

"We cannot find it in our hearts to kill you. Go where you will, only return not again to the palace."

The poor ill-fated woman again sought her mountain refuge, brooding over her sad lot; until one day the bird once more appeared, seized her and carried her off to the garden of a grand palace.

Setting down his burden, the bird shook himself, and lo! he was suddenly transformed into a handsome youth. Taking her by the hand, he led the disconsolate woman upstairs into the palace. Here a wonderful sight met her eyes. Attended by many servants, three beautiful children, all radiant and smiling, approached her. As her astonished gaze fell upon them, her eyes filled with tears of joy and her heart melted with tenderness.

Escorting the now happy and wondering Princess into a stately apartment, richly carpeted and furnished with all the art of the luxurious Orient, the youth thus addressed her: "Sultana, though I afflicted you with much grief and sorrow, robbed you of your precious children, and nearly brought you to an ignominious death, yet have you patiently borne it all and not betrayed me. In reward I have built for you this palace, in which I now restore to you your loved ones. Behold your children! Henceforth, Sultana, I am your slave." The Princess hastened with winged feet to her long-lost children, embraced them, pressed them to her bosom, and covered them with kisses.

How fared it with the Prince?

Sorrowing for his children and for his beloved wife, whom he believed to have been put to death, he grew morose and melancholy, passing the time with his old opium smoker, who beguiled the hours with indifferent stories.

One day, having no more opium, the old man requested the Prince's permission to go to the tscharschi in order to buy more. On his way thither he saw something he had never before beheld: a large and magnificent serail! "It is remarkable," thought the old fellow; "I frequent this street daily, yet have I not seen this palace before. When can it have been built? I must inspect it."

The bird of sorrow broke all the cups and saucers

The Sultana, whose palace it was, happened to be at one of the windows and caught sight of her husband's opium smoker. The slave--formerly her Bird of Sorrow--being in attendance, he respectfully suggested: "What say you, lady, to playing a trick on the Prince's old storyteller?" At these words he threw a magic rose at the feet of the greybeard. The latter picked it up, inhaled its exquisite perfume, and muttered to himself: "If your rose is so beautiful, how must it be with yourself!" So instead of returning home he entered the palace.

The Opium smoker picked up the rose

The Prince in the meantime grew concerned over the prolonged absence of the old man and sent his steward to look for him. The steward, arriving before the palace, the door of which had been left open intentionally by the slave, went in to look round. A number of female slaves received him and led the way up the stairs. At the top he was handed over to the magician slave, who requested him to remove his outer robe and precede him. The robe was taken off without difficulty, but the steward was astonished to find that in spite of all his efforts he was quite unable to remove his fez. At this the magician ordered him to be cast out "for refusing to take

203

off his fez." The steward was therefore forcibly ejected. But no sooner was he outside than--wonderful to relate--the fez fell from his head of its own accord! On his way home he overtook the old opium smoker. Meanwhile the Shahzada was troubled at the non-return of his steward and dispatched his treasurer after him. The treasurer met both on the road and demanded to know what had befallen them.

The old opium smoker answered somewhat enigmatically: "If a rose be thrown from that palace, take care not to smell it, or the consequences be on your own head." And the steward warned him no less mysteriously: "When you enter that palace, be sure to leave your fez at the door!"

The treasurer considered the behaviour of both his companions somewhat peculiar, but taking their warning lightly he entered the palace. Inside he was ordered to don a dressing-gown before proceeding upstairs. Commencing to undress for the purpose, he discovered that his schalwar refused to part company with his person. Consequently he was unceremoniously thrown out of the palace. Hardly, however, was he outside than his schalwar came off by itself!

The Prince becoming unable longer to endure the unaccountable absence of his servants, set out himself to discover, if possible, what had happened to them. On the way he met all three, who counselled him in an excited manner: "If a rose be thrown to you from the palace, be careful not to smell it; when you enter, be sure to leave your fez at the door; and before you arrive there, take off your schalwar and enter without it!"

204

The Prince was exceedingly puzzled at such extraordinary advice, yet he straightway went to the serail and disappeared from sight within the portal. Unlike his servants, the Prince was received with every mark of honour and respect, and conducted to a noble hall. Here a lady of remarkable beauty, surrounded by three lovely children, awaited him.

The lady gave to her eldest child a stool, to the second a towel, and to the youngest a tray; into the tray she put a bowl, into the bowl a pear, and beside it a spoon. The eldest set the stool on the floor, the second offered the towel to the Prince, while the youngest sat himself down in the bowl. The Prince then inquired of the children: "How long has it been the custom to eat pears with a spoon?" "Since human beings have eaten human flesh," they answered in chorus. The chord of memory was struck; the past flashed before the mind's eye of the Prince. Here the magician appeared and cried: "Oh Prince, behold thy Sultana! Behold also thy children!" Whereat all--father, mother, and children--fell on each other's necks weeping for joy.

The magician continued: "My Shahzada, I am your slave; if, however, you deign to give me my liberty, I will hasten to my own parents." Overflowing with gratitude for their reunion, they immediately set the magician slave free and prepared a new festival, happy in the knowledge that henceforth they would never be parted from each other.

Ignacz Kúnos

The Enchanted Pomegranate Branch and the Beauty

There was once a Padishah who, being very dull at home, resolved to make a journey with his Vezir. Before setting out, however, he called his Vezir and said to him: "In order that our departure may be unknown, find a man bearing a resemblance to me and set him on the throne."

The Vezir asked how such a man should be found. " Let us wander about the town for a few days," said the Padishah, " and we shall find one." Disguising themselves, they proceeded to carry the proposal into effect.

Entering an inn for refreshment, they saw there a drunken fellow who was the very image of the Padishah.

Accordingly they took the landlord aside and told him to let the man drink until he was quite dazed, and when night came to throw him out into the street. This was done, and at midnight the Padishah sent the Vezir to bring the man secretly in a basket to the palace. There the fellow was washed, clothed in royal vestments, and laid in the Padishah's own bed. Now everything was ready for the monarch and his Vezir to commence their journey.

When the drunken fellow awoke next morning he saw that he was in the King's palace. "What has befallen me?" he asked himself. "Perhaps I am dreaming, or perhaps I am dead and in heaven." After these reflections he clapped his hands, and immediately slaves brought him a washbasin and a can of water. Having washed, he drank coffee, and lighted his chibouque. "I must have become Padishah," he mused. As it was Friday the servants begged him to be pleased to say where the selamlik should be held. In the quarter where he used to live was a djami, so he decided that the selamlik should be held there, and all hurried away to make the necessary preparations.

A fortnight had elapsed since the drunkard had left his own home, and when his wife heard that the Padishah was coming to the local djami she prepared a petition, which she handed to him as he was leaving the mosque after the selamlik. The Padishah took the petition and read as follows: "Oh Padishah! I have a husband who does nothing but drink night and day. He has not been home now for fifteen days, nor sent me any money for provisions, so that we are dying of hunger." The Padishah immediately gave orders that the woman's dwelling should be pulled down and rebuilt on a better plan, and also that a monthly pension of five hundred piastres should be paid to her. This was done.

The new Padishah had three enemies: the innkeeper who threw him out into the street when he was drunk, the butcher who had beaten him because he could not pay for the meat he had bought on credit, and a restaurant-keeper who would give him no food. He gave orders that these should be beheaded, and this was done.

In the meantime the real Padishah and his Vezir had already travelled a considerable distance. One day they came to a valley, where they decided to stop and rest awhile. In the stream that flowed through the valley they found an apple, which they ate. Now the Padishah recollected that when setting out he had taken an oath to do nothing that was forbidden while on his journey. This gave him uneasiness, since he had no means of knowing whether it was permitted to eat the apple or not. " There is nothing for it," said the Padishah, " but to go to the owner and obtain permission now."

As they went along they came across a farmer ploughing. Greeting him, they told him about the apple, and when the story was finished, the farmer showed them an orchard with apple-trees from one of which had fallen the apple they had eaten. He also pointed out the house in which lived the owner of the orchard, and to this building the Padishah and his Vezir went immediately. They knocked at the door, which was opened by an old woman,

208

and to her also they related the incident of the apple. The old woman, saying that the apple-trees belonged to her daughter, went to consult her about the matter. The daughter sent back a message that if the man would marry her, permission to eat the apple was granted. The Padishah considered the question and finally agreed to make the maiden his wife.

When she heard this the old woman said: "Then I must tell you that my daughter's legs and arms are crooked, she is bald-headed, and altogether so ugly that no man can bear the sight of her." "Never mind," replied the Padishah, "I will fulfil my promise." He instructed his Vezir to arrange for the wedding that very day, as next morning they must be off again. They now went to a neighbouring hân to prepare for the marriage.

As soon as the maiden was presented to him, the Padishah was wonderstruck. " My Sultana," exclaimed he, "your mother said you were ugly; while, behold, you are the loveliest creature in the world!" The maiden said that her mother was accustomed always to speak of her in that fashion.

The wedding took place, and next day the Vezir reminded the Padishah that they must proceed. The monarch, however, replied that he had made up his mind to remain at the hân four or five days longer. As a matter of fact, he remained forty days, and on the forty-first he said to his wife: "My Sultana, I cannot remain here longer; I must go. If you should have a son, when he is grown up bind this amulet to his arm, send him into such and such a country,

209

and tell him to inquire for Ogursuz and Hajyrsyz." These were the names the Padishah and his Vezir had decided to use upon their travels.

They mounted their horses and rode away. Soon they met the farmer, of whom they took leave, stopping not again until they reached home. Having arrived at the palace, the first thing to do was to get rid of the false Padishah. Accordingly at midnight, whilst he slept, they put him into a basket and set him down by the

The innkeeper kicked him unceremoniously away

inn from which he had been fetched some months before. When the man awoke he found himself lying in the street, "I must be dreaming," he said, and closed his eyes again. Presently he clapped his hands, whereupon the new innkeeper appeared, asking: "Who is there?" The drunkard commanded him to cease jesting or he would be hanged immediately.

"Open the door; I am the Padishah," he called loudly. The landlord opened the door, and seeing the drunkard kicked him unceremoniously away. The latter in a towering rage exclaimed:

"You rascal; I am the Padishah, and I will certainly hang you for this." For answer the innkeeper took a stick and belaboured the self styled Padishah until he was insensible, after which he was taken to the madhouse.

Meanwhile the Padishah observed to his Vezir:

"Oh, lala, we brought the man to the palace, and after he had served our purpose we cast him away. Go now and see what has become of him." The Vezir went accordingly to the innkeeper and learned that the drunken fellow had gone mad and been taken to the lunatic asylum. Going next to the lunatic asylum the Vezir heard the man shouting continually that he was the Padishah, and had been nearly beaten to death. The Vezir told him he must not say he was the Padishah, or it would be the worse for him. Seeing the force of this, the man went to the overseer of the establishment and said: "Sir, I am a drunkard and not the Padishah." After this confession he was regarded as no longer insane, and accordingly set at liberty.

His first thought was to go home, but hardly had his wife set eyes on him than she cried:

"Get out of my sight, you graceless fellow. Where have you been all this time? You have heard no doubt that the Padishah has built me a new house and granted me a pension, and so now you come to share it!" The woman would not have let him in, but the Vezir happened to be passing and heard the angry altercation. Going up to her he said: "Let thy husband in, or all shall be taken from thee again." Recognising the Vezir, the woman's courage failed her and she let her husband into the house.

211

Leaving this worthy couple in peace, we will now return to the proprietress of the orchard. In due time a son was born to her. When he grew up his mother, remembering the Padishah's instructions, called her son to her. "Your father," she said, "left you this amulet, saying that when grown up you were to go to his country and inquire for Ogursuz and Hajyrsyz." Hearing this the youth took the amulet and prepared for the journey.

On the way he met the farmer, with whom he rested a little. During their conversation the farmer told the youth that Ogursuz was his friend, and he counselled him not to go alone. The boy consented to take the farmer's son with him, and the two set out again. By and by they came to a well, and being overcome with thirst the farmer's son said to the youth: "I will first let you down the well that you may drink; afterwards you shall let me down." The Shahzada accordingly was lowered into the well, but when he had quenched his thirst and was ready to return to the top, the farmer's son called down to him: "Swear you will say that I am the son of Ogursuz and that you are the son of the farmer, also promise never to reveal the truth, or you shall remain where you are." As he was helpless, the Shahzada swore accordingly and was drawn to the surface.

They proceeded farther and in a few weeks arrived at the capital of the Padishah's kingdom. They wandered about the town inquiring for Ogursuz and Hajyrsyz, and when this came to the knowledge of the Padishah he ordered both boys to be brought before him. They were taken to the palace, and when the King asked which was his son, the Shahzada pointed to the other and named himself as the son of the farmer. So the one was taken into the palace as a prince, and the other given employment in the court.

Once in a dream the false Prince saw a dervish who presented to him the Princess Beautiful and gave him to drink of the chalice of love. From that time he was a changed man. Neither eating nor drinking, sleep nor rest, contented him; he became pale and weak. Physicians and hodjas, one after the other, were called in, but none did him any good; they did not understand his illness, and therefore could prescribe no remedy.

One day the false Prince said to the Padishah: "My father, physicians and hodjas cannot help me. Love for the Princess Beautiful is my malady." The King was frightened at the youth's strange words and feared for his reason. "You must not think of her; it is dangerous," said the monarch; "her love would bring only death." But the young man continued to get thinner and paler and had no joy in life. The Padishah asked him continually whether he desired anything, and the answer was invariably the same: "The Princess Beautiful." The King felt that his son would surely die if he refused to let him go away, and that he would be the cause of his death. So trusting that the righteous Allah would have mercy upon him, he was about to consent to his son's departure, when the false Prince said: "I do not wish to go myself; let us send the farmer's son to fetch the maiden for me." The Padishah immediately sent for the farmer's son, and commissioned him to go in quest of the Princess Beautiful and bring her home to be the bride of the Shahzada.

On the following day the youth set off over hill and down dale, across plains and through ravines, in quest of the Princess Beautiful. After some time he came to the seashore, where he saw a little fish floundering on the sand. The creature implored him to cast it into the water, and he consented; but first the fish offered him three of its scales, saying: "When in trouble burn one of these scales." Accepting them gratefully, the youth threw the fish back into the sea and went his way.

He saw a little fish
floundering on the sand

Coming to a great plain he met an ant, who begged his aid, as it was going to a wedding and would be too late to join its companions. The young man took up the ant and carried it to its companions. Before taking leave of its helper, the insect offered him a piece of its wing, saying: "When in trouble burn this piece of my wing."

Dispirited and weary, the reputed farmer's son at length reached a thick forest, where he saw a small bird struggling with a large snake. The bird besought the aid of the youth, who promptly struck the snake with his sword and cut it in two. In reward the bird gave him three of her feathers, saying: "When in trouble burn one of these."

Once more he took his pilgrim-staff and went o'er mountain and sea until he came to a large city. He was now in the kingdom of the father of Princess Beautiful. Going directly to the palace, he begged in the name of Allah that the Padishah would give him his daughter in marriage. "First you must accomplish three tasks," said the Padishah, "and then you may speak to my daughter." The monarch then took a ring, cast it into the sea, and told the Prince to bring it back again in three days or his life would be forfeit.

The Prince thought deeply, and recollecting the three fish-scales he burnt one of them. Immediately the little fish appeared and said: "What is your command, my Sultan?" "The ring of Princess Beautiful has fallen into the sea; fetch it to me," replied the Prince. The fish went after the ring, but could not find it; down it went a second time, without success; diving a third time, it went right down, down to the bottom of the seventh sea and brought up a fish. The Prince slit its stomach and found the ring inside. He gave it back to the Padishah, who handed it to his daughter. In the neighbourhood of the palace was a cave, filled with a mixture of ashes and millet. "Your second task," said the Padishah, "is to separate the ashes from the millet." The Prince went to the cave and burnt the ant's wing, whereupon all the ants in the world appeared and set about the work. The task was thus finished that very day, and in the evening the Padishah came and satisfied himself that not a grain had been overlooked.

"One other task remains to be done," said the Padishah, "and then I will take you to my daughter." Calling a female slave to him, the King split her head open and said to the youth: "Thus shall your own head be split if you cannot restore her to life." The youth left the palace wondering whether the bird's feather would help him. He burnt one, and straightway the little bird appeared and awaited his commands. With a heavy heart the Prince related the difficult task that had been set him. Now the bird belonged to the Peris, and flying up in the air out of sight it soon reappeared with a vessel of water. "Here," said the bird, "is some water of Paradise which will restore the dead to life." Taking it to the palace the Prince sprinkled some over the corpse, and the maiden arose immediately as though just awakened from sleep. The Princess Beautiful was informed of the youth's exploits, and she prepared herself to receive him. The maiden resided in a small marble kiosk, before which a golden reservoir, and into this water poured from four sides. In the court was a magnificent garden, filled with trees, flowers, and singing-birds.

The Princess appeared.

When the Prince saw all this it seemed to him as though he were at the gate of Paradise. Suddenly the door of the kiosk opened, and the garden was suffused with an effulgent light that quite dazzled the Prince. The Princess now appeared in all her radiant beauty. She approached the Prince to address him, but no sooner did she look at him than she fell in a swoon. She was carried to the kiosk, the youth following, and when she came to herself she said: "Oh, Prince, you are the son of Shah Suleiman, and you can aid me. In the garden of the Reh-Dew sings a pomegranate branch; if you will bring it to me I am yours eternally!"

The youth went far away to fulfil the Princess's behest. For a month he wandered up hill and down dale. "Oh, Allah, Creator of all things," he prayed," show me the right way." Presently he reached the foot of a mountain. Here he heard a terrible noise, as though the Judgment Day had come; the rocks and mountains trembled, and pitch darkness fell. As the youth went bravely forward the noise increased and became more terrifying, while he was enveloped in a whirlwind of dust and smoke. He could not tell whether he was on the right road, but he knew that a six months' journey should bring him to the garden of the Reh-Dew and that the awful noise was created by the talismans of the Dew.

Continuing his onward way, the little garden at length came in view. At the gate were the shrieking talismans and also the guard. The Prince went to him and told him what he wanted. "Why were you not terrified by the great noise?" asked the guard in astonishment.

"All the talismans were aroused on your account; they alarmed even me." The Prince enquired about the pomegranate branch. "It is a difficult matter to procure it," said the guard gravely; "but if you are not afraid you may perchance succeed. At the end of a three months' journey you will arrive at another place similar to this, with other talismans; there you will

The old woman was about ninety years old

find another garden, the guardian of which is my mother. But go not near her; wait until she comes to you. Give her my greeting, but do not relate your business until she questions you." The youth now took the road pointed out to him, and after journeying for three months he heard an awe-inspiring sound which it would be impossible to describe. Here was the large garden of the Reh-Dew, and the noise proceeded from his talismans. The youth hid himself behind a rock, and presently saw a human form which proved to be that of an old woman about ninety years old. Her hair was snow-white, her eyelids red, her eyebrows like two arrows, her eyes gleamed fire, her fingernails were two yards long; and leaning on a staff she sniffed the air, sneezed at every step, and her knees knocked together. Such was the guardian of the large garden. Coming up to the youth she demanded to know what he was doing there. The Prince gave her greeting from her son. "The good-for-nothing fellow!" she wheezed; "So you have met him, eh? Did my miserable son think I should have mercy on you that he sent you to me? I'll soon make an end of you." So saying she seized the youth and shook him fiercely.

The Creature was making off with him

The Prince knew not what had happened; he saw only that he was on the back of something which had neither eyes nor ears, and was shrivelled up like a toad. This creature was making off with him, taking gigantic strides and springing overseas at a single bound. Suddenly the hideous thing set him down, and said: "Whatever you hear, whatever you see, be careful not to speak thereof, or you are lost!" In a moment it was gone,

As in a dream the Prince now saw a garden of endless extent, with rippling streams and waterfalls, and trees, flowers, and fruits, whose like could be found nowhere in the world. All around was the sound of singing-birds as though the air itself were song. Taking a glance around the youth entered the garden, and heard a heartrending sound as of weeping. Remembering the pomegranate branch he began to seek it. In the midst of the garden was a small conservatory, and in this hung, like lamps, a number of pomegranates. He plucked a branch, and at once a fearful cry was heard: "A mortal is taking our lives! A mortal is killing us!" Seized with dread, the youth fled from the garden.

"Quick! Run!" shouted the nameless thing waiting at the gate. He jumped on its back, and with one bound he was on the other side of the sea. Now for the first time the youth looked at the pomegranate branch. He saw there were fifty pomegranates thereon, each of which sang a different song, as though all the music of the world were brought together there. Now he met the old woman who was ninety years old.

"Take good care of the pomegranate branch," said the old woman; "never let it out of your sight. If you can listen to it throughout your wedding day the pomegranates will love you; you need fear nothing, for they will protect you in any distress."

Taking leave of the mother the Prince went to her son, who exhorted him to bear the old woman's advice well in mind. Then the youth made the best of his way to the Princess Beautiful.

The maiden awaited him anxiously, for she loved the Prince so fondly that her days were filled with fear on his behalf lest any misfortune might befall him. Suddenly the sound of music was heard, the different melodies of the fifty pomegranates. The maiden hastened to meet the

221

Prince, and the pomegranate branch chanted the union of their two hearts in such exquisite strains that they seemed to be lifted up from this earth to the Paradise of Allah. Their wedding-feast lasted forty days and forty nights, and all the time they listened to the singing of the pomegranates. When the feast was ended the Prince said: "Like yourself, I have a father and mother. We have already celebrated our marriage here; we will now go to my parents and celebrate it there also." Accordingly they set out on the following day.

When they arrived at the end of their journey the youth went to the Padishah and reported that he had succeeded in bringing the Princess Beautiful with him. The King praised him for his bravery and skill, gave him a valuable present, and made preparations for the Princess's marriage to the false Shahzada. When the maiden saw that it was intended to unite her to the false Prince, she struck him in the face. He ran to the Padishah to complain, and the monarch, suspecting there was more in the matter than appeared on the surface, went to the maiden and begged her to explain such conduct.

The Princess implored the Padishah not to allow the marriage to take place until the farmer's son had been put to death. Accordingly the King ordered the youth to be brought before him, and he was beheaded in his presence. Immediately the Princess took Paradise water, sprinkled the body of the youth therewith, and at once he arose to new life.

"Now," said the Princess, "you have died and risen again; thus you are released from your oath, and can tell all that has befallen you." On this the youth related how, after leaving his mother, he met with the farmer's son, He spoke of the incident at the well, and of everything connected with his perilous quest for the Princess. He also established his identity by showing the amulet he had received from his mother.

Being convinced that the youth was truly his son, the Padishah embraced and kissed him repeatedly. The impostor was executed, and the Prince's mother was brought to the palace in time for the wedding of her son with the Princess Beautiful.

The Majic Hair-Pins

There was once a Padishah whose daughter was so beautiful that her loveliness was without equal in the world.

Now the Padishah's wife had an Arab slave whom she kept locked up in a room, and to whom every day she put the following questions: "Is the moon beautiful? Am I beautiful? Are you beautiful?" "Everything and everybody is beautiful," was invariably the answer. After this entertaining dialogue the Sultana would lock the door again and go away.

One day, as the Padishah's daughter, by name Nar-tanesi or little Pomegranate, was making a tour of the serai, the Arab caught a glimpse of her and immediately fell in love with her. Thus on the next day the Arab modified his usual answer as follows: "The moon is beautiful, you are beautiful, I am beautiful, but Nar-tanesi is the most beautiful of all."

224

The Sultana was exceedingly angry. Now that the Arab had seen her daughter, probably he would no longer admire the mother. So she went to the Princess and proposed that they should take a walk together. During the promenade they came to a meadow, where the maiden, being fatigued, lay down in the shade of a tree. When she fell asleep the mother left her there and hastened back to the palace.

When the Princess awoke and could not see her mother she began to weep, running hither and thither in fear, seeking her mother everywhere. It was of no avail, however, and soon her cries of despair echoed through wood and field.

Three brothers were by chance hunting in the forest, and came upon the distressed maiden. When she saw them she was still more afraid, and implored their grace and protection, requesting them to accept her as a sister. Overcome with pity the three hunters agreed to be her brothers, and she accompanied them to their home.

Henceforth the three youths went hunting every day, and when they brought home the game, the Princess prepared it for eating. Thus the days passed merrily away.

But the news of the maiden's extraordinary loveliness spread far and wide. The story was told of her discovery by the three brothers in the forest, and how they had taken her home to be their sister. This came to the ears of the Sultana, her mother, who was enraged to find her daughter still living. She thought the girl had long ago been torn to pieces and devoured by wild beasts.

She went accordingly to a witch and asked what she should do further to get rid of her daughter. The witch gave the Sultana two magic hairpins, saying that if she stuck them in the Princess's head the girl would surely die. The woman took the hairpins, and disguised herself as a poor beggar by means of an old feredje. Packing various articles in a bundle, she went to the maiden.

Whenever the three brothers were away hunting, the Princess kept the door locked; and when the woman knocked she made no answer. "Oh, my child," cried the woman, " why do you not open the door? I have come all the way from Anatolia with presents for my sons; at least receive them from me." Then the maiden answered through a crack in the door: "The door is locked." "My daughter," returned the woman, "having heard that you are their sister, I have brought you also a present of some hair pins; hold your head close to the keyhole that I may stick them in." Suspecting no evil the girl put her head to the key. hole. The woman stuck the pins into the Princess's head, and she fell down dead immediately. Having thus accomplished her revenge, the Sultana went straight back to the serai.

When towards evening the brothers returned from hunting and entered the house, they saw the dead body of the maiden lying by the door. They raised loud lamentation and wrung their hands in despair. When their grief was somewhat calmed they began to prepare for the funeral. Laying their sister in a golden casket, they took it up a hill and hung it between two trees.

It came to pass soon after this that the son of a Padishah went hunting and saw the golden casket hanging from the

The woman stuck the pins into the Princess' head

trees. Taking it down he opened it, and when he saw the lovely maiden lying within he fell deeply in love with her. The casket was carried to his home and put into his own apartment, and whenever he went out he took care to lock the door. The Prince spent his days in hunting, and the nights in looking at and sighing over the dead maiden.

In the meantime the Padishah intended to take part in a war that had broken out; but the Vezir dissuaded him, advising him to send his son the Shahzada instead. Therefore the King called his son and ordered him to go to the battlefield. The youth returned to his apartment, opened the casket and took a last fond look at the serene countenance of the maiden. He then locked up the room, and ordering that none should enter it during his absence, he departed for the war.

We have omitted to state that the Shahzada was betrothed. The Princess he was going to marry chanced to hear of the Shahzada's locked apartment, and she determined to discover what secret he hid therein. It availed nothing to tell her that the Prince had forbidden anyone to enter it during his absence. She shook the door with such force that it opened, and she entered the room. Seeing the dead girl in the casket, she exclaimed in great irritation: "Who is this maiden that the Prince guards day and night!" Looking at her more closely she saw the hairpins sticking in her head. Putting forth her hand she drew them out; and hardly had she done so than the maiden was transformed into a bird and flew away.

A long time passed; the war was over, and the Shahzada came home again. Hastening to his apartment, he found to his sorrow and dismay that the casket was open and empty. In great wrath he asked his slave: "Who has dared to enter my apartment?" "The Princess who is to be your bride," was the reply. "What can she have done to her!" groaned the Prince, and from that time he became ill and grew worse every day.

Now that the war was ended the Padishah began to make preparations for his son's marriage, and in due time the wedding took place.

Every morning the bird came to the palace garden, and sitting on a tree said to the gardener, "How is my

Shahzada?" "He sleeps," was the answer. "May he sleep and enjoy good health," said the bird, "and may the tree, on which I sit, wither!" This dialogue continued daily for several days, and every day a tree withered. The gardener called the attention of the Shahzada to the matter, observing that if the thing went on much longer there would not be a tree alive in the whole garden. The Prince's curiosity being excited he set a trap to catch the bird. The bird being duly caught, the Prince put it in a golden cage and took a delight in regarding its wonderful plumage.

The woman was startled

When first the Prince's wife saw the bird she recognised it as the maiden of the casket, and made up her mind to destroy it as soon as possible. Her opportunity came when one day the Shahzada had to go on a journey. No sooner had he set off than she wrung the bird's neck and threw it into the garden; and on his return home she told her husband the cat had devoured it.

The Shahzada was very sorry for the accident, but it could not be helped. When the dead bird was flung into the garden rose bushes sprang up wherever its blood-drops fell. One day the gardener's wife came for some flowers, and among those the gardener plucked was one of these roses. They were put all together in a vase, but soon faded, with the exception of the rose, which remained as fresh as

229

when it was growing on its stalk. "What wonderful flower is this?" exclaimed the woman.

"It does not fade!" And while she was sniffing its delightful odour it suddenly changed into a bird, and flew hither and thither about the room. The woman was startled, thinking it must be either an in or a jin. However, after she had recovered herself somewhat, she took the beautiful creature and caressed it, and in doing so she remarked on its head something resembling a diamond. Examining it, she saw it was a pin. She drew it out, and behold! the bird was transformed into a maiden, who related to the astounded woman the story of her adventures.

Without delay the old woman went to the serai, stole into the private apartment of the Shahzada and told him all. His joy was unutterable; he bade the woman go home and take care of the maiden until he himself should come in the evening.

Twilight was scarcely past when the Shahzada was on the spot. At sight of the maiden he swooned away, and when he came to himself he requested her to relate her story with her own lips. When he left the gardener's house he took the maiden with him, but while on the road to the palace a monkey sprang out upon them. The Prince started in pursuit of it, and he was away so long that the maiden, being tired, fell fast asleep. Now it had come to the knowledge of the maiden's mother that she had disappeared from the casket, and in order to make certain that she would not annoy her again, the Sultana left the

The Prince started in pursuit of it.

serai in search of her, meaning to kill her. After long wandering the woman chanced upon the spot where her daughter lay sleeping. With suppressed glee she muttered: "Oh! you have fallen into my hands once more!"

Meanwhile, failing to catch the monkey, the Prince hurried back to the maiden, anxious lest any further harm should come to her. On arriving at the spot he saw the maiden asleep and a woman by her side. When the Prince demanded her intention, the woman said she was only keeping watch over the girl, who might otherwise have suffered some ill.

Suddenly a thought struck the Shahzada, and he asked the woman who and what she was. She replied that she was a poor forsaken creature, who had nothing, and who was alone in the world. Then said the Prince, "Come with me, and I will repay your kindness." The maiden, however, being now awake, recognised her mother, and secretly informed the Prince.

All three set off together towards the serai, the woman rejoicing over the opportunity thus afforded her of putting her daughter out of the way for ever. But as soon as they arrived at the palace the Prince ordered the woman, as well as his wife, to be hanged, as a punishment for their treacherous cruelty, and made preparations for his wedding with the maiden of the golden casket. Thus they lived happily ever afterwards.

Patience-Stone

and

Patience-Knife

There was once a poor woman who had a daughter. While the mother went out washing, the daughter remained at home making embroidery. One day as the maiden was at work by the window, a little bird flew in and said: "Oh my poor maiden, your kismet is with a dead person," and immediately flew off again. The girl's mind was now completely disturbed, and when her mother came home in the evening she told her what the bird had said. "Always be sure to fasten the door and window while you are at work," advised her mother.

Next day the girl secured the door and window, and commenced her work, when suddenly, purr!--and the bird perched itself on her embroidery table. "Oh my poor maiden, your kismet is with a dead person," it said as before, and flew away. The girl

was more frightened than ever and told her mother when she came home. "Tomorrow," advised her mother, "fasten door and window, creep into the cupboard, and work by candlelight there."

As soon as her mother had taken her departure next morning, the girl fastened up the house, crept into the cupboard, lit a candle and began her work. She had only made a few stitches when purr!--and the bird was before her. "Oh my poor maiden, your kismet is with a dead person," it repeated, and flew away. The poor girl had no mind to work that day, the embroidery was cast aside, and she could do nothing but brood over what the mysterious words might signify. Even the mother was perturbed when in the evening she heard of the bird's third visit, and she resolved to remain at home herself on the following day in order to see the ill-omened creature. But the bird never came again.

Henceforth neither mother nor daughter quitted the house, but waited constantly lest the bird should return. One day some girls belonging to the neighbourhood came on a visit, and requested the woman to let her daughter go out with them to enjoy herself and try to forget her sorrow. The mother was afraid to let her daughter go, but as they promised not to let her out of their sight for a moment, she eventually consented.

The party went into the meadows, and danced and made merry till sunset. On their way home they stopped at a spring to quench their thirst. The poor woman's daughter also went to the spring, and while she was drinking, a wall rose up by magic and cut her off from her companions. Such a wall had never been seen before; it was so high that none could scale it, and so broad that none could cross it. All the girls were terror-stricken; they moaned and wept and ran about in confusion uttering cries of despair; what would become of the poor maiden and of her poor mother!

"I told you," said one, "that we must not take her with us."

"What are we to say to her mother?" asked another. "How can we face her?"

"It's your fault--you proposed it," said a third; and thus they disputed while gazing helplessly at the gigantic wall.

The mother, standing at the door, was anxiously awaiting her daughter's return. The girls came weeping loudly, and could hardly find the courage to tell the poor woman what had happened. When she under stood, however, she ran to the wall, and there the air was filled with lamentations-- from the mother on the one side and the daughter on the other.

Exhausted with weeping, the maiden fell asleep, and when she awoke next day she espied a large door in the wall. Opening the door she saw a splendid serai, more beautiful than she had ever dreamt of. She entered the antechamber and saw forty keys hanging up on the wall. She took them down, and opening each room in turn, she saw in one silver, in another gold, in another diamonds, in a fourth emeralds, in each room a different kind of

235

precious stone till her eyes were aching with their brilliance.

When she came to the fortieth room she saw there a handsome Bey on a bier, a pearl fan beside him; on his breast was a document which read: "Whoever for forty days will fan me and pray by me shall find her kismet." The maiden now remembered what the little bird had said, that in a dead person she should find her kismet.

She commenced to pray, and, with fan in hand, she sat down by the body. Day and night she fanned and prayed until the fortieth day dawned. On this last morning she glanced through the window and saw an Arab girl before the palace. She called her in and instructed her to continue to fan and pray while she, the white maiden, washed herself and put the room in order.

Seeing the paper the Arab girl read it, and while the white maiden was away the youth woke up. Looking about him he saw the Arab, embraced her, and called her his promised wife. The poor maiden could scarcely believe her own eyes when she returned to the apartment, and her astonishment was complete when the Arab woman addressed her: "I, a Sultan's daughter, am not ashamed to go in this dishabille, and yet this domestic dares to appear before me in such finery!" She drove her forth from the room, and told her to go to the kitchen and mind her work. The Bey could not help wondering what it meant, but he could say nothing; the Arab was his wife and the other--the cook!

The feast of Bairam was approaching, and in accordance with custom the Bey desired to make presents to all his servants. He inquired of the Arab what present she would prefer. She requested a garment which neither needle had sewn nor scissors cut. Then the Bey went to the kitchen and asked the maiden what she would like.

"A yellow patience-stone and a brown patience-knife-- please bring me both," said she.

The Bey departed and bought the garment, but the patience-stone and patience-knife he could find nowhere. He would not return without them if he could avoid it, so he entered a ship.

When the ship had accomplished it came suddenly to a full stop, and would go neither forward nor backward. The captain was alarmed, and calling the passengers together he informed them that there must be a man on board who had failed to keep his word; that was why they could

The Arab girl read the paper

not proceed. Then the Bey stepped forth and confessed that he was the man. He was accordingly put ashore, that he might fulfil his promise and then return to the vessel. The Bey went from one place to another till at length he stopped at a large spring. Hardly had he leaned against

237

the stone when a thick-lipped Arab appeared and asked what he wanted. "A yellow patience-stone and a brown patience-knife," he replied. The next moment the two articles were placed in the Bey's hand, and he went joyfully back to the vessel, and in due course returned home in time for the Bairam festivities. He gave his wife the garment, and took the patience, stone and patience-knife into the kitchen.

The Bey became curious to know what the maiden would do with the things, so one night he stole into the kitchen and hid himself to await developments. Presently the maiden took the knife in her hand, set the stone before her, and began to relate her life, story. She repeated what the little bird had told her and described the terrible anxiety she and her mother had endured. As she proceeded the stone began to swell up, to gasp and splutter, as though it were an animate being. The maiden further related how she came to the palace of the Bey, how she had prayed by him and fanned him for forty days, and how finally she had asked the Arab woman to relieve her for a few minutes while she went to wash herself and put things in order. The stone swelled up still more, and gasped and foamed as though it were about to burst.

Proceeding, the maiden related how the Arab woman had deceived her, and how the Bey had taken the Arab woman and not her, self to be his wife. As though the stone had a heart, it gasped and swelled, and when the maiden had finished her narrative it could endure no more, but split asunder.

238

The girl began to relate her life story

Now the maiden took up the knife and cried: "O yellow patience stone, though you are stone you cannot bear it; must then I, a weak maiden, bear it?" She would now have plunged the knife into her own body had not the Bey sprung from his hiding-place and stayed her hand. "You are my true kismet!" exclaimed the youth, and he took her to the place of the Arab woman. The false one was put to death, and the maiden's mother was sent for to the palace, where they all lived happily ever after. Sometimes a little bird flies in at the palace window and joyously sings: "O maid! O happy maid! you have found your kismet."

Ignace Kúnos

The Dragon Prince and the Stepmother

There was once a Padishah who had no children, When out walking one day with his lala he saw a dragon accompanied by five or six young ones.

"Oh, my Allah!" he complained, "Thou hast blessed this creature with so much offspring. Would that this dragon had one less, and that Thou hadst given me one child!" They continued their walk until it began to get dark, and then re turned to the serai. Time passed, until one night the Sultan's wife was taken seriously ill. In all haste messengers were dispatched here and there in search of skilled nurses.

There was no difficulty about securing one, but the woman, as soon as she arrived at the sickbed, fell down dead. Immediately another nurse was sent for, who also died as soon as she arrived, In short, all those who approached were instantly seized with a mysterious malady which had a fatal termination.

In the royal palace was a servant who had a stepdaughter whom she hated, This event, the woman thought, presented a good opportunity to get the step-daughter out of the way. Hearing that all the nurses were dead, she went immediately to the Padishah and said: "My Lord and Shah, I have a daughter who is skilled in nursing. If thou wilt permit her to come, the Sultana may perchance be cured."

Accordingly the Padishah ordered a carriage to be sent to fetch the step-daughter. But the girl was quite ignorant of nursing, and asked her father whatever she should do. Her father answered: "Fear not, my daughter. On thy way to the palace, stop awhile at thy mother's grave and offer up a prayer, for Allah always helps those that are in need. Afterwards go in confidence to the serai."

The maiden entered the carriage, drove to her mother's grave, and shed scalding tears in her grief and despair. While calling on the Creator to aid her, a voice was heard proceeding from the grave: "As soon as thou arrivest before the Padishah, ask for a kettle of milk; then canst thou reach the Sultana."

241

The maiden now reentered the carriage, arrived at the palace, and asked for a kettle of milk, with which she entered the chamber of the Sultana. She returned shortly with the news that a Prince had been born, whose form, however, was that of a dragon. The monarch was not particularly pleased, but contented himself with the knowledge that he now had an heir. To celebrate the auspicious occasion lambs were sacrificed and slaves given their freedom.

The time soon arrived when the young dragon must commence his instruction. Hodjas were summoned, who however, one after another, were killed by the dragon before they had a chance to commence their lesson. In this way there was hardly a hodja left in the land. Hearing this the stepmother went again to the Padishah and said: "My Lord and Shah, the maiden who assisted at the birth of the dragon can also impart the desired instruction."

The Padishah accordingly ordered the maiden to be fetched. Before coming to the royal palace, however, she visited her mother's grave. While she was praying for divine protection and deliverance, her mother reached out her hand from the grave and offered her a staff, saying: "Take this staff, my daughter, and should the dragon attack thee, thou hast only to show him this staff and he will retreat." So the maiden took the staff and went to the serai. When she approached the Shahzada to commence the instruction, he attempted to bite her, but at sight of the staff he refrained from his intention. After a time her efforts to instruct the Shahzada showed such satisfactory results that the Padishah rewarded the maiden with a pile of gold, and permitted her to go home.

Years passed away, and the Dragon. Prince was now old enough to get married. The Padishah pondered the matter,

grieved considerably, and finally came to the conclusion that there was nothing for it but to seek a wife for his heir. A bride was eventually found and the marriage took place, but on the wedding-night the dragon devoured his bride. The same fate overtook a second bride; in short, every maiden that was given him to wife was

Her Mother reached out her hand from the grave and offered her a staff

forthwith killed and eaten. Now the step. mother went to the Padishah and said: "My King and Shah, the maiden that assisted at the birth of the Prince, and who has since instructed him, can also make him a good wife." The Padishah rejoiced at the suggestion, and immediately sent for the maiden. Before obeying the royal summons the maiden once more poured out her sorrow at her mother's grave. The voice of the dead was heard from the tomb: "My daughter, take the skin of a hedgehog and make a mask thereof. When thou goest to the dragon he will seek to harm thee and the prickles will wound him. He will then say, 'Take off the mask', answer, 'I will take off the mask if thou wilt take off thy clothing.' When he has taken off his clothes, seize them and cast them in the fire. On

243

that he will lose his dragon form and appear as a human being."

In due course the maiden arrived at the palace and was ushered into the private apartment of the Dragon Prince, where the marriage ceremony took place. As soon as they were alone the Dragon essayed to attack his bride, but the

"Take off thy mask" snapped the Dragon-Prince

prickly mask prevented him. "Take off thy mask," he snapped. "I will only take off the mask if thou wilt take off thy clothes," she answered with as much courage as she could command. With, out hesitation the Dragon undressed; as the last article of attire was discarded, the maiden threw them all in the fire and lo! instead of a horrid Dragon a handsome youth stood before her. They fell into each other's arms and embraced and kissed unceasingly.

When the slaves entered the apartment next morning they found the newly-wedded pair in the best health and joy.

They hastened to carry the joyful news to the Padishah, who ordered a grand feast in honour of the occasion. The maiden who had happily delivered the Prince from the magic spell was received by everyone in the palace with the highest honour and respect.

Sometime after these events, war was declared between our Padishah and the Padishah of a neighbouring country. The King himself desired to take part in the campaign, but the Shahzada begged his father to allow him to go instead. As he persisted in his request, in spite of discouragement, the Padishah finally yielded and the Prince went to the war.

While he was absent in camp the cruel stepmother considered what steps she should take to destroy the Shahzada's wife. She wrote a letter in the Prince's name to the Padishah in which he requested his father to put his wife away. When the Padishah received the letter the Prince's wife was present, and as soon as she was acquainted with the purport of the missive she said: "Knowing that the Shahzada no longer loves me, there is nothing for me to do but to leave this palace." The Padishah endeavoured to calm her, assuring her that in his belief the letter was the work of some secret enemy; but it was of no avail, she could not be turned from her purpose. "I will go," she said, "for my husband has certainly found some one more beautiful than I, or he would not have written such a letter."

With these words she quitted the palace in tears. Wandering through wood and field, up hill and down dale, across land and sea, she came one day to a spring where she saw a coffin in which a beautiful youth lay dead,

"What can be the meaning of this?" she asked herself, and while absorbed in reflection and trembling with fear the darkness came on. She sought and found a hiding-place in the neighbourhood of the spring, and about midnight she saw forty doves flying towards the spot. Watching them, she saw them all alight on the crest of the water and shake themselves, on which they immediately changed into maidens and proceeded to the coffin. One of them took a wand, and touching the dead youth three times with it, he rose up as though from sleep. All night long they played together with him, and when morning dawned the youth lay down again in the coffin, the maiden touched him three times with the wand, and he was dead; then all the maidens went back to the spring, shook themselves, and resuming the form of doves, flew off.

All this the Prince's wife saw from her hiding-place. As no one was to be seen, she stole to the coffin, picked up the wand which the fairies had left behind, touched the dead youth three times with it, and he woke up immediately. Seeing the maiden he asked: "Who art thou?" "Who art thou, and what were the maidens who visited thee during the night?" returned she. Then said the youth: "They are forty peris who stole me away in my childhood."

She touched the dead youth three times

The restored youth and the forlorn maiden swore eternal friendship and resolved to marry one another. He loved her on account of her fidelity, and for some time they lived very happily together. Then the youth began to look pale

and anxious, until one day he said: "Hitherto the forty peris have ignored you, but if they should hear of our marriage they will come and kill us. It would be best for you to go away from here to my mother. There you may live in safety, and we shall see what favour Allah will grant us." So with a heavy heart the maiden set out for the dwelling of the youth's mother.

Knocking at the door, she begged admittance and shelter in Allah's name, telling her story, and saying further that she had been driven from home and had not a

247

friend in the world. The youth's mother, who had lived in continual grief for her son, took pity on the maiden and received her into the house. That same night a son was born to her.

Some days afterwards, the youth appeared in the form of a bird at the window of her chamber, and inquired: "How art thou, and how is the child?" The woman answered, "We are both well." The young man's mother, chancing to overhear the dialogue, asked the woman who the bird really was. The young woman now told her all she knew and what had happened. "Oh, that is my son indeed!" exclaimed the mother, beside herself with joy.

From this moment she loved the young woman and could not do enough for her; she had better clothing made for her, and surrounded her with all possible care and attention. "My dear daughter," said she one day, "if this bird should come again and ask what the child is doing, tell him it is angry with its father because he does not come to see it. If then he should enter the room ask him in what way he can obtain deliverance from the power of the peris."

Next day the bird appeared again, and when he made the usual inquiries the woman answered: "The child is angry with you." "Why?" asked the young man. " Because you have never seen it," answered the young woman. "Very well, open the window and let me come in," said the bird. The window was accordingly opened, the youth put off his bird form and stepped into the room. While he was fondling the child the old woman said to him: "My son, is

248

there no means of delivering thee from the forty peris?"
"Yes," answered the youth, " there is a means that is easy
and yet difficult." He then explained that, to accomplish
the desired purpose, his bird-form must be thrown into a
hot oven; the peris would know of it, and crying "Our
Shah is burning!" would cast themselves into the oven to
rescue him; if, on this, the oven door could be shut fast,
the peris would all be burnt up and then he would be free
from their spell.

HE maiden accordingly gave the servants instructions to
get the oven ready; and no sooner had she thrown in the
youth's bird-form than the forty peris came crying "Our
Shah is burning!" and flew straight into the oven. The door
was quickly shut and fastened up, and thus the forty peris
all perished. The youth was now free, and there was much
embracing and kissing and weeping and laughing for joy.

While the young woman and the young man now
spent their days in peace, the Prince, the rightful
husband of the young woman, came home from the
war, and his first words were: "Where is my wife?"
The Padishah informed him that she had left home on
account of the letter he had sent. In his despair the
Prince resolved to set out at once in search of her.

Carrying a knapsack light in weight but heavy in
value, he wandered for six months, up mountains,
through valleys, across fields, drinking coffee,
smoking his chibouque, and picking flowers, until one
day he arrived at the spring where his wife had
stopped. He noticed that all around it was burnt up,

249

The youth appeared in the form of a bird

as though there had been a recent conflagration. From thence he wandered into the town where his wife was living. He entered a coffeehouse, and while he was resting the proprietor accosted him, inquiring whence he came and whither he was going. The Prince said he was seeking his wife, who had run away from him. On this the coffeehouse keeper related that there was a young man living in that town who had been delivered from the power of the peris by a very beautiful young woman. "Perhaps that is thy wife," suggested the coffeehouse keeper.

He had scarcely finished speaking when the young man referred to entered the coffeehouse. The Shahzada turned to him and inquired after his wife. The man related all that had happened, which was sufficient to convince the Prince that the woman was indeed his wife. Now said he to the young man: "Go home and tell thy wife that I am here, and ask her also which of us she prefers--thee or me. Thou hast but to mention that I am her first husband, Black-eyed Snake" (that was the Prince's name when he was in dragon-form).

The young man accordingly went back home and told his wife of the occurrence, and when he put the question, "Whom wilt thou have--me or thy first husband?" she answered: "By thee I have two roses, but Black-eyed Snake possesses my heart." So saying she flew as on the wings of the wind to her first husband. They rejoiced at finding each other again, and set off on their return journey.

As soon as they arrived at the palace the Prince inquired who was the cause of all the suffering they had both endured, and it was found to be the work of the stepmother. Called into the presence of the Prince the woman was given her choice of forty mules or forty sticks. "Forty sticks are for my enemies," answered the woman; "for myself I prefer forty mules." Accordingly she was tied to the tails of forty mules and torn limb from limb.

The reunited pair now celebrated their wedding anew, and they lived the rest of their lives in unalloyed bliss.

The Magic Mirror

There was once a Padishah who had three sons. He also possessed a mirror, in which he looked every morning on rising, seeing therein everything that was to happen during the day. He got up one morning and went about his affairs without remembering to look in the mirror. When he had finished his duties he recollected the omission, and hastened to repair it; but to his sorrow the mirror was not to be found. Search was made everywhere, but all in vain.

Worrying over his loss brought on an illness, and, seeing their father's condition, his sons inquired the cause. " I am grieving for the loss of my fine mirror," he answered them. Then said his sons: "Do not give yourself so much pain, father, but grant us permission to seek the mirror." His sons' request caused the Padishah much happiness, for if the mirror was not soon found he felt he would die of grief. He gladly gave the desired permission, and the three brothers set out on their journey.

The Dew-Mother was about to make Helwa

After long travelling they came to a place where three roads branched off. In the midst of the place was a stone, on which was inscribed the direction of the several roads. The first was the strollers' way, the second the way to the inn, and the third the way by which none ever returned. The eldest brother chose the first, the middle brother the second, and the youngest brother the third road. Before parting they agreed to leave their rings under the stone, and to take them up again when and if they returned. We will now let the two eldest go their respective ways, and follow the ad ventures of the youngest brother. On arriving at the top of a mountain he caught sight of a Dew-mother, who was about to make helwa. Hastening up to her he embraced her, calling her "Mother."

"Oh, little son," said the Dew-woman kindly, "if you had not called me 'Mother' I should have torn you asunder." "And if you had not called me 'little son,'" retorted the youth, "I should have cut you down with my sword." Then the Dew mother asked him whence he came, whither he went, and wherefore he was there. He told her he was a Padishah's son, seeking a mirror which his father had lost. "Oh, my son," said the woman, "this mirror has been carried off by the Dews. They have taken it to their garden, where it is jealously guarded.

When you arrive there you will find all the Dews. If their eyes are open you may be quite certain they are asleep. Fear not; go forward in confidence and fetch the mirror. Every tree in the garden is covered with diamonds and precious stones; take care not to touch them, or you are lost."

The youth was grateful for the woman's instructions, and went his way. After long wandering he came to the garden of the Dews, and as he approached he saw them all asleep with their eyes wide open. Remembering the words of the Dew-mother, he went boldly into the garden, took the mirror, and started back. "Now," thought he to himself, "as they are all asleep, they would be none the wiser if I broke off a branch of these bejewelled trees." No sooner did he stretch forth his hand to pluck a branch than the Dews all rose up as one man and demanded: "By what right have you dared to come here?" The youth, now terrified, implored them to be merciful to him. They agreed to set him free and let him keep the mirror on condition that he brought them as a ransom the sword of Arab-Uzengi.

Pledging his word, the youth was allowed to return to the Dew-mother, to whom he related his difficulty. "Did I not warn you not to touch their property?" scolded the old woman. "What is to be done now?" Expressing deep sorrow for his fault, he implored the Dew-mother to advise him further. Pitying the youth, she instructed him as follows: "By following a certain path you will arrive at a serai with two doors; the one open, the other shut. Shut the open door, open the closed door, and enter. On your right hand you will find a lion with a piece of meat beside him; on your left a dog with grass near him. Give the grass to the lion and the meat to the dog, then ascend the stairs. In his chamber you will find Arab-Uzengi asleep, his sword hanging on the wall. Take it quickly, and lose no time in returning here. But beware of withdrawing the sword from its sheath."

He suddenly found himself in the Hands of Arab-Uzengi

The youth now set out again, and in due course reached the serai. Opening one door and closing the other, he entered. Giving the grass to the lion and the meat to the dog, he mounted to the giant's chamber. When he entered the apartment of Arab-Uzengi he saw the sword hanging from the wall; to take it down and flee from the palace was the work of a moment.

When he was drawing nigh to the dwelling of the Dew-mother he thought he was quite out of danger, so he drew the sword from its sheath, and suddenly found himself in the hands of Arab-Uzengi. "Now I will make you feel my power!" roared the giant, as he dragged the youth back to his palace.

The Dew-woman had prepared the youth for what he might expect if he should have the misfortune to be taken prisoner by Arab-Uzengi. Every day for forty days the giant would give him a lesson on transformation, and at the close of the lesson, when he was asked, "Dost know it?" he must unfailingly reply, "I know it not."

Thus it came to pass that for forty days the youth underwent instruction from the giant, who at the end of every lesson beat him and asked, "Dost know it?" The youth remembered always to answer, "I know it not." When the forty days had expired Arab-Uzengi set him free on condition that he would bring him the daughter of the Peri-Padishah.

The youth went back to the Dew-mother and told her what had happened to him. "Did I not warn you not to draw the sword!" she screamed, and scolded him more severely than before. Nevertheless she yielded to his earnest prayers to help him still once more. She informed him that the Peri-Princess lived in a certain town where there were no men and where it was impossible for any man to approach her; besides which the maiden had a talisman. If any man should succeed in entering the town, however, her talisman would cease to be effective, and thus he could do whatever he desired with her. "Not only Arab-Uzengi but also the Dews are in love with the Peri-Princess," said the Dew-woman; "and these latter would have carried her off years ago but were unable to overcome her talisman."

"Then how is it possible for me to come near her?" sighed the youth despairingly.

"Hast learnt nothing at all, then, from Arab-Uzengi?" demanded the Dew-woman.

"I have certainly learnt how to transform myself into a bird," he answered.

"Then it is well, my son," said the woman. "Change yourself into a bird and fly into the maiden's palace. In the garden is a stone cage; by getting into that you will destroy the Princess's talisman and she will be at your mercy. Then take her and deliver her to Arab-Uzengi."

So the youth changing himself into a bird, flew straight to the town, and from thence to the garden of the serai. Finding the stone cage he entered it, and from that moment the Princess's talisman was of no effect. By that token she knew that the bird was really a man.

"Now, son of earth," said the Peri-Princess to the youth, "I have become a mortal creature like yourself; you have nothing to fear; henceforth I belong to you entirely." Upon this the bird shook himself and resumed his human form. Now the Princess proclaimed that there was no longer any restriction surrounding her, men and women might enter the town freely. She also notified her father of what had happened, and that she had become the bride of a mortal. The youth told her that he was the son of a Padishah and that their wedding should take place with suitable pomp at his father's palace. He then prepared to return, taking the maiden with him.

As they came nigh to the palace of Arab-Uzengi, the Princess divined the youth's intention and began to weep bitterly. He calmed her, however, explaining that he was obliged to take her there to save his own life, but promised not to leave her with the giant--rather he would perish first.

When they reached the palace gates Arab-Uzengi, seeing them, cried with a loud voice: "Away, away! come not here! As you were able to take the Princess you are capable of anything--all things are possible unto you. Keep the maiden and the sword; only come not near me!

Thence went the youth with the maiden and the sword to the garden of the Dews; and as soon as the Dews saw that he had the sword, they shouted: "Away, away! Come not here! We fear you, for if you could take the sword of Arab-Uzengi and also the Peri-Princess, all things are possible unto you. As you have the maiden, the sword, and the mirror, keep also the branch you broke from the tree in our garden."

Having now done all that was expected of him, the youth escorted the maiden to the Dew-mother's house, where, after resting awhile, they bade farewell and proceeded on their homeward journey.

After long wanderings they came to the spot where the three brothers had parted many months before. Examining the stone the youngest saw that all the rings were still there. " What can have happened to my brothers?" he asked himself; and while he was musing he saw them in the distance, but in such a disreputable and forlorn condition that they hardly resembled human beings at all. He was nevertheless glad to see them safe, and they related how it had fared with them. Seeing that their youngest brother had the beautiful maiden and the magic mirror, jealousy and rage entered the hearts of the two elder. They pursued their way, and, thirst overcoming them, they sought a means of quenching it. Ere long they came to a well with an iron cover, and the two eldest suggested that the youngest should be let down by means of a rope to fill the jug with water. When he had done this, however, he found that his brothers had abandoned him to his fate at the bottom of the well. They left behind his horse, but took the maiden with them, saying to her that their brother would follow a little later.

The horse stamped continually with his hoof on the lid

When the youth realised that his brothers had forsaken him he wept and lamented bitterly. The elders in due course arrived at their royal father's palace and gave him back the magic mirror which they said they had recovered. As for their youngest brother, they denied having seen him again since they parted to go their several ways. The Padishah, in his exceeding joy at the restoration of his mirror, soon forgot the loss of his youngest son, and ordered preparations to be made for the marriage of the Peri-Princess with the eldest Prince.

Let us now return to the youth in the well. His horse, suffering terribly from hunger and thirst, stamped continually with its hoofs on the lid of the well, which at length broke. Hearing the neighing of his horse the youth made one supreme effort, and with indescribable difficulty succeeded in climbing to the top.

He now made the best of his way to the palace of his father, whose joy at seeing his long-lost son knew no bounds. Wrathful at the perfidious cruelty of the two eldest towards their youngest brother, the Padishah had them both put to death, after which he betrothed the Peri-Princess to her real lover, who had won her and rescued her from so much peril. The marriage feast lasted forty days and forty nights, and they lived happily ever after.

The Imp of the Well

The incident I am going to relate happened a very long time ago. We were on a journey, and we went up hill and down dale six months without interruption, and on looking backward we found we had travelled the length of a barley-stalk. Setting off again, we wandered on until we came to the garden of the Padishah of Chinimatchin. We entered; there stood a miller grinding meal, a cat by his side. The cat--oh, its eyes! The cat--oh, its nose! The cat--oh, its mouth! The cat--oh, its forelegs! The cat oh, its hind-legs! The cat--oh, its throat! The cat--oh, its ears! The cat--oh, its whiskers! The cat--oh, its long tail!

Nearby lived a wood cutter who, besides his poverty, had nothing but a most cantankerous wife. All the money this poor man earned, his wife took from him, so that he had never a single para for himself. When the supper was too salt--and this happened very often--if the man dared to say, "You have oversalted the food, mother!" he might be quite certain that the next day there would not be so much as a pinch of salt in it.

Now if he dared to say, "You have forgotten the salt, mother!" on the following day it would be so salt that he would be unable to eat it. It once happened to this poor man that he kept back a piastre from his wages, intending to buy a rope. His wife found this out, and began to scold him furiously. "But, my dear," said the woodcutter gently, "I only wanted the money to buy a rope. Do not be so violent." "What I have done to you hitherto is as nothing to what I intend to do," snapped the woman, and sprang at him, whereon a great uproar ensued, and how either escaped with their life is more than I can understand.

She got upon an ass and set off after him

Next morning the husband, determined to endure it no longer, saddled an ass and went into the mountains. All he said to his wife was that she must not follow him. He had not been gone long, however, before she also got upon an ass and set off after him. "Who knows," she mumbled to herself, "what he will be up to if I am not with him?" Presently the man became aware that his wife was behind him, but he pretended not to notice her. When he arrived in the mountains he immediately set to work woodcutting. The woman walked to and fro restlessly, examining every nook and corner; only an old well escaped her vigilant eye, and she was upon it before anyone could have stopped her. "Take care!" shouted her husband; "mind the well! Come back!" But the woman paid no heed to the warning, though she heard well enough. Another step, she last her balance, then presto! she found herself at the bottom of the well. Her husband, deciding she was not worth troubling about further, bestrode his ass and went home.

Next day he returned to his work in the mountains, and, thinking of his wife, he said to himself: "I will just see what has happened to the poor woman." Going to the top of the well he peeped down, but could see no trace of her. He now repented his unfeeling conduct of the previous day, reflecting that, though a shrew, she was after all his wife. What could have become of her? He took a rope, let it down the well, and shouted: "Take hold of the rope, mother, and I will pull you up." Presently the man perceived by the tightening of the rope that some one had grasped it, and he commenced to haul with all his might. He pulled away until he was nearly exhausted, and brought to the surface---a horrible imp! The miserable woodcutter was terribly frightened. "Fear me not, poor man," said the imp. "May the Almighty bless you for your deed. You have rescued me from great peril, and I shall always remember your kindness." Astounded, the poor man inquired the nature of the peril from which he had chanced to rescue the imp.

"For many years," answered the imp, "I had lived peacefully in this old well. Until last night nothing had ever happened to disturb the calm of my existence. Then an old woman fell down upon me. She seized me by the ears, and held on so tightly that I could not free myself from her grasp. By good fortune, when you let down the rope, I was the first to seize it--praised be the most merciful Allah! For your kindness I will reward you."

So saying, the imp brought forth three leaves, and gave them to the woodcutter. "I will now creep into the Sultan's daughter," he proceeded. "She will then become very ill. They will send for physicians and hodjas, but all will be in vain. When you hear of it, go to the Padishah, and produce these three leaves. As soon as you touch her face with them I will come out of her; she will be restored to health, and you will be richly rewarded."

The woodcutter, who considered this a capital plan, now parted from the imp, and gave no further thought to his wife in the well.

No sooner had the imp left the woodcutter than he went direct to the palace of the Padishah, and crept into the Sultan's daughter. The poor Princess broke out into loud and constant cries of "My head! Oh, my head!" The monarch, being told of this sudden malady, visited his afflicted daughter, and was grieved to find her in such dreadful pain. Physicians and hodjas without number were sent for, but all their skill was of no avail; the maiden continued to shriek, " Oh, my head!" "My darling," said her father, "hearing your cries of suffering causes me pain almost as great as your own. What can be done? I will call the astrologers perhaps they can tell us." All the most famous astrologers of the land came, consulted the stars, and prescribed each a different medicine; but the Princess grew worse and worse.

She seized him by the ears

To return to the woodcutter. He managed quite well without his wife, and soon forgot her. He had nearly forgotten the imp and the leaves as well, when one day he heard the Padishah's proclamation. "My daughter is sick unto death," it ran. "Physicians, hodjas, and astrologers have failed to heal her. Whoever can render help, let him come and render it. If he be a Mussulman he shall receive my daughter in marriage now, and my kingdom at my death; or, if he be an unbeliever, all the treasures of my kingdom shall be his."

This reminded the woodcutter of the imp and the three leaves. He went to the palace and undertook by the aid of Allah to cure the Princess. The Padishah led him without delay into the chamber of his sick daughter, who was still crying, "Oh, my head! my head!" The woodcutter produced the three leaves, moistened them, and pressed them on the patient's forehead, when the pain instantly departed and she was as well as though she had never known illness. Then there was great rejoicing in the serai.

The Sultan's daughter became the bride of the poor wood cutter, who was henceforth the Padishah's son-in-law.

Our Padishah had a good friend in the Padishah of the adjoining kingdom, whose daughter also was in the power of the Imp of the Well. She suffered from the same complaint, and the physicians and hodjas were just as helpless in her case as in the other. Now our Padishah informed his friend of his own good fortune and offered to send his son-in-law, who, by the grace of Allah, would no doubt be able to restore the daughter of his friend.

Accordingly the Padishah made known to his son-in-law what he desired. Though the latter had great misgiving, he could not well refuse; so he set forth on his journey to the court of the neighbouring country. Immediately on arrival he was taken to the sick Princess, and soon realised that he had again to do with the Imp of the Well.

"Once you did me a favour," said the imp, "but now you cannot say I am your debtor. I delivered the Sultan's daughter into your hands and sought another for myself;

would you take this one also from me? If you do, I will take your Princess from you."

The poor man was terribly perplexed, but resolved to try the effect of a trick. "I have not come for the maid," said he, "she is your lawful property; if you wish you may have mine also." "Then what do you here?" demanded the imp. "The woman--the woman in the well," groaned the former woodcutter, "she was my wife; I left her in the well to be rid of her." The imp showed signs of uneasiness, and asked: "Has she got out of the well?" "yes, more's the pity!" sighed the man. "She follows me about wherever I go. Now she is there behind the door!" That was enough to frighten the imp; he lost no time in quitting the Sultan's daughter. He left the town in all haste, without waiting to learn if the woodcutter spoke the truth, and was never heard of again. Thus the Princess recovered and henceforth lived very happily.

That was enough to frighten the imp.

The Soothsayer

There was once a man between forty and fifty, whose grey hairs and beard might have caused him to be mistaken for sixty or seventy. Being skilled in various branches of industry, he managed tolerably to provide for the needs of himself and his wife.

One day on going to the bath his wife saw a great crowd of people. She was informed by the other women, who like herself had come to bathe, that on that day the chief soothsayer's wife was coming to the establishment; that was why there was so much confusion and excitement. While they were speaking the sound of song and music betokened the approach of the wife of the chief soothsayer, and as her husband was a great favourite of the Padishah she had a numerous escort. The bath-woman, in the hope of receiving a valuable present, paid the lady great honour and respect and begged her to choose her place.

Our poor woman, an eye witness of all this favouritism, took her bath and returned home. Chafing at the slight which she, in common with the other women, had experienced, she sought out her husband and said to him: "Either thou must become a soothsayer or I will leave thee!" The man replied: "Woman, it is as much as I can do to procure our daily bread; I have no time to study the soothsayer's art. How could I carry out thy wish?" But the

271

woman repeated her resolve--either he must become a soothsayer or she should leave him.

His wife being of exceptional beauty he did not like the thought of losing her, so he began to consider whether anything could be done. He went to a coffeehouse, and while he was absorbed in thought over the difficulty a friend came up and asked what was the matter. Our man related his trouble. Now the friend was intimate with the bath-woman, and he answered: "Be consoled, brother, I will help thee." With these words he went straight to the bath-woman and put the situation clearly before her. The woman rejoined: "Tomorrow let the man post himself at the gate of the bath, armed with paper, pen, and inkpot, and scribble away like a soothsayer. The rest shall be my affair."

Our man, though he could neither read nor write, went to the stationer's and bought all the necessary materials, after which he took up his stand at the gate of the bath, where everyone who passed mistook him for a hodja. The chief soothsayer's wife came as usual to the bath. While the attendants were occupied with her they, on the instructions of the bath, woman, took a costly ring secretly from the lady's finger, and this the bath-woman hid in the mud collected in the gutter, advising the man at the gate of what had taken place.

Soon the chief-soothsayer's wife raised a great clamour over her lost ring. The bathers ran hither and thither in confusion, and while the uproar was at its height the bath-woman said: "A hodja is at the gate who is skilled in revealing the whereabouts of

"O best of Hodjas"
I have the ring

missing articles." Immediately the hodja was fetched in and informed of what was required. Looking very wise and with knitted brows reflecting, he presently said: "The ring will be found buried in the mud in the narrow part of the gutter." The place indicated was searched and behold! there the ring was indeed. The lady, now happy in the recovery of her treasure, gave the hodja much baksheesh, and he went home highly satisfied with his first success as a soothsayer.

A few days later it was reported that the Sultana had lost her ring in the serai. It was believed one of the slaves had stolen it. Every. body and everywhere were searched, but the missing jewel could not be found. When it came to the ears of the Chief soothsayer's wife, she mentioned the hodja as the most likely person to be of use in the matter.

273

He was accordingly sent for, and when he came into the Sultana's presence she said: "Hodja, thou must discover my ring wherever it be. I give thee until tomorrow morning; if by then it is not forthcoming thy head falls."

"O King, kill this goose," said the hodja

They led him away and locked him up in a room by himself, where he flung himself on the floor crying in the agony of despair: "O Allah, who knowest all things, tomorrow my soul will be in thy hands!"

Now it happened that the slave who had stolen the ring was also suffering indescribable agony at the fear of her crime coming to light. She could not sleep, and at length resolved to risk consequences and make confession to the hodja. In the dead of night she got up and went to the room in which the hodja was confined. Hearing the sound of the key turning in the lock, his fear increased, for he thought it must already be morning. One may imagine his surprise then when the slave fell at his feet and implored: "O best of hodjas, I have the ring; if it becomes known I am a dead woman. O save me! Save me!"

Now thought the happy hodja to himself: "As Allah has delivered me, I must also help this poor creature in her distress." The slave told him everything; then said he to the woman: "Go, my daughter, and without any person seeing thee, let a goose swallow the ring and afterwards break its leg. Do as I command thee and fear not."

When morning broke the hodja was brought before the Padishah, to whom he said: "My Shah, all night I have pondered this thing. Animals are visible in sand. Let all the poultry, cocks, hens, geese, turkeys, and other fowls be gathered together in the garden."

The monarch ordered this to be done without delay, and the hodja followed by the whole court proceeded to the garden. Surveying the assembled fowls and scribbling the while, the hodja espied a goose which limped. Pointing it out he announced triumphantly: "O King, kill this goose and the lost ring will be found inside." The goose was quickly killed, and to the astonishment of every one, there was the ring in its stomach just as the learned hodja had predicted.

He was promoted to be chief soothsayer, besides receiving several konaks as presents. Thus the poor artisan became a very famous hodja.

Ignacz Kúnos

The Daughter
of the
Padishah of Kandahar

In olden time there was a Padishah who had no children. One day he said to his Vezir: "Behold, we are both childless; let us go on a pilgrimage, then perchance Allah will show us his wonders."

They accordingly set out, and after many days came to a spring in the midst of a great plain. " Let us sit here and rest a little," suggested the Padishah. So they sat down under a tree, and while they were resting a dervish suddenly appeared and greeted them. "Essalaam alejkum, Padishah!" "Ve alejkum salaam, father," they answered, and bade him sit down beside them. Then said the Padishah to the dervish,

276

"If you know that I am the Padishah, you know also my sorrow." The dervish answered: "Because you have no children you take this pilgrimage." Speaking thus, he took two apples from his breast, gave one to the Padishah and the other to the lala, saying: "Take these apples, and when you are both at home in your palaces eat one half yourselves and give the other half to your wives. Allah will then bless you with children." A moment later he was gone.

Now the Padishah and his lala returned home. They ate each half an apple, giving the corresponding halves to their wives; and soon afterwards each had a son. The double event was celebrated with great rejoicing and public festivity. The boys thrived, and up to their thirteenth year they were never separated day or night.

Going to the tcharchi one day, they saw a tellal with a box which was offered for sale for a hundred lira. "I am going to buy that box," said the Prince. So the box was bought, and they carried it to the palace and put it in their apartment. During his lala's absence the Prince, to satisfy his curiosity, opened the box, and saw that it contained the portrait of a maiden. At the very sight of the picture he swooned away. The lala, returning, was alarmed for his friend, and sprinkled water on his face to restore him. As the Prince opened his eyes the Vezir's son asked: "What has happened, my Prince?" "Oh, lala," he replied, "I am in love with this portrait. According to the inscription it is a portrait of the daughter of the Padishah of Kandahar. If she is living I will endeavour to find her."

277

"Let me dissuade you, my Prince. Much unhappiness might result to you from such a quest." But the Prince refused to listen, and began preparations for the journey. Then said his companion: "If you are indeed resolved to go I cannot remain behind alone; we will go together." So they both saddled their horses, and without telling anyone of their intention, set out.

They travelled for weeks and months until they reached a city, where they met with an old woman, of whom they demanded lodging for the night. "My children," said the woman, "I have but a kuliba, in which I myself can hardly stir. How then can I accommodate you?" When, however, the youths gave her a handful of gold, she said: "Well, enter, my sons." And she led the way into the house.

The Prince was sighing continually after his loved one. The woman, perceiving his sadness, inquired the cause; whereupon the Prince showed her the portrait. "Look, mother, I am in love with this maiden," he said. "On her account I am here in this strange land, and if I cannot win the object of my love I cannot live." "My son," returned the woman, "this is the daughter of our Padishah. This week her betrothal takes place. I go in and out of the King's palace constantly. Calm yourself; tomorrow morning I will endeavour to point out to you the Sultan's daughter." The youth was most grateful for the old woman's kindly interest; he kissed her hand, and begged her to arrange a meeting with the Princess for him.

Next morning the woman went early to the palace. The Princess's ladies-in-waiting received her kindly, inquired after her health, and conversed on various topics. At length by chance she found herself alone with the Sultan's daughter, and she seized the opportunity to tell the Princess of the Prince's love for her. "But, dear mother," returned the Princess, "know you not that my betrothal takes place this week?" The old woman, however, was not content. She pleaded and persuaded, describing how bitterly the Prince wept, and that he desired to see her but once. At last the maiden's sympathy was touched, and she said: "Tomorrow I go with the wedding party to my bridegroom's capital. On the way is a black türbe. The youth may await me there and I will meet him." The old woman now went home and related to the Prince all that the Sultan's daughter had said. He was very happy, and, taking his lala, they set out toward midnight for the appointed spot.

The Princess rose betimes, dressed, and took her seat in the carriage, and the procession started. When they reached the tomb she ordered her carriage to stop, saying: "I wish to visit this tomb for a short time; wait until my return." As soon as the two young people met they fell in love with one another, and they found so much to say that time passed more rapidly than either of them suspected.

Meanwhile the lala kept guard over them, and when he thought the wedding party were becoming impatient he took clothes belonging to the Princess and dressed himself therein and went to the carriage. Thinking he was the Sultan's daughter the guests reproached him for keeping them waiting so long, saw him safely into the carriage, and proceeded on their journey. Presently the youth and

279

the maiden in the türbe began to realise how late it was growing, and the latter, discovering the loss of her garments, was seized with despair. The Prince endeavoured to soothe her. "Fear not, my Sultana," said he, "my lala has taken thy place at the wedding. Let us go hence; the lala will find us later," So they made up their minds to go to the dwelling of the old woman.

During this time the lala was travelling in the wedding procession to the palace of the Padishah to whom the Princess was to be given in marriage. As the "bride", the lala was taken to the bridal chamber, where he said: "I am fatigued with the journey; let the wedding be postponed for forty days that I may recover from my indisposition." This was agreed to, and the Padishah's sister undertook to be the "bride's" constant companion.

One day when they were in the garden, seated beside a pond, a bird which had been singing lustily on a tree flew away. The lala was observed to smile. "Why do you smile?" asked the maiden. "At nothing of importance," answered the lala. "Then tell me," persisted the maiden. "That bird said just now," replied the lala: "'If these two young people were to jump into the pond and bathe, one of them would be transformed into a man who would marry the other.'" "Is it possible?" exclaimed the maiden, and proposed that they should put the statement to the test forthwith. "It cannot be," answered the lala sadly, "for if I were a man you would not marry me." "Wallahi," returned the maiden, "indeed I would marry you," "But how if you should become the man, would you then marry me?" asked the lala. The maiden swore that nothing less was her inclination, and urged the matter so long that they jumped into the water. When they emerged the lala was in very deed a man! The maiden was delighted beyond description, and declared that Allah had changed him into a man that they might marry each other. If it became known, however, their marriage would be forbidden; therefore they must flee for safety.

"I will find your daughter," said the witch

They took a horse and made their escape, arriving after many days at the old woman's, where they rejoiced to find the Prince and the young Sultana already before them. Next day, rewarding the old woman with another handful of gold, they mounted their horses and rode away.

While this was happening the Padishah was overwhelmed with surprise and grief at the mysterious disappearance of both his bride and sister. He went to his bride's father, and the two made search everywhere, without success. The only result of their efforts was the appearance of a witch, who said to the Princess's father: "I will find your daughter and bring her back to you, together with the three others who have fled with her." "Do so!" said the Padishah; "bring back the fugitives and I will reward you well."

After much wandering the fugitives reached a spring, where they sat down to rest in the shade of a tree. The lala kept watch while the others slept. Suddenly two doves flew on to the tree, the one laughing and the other weeping.

The weeping bird, addressing the other, said: "Why do you laugh? You should rather pity the poor sleepers." At this the laughing bird laughed all the more, and asked its companion why it wept. "Why should I not weep, indeed, when I see these sleepers? Do you not know that when they reach the other side of the hill a beautifully formed horse will appear to them out of the forest. They will try to catch it, and in doing so lies their destruction; for this horse is no other than a witch who is resolved to capture them and deliver them all over to the Padishah, who will put them to death. Wherefore I weep."

The other dove could not stop laughing, and said: "There is no need to weep; all they have to do is to kill the horse at a single blow." Still the bird would not stop weeping, but continued: "Even should they settle with the horse they have still to encounter a little dog on the opposite side of the farther hill; this also is a witch set to capture them and deliver them to the Padishah."

Still laughing, the other dove replied: "That is of no importance either if they kill the dog with a single blow they are freed from that danger also." Said the weeping dove: "When they have settled with the dog there is still another peril hovering over them. On their bridal night a monster will appear and drag them out of bed." "Then they must kill him also," returned the bird, still laughing, and adding: "If anyone overhears our conversation and repeats it to another he shall be turned into stone." With this they flew away.

The lala, who had listened attentively to this dialogue, now woke up his companions; they mounted their horses and rode farther. After a long ride they reached the other side of the hill, where they saw a beautiful horse approaching them and whinnying. The Prince cried out in great glee: "Look at that lovely creature! Let us catch it." "Stop!" said the lala; "I will catch it," and as soon as he came up with it he drove his sword clean through it and it fell dead. Though considerably astonished at the lala's strange action, his companions said nothing, but proceeded on their way.

Having crossed the second hill a little dog greeted them with loud barking and much wagging of its tail. The Padishah's son would have caught it, but he was prevented by the lala, who cut it in two by a blow of his sword. "Both were our enemies," he observed, and they continued their flight.

After overcoming many dangers and obstacles they arrived safely in the capital, their return being celebrated with brilliant festivities and great public rejoicings. The Padishah, overwhelmed with joy at the reunion with his son, betrothed the two youths to their respective lovers, and at the expiration of forty days they were married with much pomp and circumstance.

Before night came, however, the lala stole into the bridal chamber and hid himself. Later came his own bride and also the Prince with his bride, and all three lay down to rest. The lala kept his lonely vigil, and towards midnight the ceiling shook and opened with a loud crash, and a monstrous beast came through and crept toward the bed. The horrid creature was so frightfully ugly that one could not look upon him without disgust.

He cut the dog in two by a blow of his sword

When the monster had reached the bed and was about to pick it up in his shaggy arms, the lala stole behind him and ran him through with his sword. This done, he got into bed, lay down, and went to sleep.

When the others awoke next morning and their eyes fell on the dead monster lying at the foot of the bed, they were seized with fear. They pulled the bed cover over their faces and re fused to stir. After a while there came a knocking at the door, and a voice informed them it was late. "We are afraid to get up," they answered, "for there is something in the room." Then the door was opened, and those who entered the room ran quickly out again at the sight of the awful creature lying on the floor.

The Padishah himself came and saw the body of the ifrid. "Who has brought this in here?" he demanded. Now one of the vezirs, who was envious of the preference shown to the lala, answered: "This is the lala's deed. Who but he could have done it?"

The lala ran him through with his sword

The Vezir persuaded the monarch that the lala coveted the Sultan's daughter, and thus had sought to frighten the Prince, his son, to death. The Padishah commanded; the youth to be brought before him, and though the latter protested his innocence he was condemned to death.

She was being led to execution the Shahzada pleaded for his friend's life, saying: "O father, let not my lala die. He cannot be my enemy. I am indebted to him for many benefits." All these words were vain, however, for the Padishah refused to listen, Seeing that he must die, the lala resolved to reveal everything, for he would rather be petrified than die by the sword. He begged to be taken to the Padishah, having something of importance to tell him. His wish was granted, and he began a complete account from the hour when he and the Prince left the palace to the conversation of the laughing and weeping doves. Behold! half his body was already turned to stone. Seeing this, the Padishah exclaimed: "Say no more, my child, I believe thee!" But the lala continued: "As I am already half stone my further fate does not trouble me," and finished his narrative, when he was seen to be completely turned into stone.

Neither the Padishah's sorrow nor that of his son could avail anything now. The Shahzada lamented bitterly, and had a stately türbe erected for his friend in the garden, where he passed his days and nights, completely neglecting his wife.

286

He Greeted him respectfully.

Seven years had passed away since the events recorded, when one day, as the Padishah's son was standing at the entrance to the palace, the door opened, and a grey-bearded old pir appeared. When the Prince saw him he greeted him respectfully and kissed his hand. The pir then asked: "Why are you so sad?" The Prince opened his heart to the old man, and told him his grief. "My son," said the pir, "there is a way to rectify this matter." "How?" asked the Prince eagerly. "Take a seven-year-old child, lay it upon the petrified body of your friend, and slaughter it there, letting its blood flow over the body. Then will the stone dissolve, for it is but a casing, and the human body within is not dead. Thus will your friend be restored to you."

"Where shall I find the seven-year-old child?" asked the Prince in great perturbation, for he himself was the father of a boy of that age. "Your own child will answer the purpose," replied the pir "I will do it," said the Prince with fierce resolution, and entering the palace, he called for his son. "The Prince seems in better spirits today," observed the courtiers, as they arrayed the child in fine raiment and led him to his father.

He took the child, and, laying him on the stone, did as the pir had instructed him. Lo! the stone was seen to melt gradually, and soon the lala rose up to life. "O my Shahzada, why did you kill your child? I was quite at my ease in my petrified state," he said. Then answered the Prince: "My faithful lala, if I had a hundred children I would have given them all to have restored you."

While the Prince was speaking the pir came up and said: "Come, my children, I will pray, and you shall say amin; who knows but Allah may raise up the infant again." The pir prayed, and passed his hands over the face of the dead boy, when behold! the child opened its eyes and smiled as though just awakened from sleep. They looked round, but the pir had vanished. The Prince now took his child in his arms, and together with the restored lala they returned to the palace. The old Padishah embraced and kissed them all three. The lala was reunited to his faithful wife, and the happy event was celebrated with feasting and rejoicing, lasting forty days and forty nights. Ever after they passed their time in perfect bliss.

Ignacz Kúnos

Shah Mermam
and
Sultan Sade

There was once a Padishah who had three sons, and when the Padishah their father died the three brothers disputed for the succession to the throne. At length the youngest made the following proposition: "Let each of us take bow and arrow, and whichever shall shoot farthest to him shall belong the throne." This met with favour from the others, so all three repaired to the open plain and shot their arrows. The arrow of the eldest fell at a certain part of the plain, that of the second brother at a point somewhat more distant, and the youngest brother's came down into a bush.

290

While they were engaged in recovering their arrows darkness came upon them, and not only was the search for the arrows futile, but they could not even find each other.

The youngest, however, espied a small light in the distance, and as he was benighted and unable to find his way home, he went in its direction. In course of time he came to a serai, around which forty men were gathered. Accosting them and asking what they were doing, he was answered: "We are robbers who for many years have been trying to get into this serai, but so far we have been unable to accomplish our purpose." After some investigation the young man discovered a place where he could scale the wall. He climbed up, and when he had reached the top he invited the others to follow him one by one. As they came up he cut off their heads and threw their bodies into the courtyard. When all the forty had been destroyed in this manner he entered the serai and began to wander through the halls and corridors.

While engaged in this manner he came upon three rooms, in each of which was a beautiful maiden asleep. These he disposed of in his mind, intending to marry one himself and give the others to his elder brothers. Then he stuck his handschar in the door of the apartment occupied by his chosen one and departed.

Morning broke and found him near the spot where his arrow had fallen. All three arrows were eventually recovered, and as it was seen that the youngest brother

had shot the farthest he was set upon the throne with suitable pomp and ceremony.

On the morning following the youth's adventure with the robbers, the old Padishah of the serai arose and found the handschar sticking in the door of his youngest daughter's apartment. He attempted to withdraw the weapon, but could not. He called his servants, but they had no better success. Then he issued a proclamation that whosoever should be able to withdraw the handschar from the door should receive the Princess in marriage. Suitors came from many lands, but none could be found to pull the weapon from the door. Only the three brothers remained, and these were now invited to come and test their strength and skill. First the eldest tried but without success; the second brother was equally unfortunate; but when the youngest grasped the handschar he released it without apparent effort and replaced it in its sheath.

Then said the Padishah: "My son, my daughter is yours." "But I have two brothers," observed the young man. "Then they shall have my two eldest daughters," rejoined the Padishah. The triple marriage ceremony was performed forthwith, after which the three brothers with their wives mounted their horses and rode away.

As they went along something came like a lightning-flash from the cloudless sky, tore the maiden from the lap of the youngest brother, and disappeared with her. It was a Dew; and the forty robbers whose heads the youngest brother had cut off were his servants, who had undertaken the

293

task of carrying away the maiden at the behest of their master.

Now the young man said to his brothers: "Go home with your wives, and when I have found mine I will follow you." With these words he parted from them to prosecute his difficult and dangerous enterprise.

Wandering up hill and down dale, over forest and meadow, he met a Dew-woman, the mother of the Dew who had carried off his bride. When he saw her he was afraid and said to himself: "She will surely cut me to pieces." Nevertheless he approached her with apparent boldness, embraced her, and accosted her as "Mother."

The Dew disappeared with the girl

"My son," returned the Dew woman, "whence do you come, and whither do you go?" He informed her of the object of his journey, and the woman said: "The Dew who bore away your wife is my son, who has for years been seeking an opportunity to carry her off. It will be very difficult to take her from him, but nevertheless you can try. Go the way I will show you, and you will meet my elder sister. Greet her from me, and perhaps she may be disposed to help you."

He embraced the Dew-Mother

The youth accordingly set out; and when he found the Dew-woman's elder sister, he embraced her, addressed her as "Mother," and delivered his message. Afterwards he recounted his trouble and begged her aid. This Dew-woman now dispatched him to another elder sister, who might be able to help him.

Again he set off, came to the eldest sister, and having exchanged greetings, related his trouble and begged for help as before. The old woman then said: "It is a hard task to reach the Dew's abode, but I will tell you of a means whereby you may succeed. Seek a certain place by the sea

295

shore and wait there for a space of forty days. Once only
in that period the young sea. horses come to the shore.

Take a skein of wool in your hand, and should you
succeed in catching one of the creatures bring it here. We
will then feed it and train it for forty days, after which you
may mount it and it will convey you wheresoever you
desire to go."

So the young man set off once more, and, arriving at the
seashore, he prepared for his forty days vigil. On the
fortieth day the little sea-horses made their appearance.
He caught one with his skein of wool and returned with it
to the Dew-mother. When the forty days had nearly
expired she said to the horse: "Can you take this young
man whither he would go?" The horse answered: "I am
still small, and the Dew who has carried off this young
man's wife is my father, however quickly I might run, my
father would surely overtake me. However, if when I am
returning, with the youth and the maiden on my back, he
would stick a pin in my neck, the pain might make me go
faster. Should the Dew catch us we are all lost."

At these words the youth
mounted the horse and set
off directly for the abode
of the Dew. Arrived there
they found him sleeping.
When the Princess saw
her husband she cried:
"O my Shahzada, now
is the time to rescue me

*The youth mounted
the Sea Horse*

and to escape for when the Dew awakes he will kill us." Quickly the Prince seized his wife, lifted her beside him on the horse's back, and away they went.

After they had gone, the Dew's horse neighed and woke the sleeper, who locked round and saw that the maiden was missing. Like a lightning-flash the Dew bestrode his horse and gave chase.

By constant pinpricking the youth endeavoured to increase his horse's speed. The horse himself was in despair. "O my Shahzada," he exclaimed, "my father is coming; he will surely catch us." At this the Prince buried the pin up to its head in the horse's body, and the brave animal made a frantic effort to reach the Dew-mother. As soon as she saw them she shouted: "Now you have nothing further to fear; otherwise he would have caught you both before this and torn you to pieces. You can now depart with your wife, but forget not to send me a man every day. If you fail in this, I shall visit you at night while you sleep and devour both you and your wife."

In the meantime his brothers awaited their arrival. They rejoiced to see them both, and celebrated their homecoming with forty days and forty nights of feasting and revelry.

No wonder that in the midst of all this merrymaking the Prince forgot one day to send a man to the Dew-woman. The result of this negligence was that the Dew-woman appeared that same night, as the Prince and his wife slept; she carried off the bed with its occupants, and next morning they woke to find themselves in her clutches. The Prince's despair was deepened by the melancholy reflection that the misfortune was due solely to his own thoughtlessness. The Dew-woman, moreover, reproached him for his ingratitude, and made preparations to eat them both. He wept and implored her mercy so piteously, however, that at length the Dew-woman pardoned him on condition that he should repair the omission as soon as he arrived back home. Promising to do so, they were set at liberty. While on the way home, being tired, they sat down to rest, and the Prince, with his head on his wife's knees, fell asleep. Suddenly the Dew appeared and carried off the Princess before the youth was sufficiently awake to make any attempt to prevent him.

For the second time bereft, gazing around in despair he saw a well from which he was astonished to hear an earsplitting noise and uproarious singing. "I wonder what can be the matter down there?" he said to himself, and while thus musing a bird flew out of the well. Seeing the Prince it addressed him: "What seek you here, young man?" "I am a stranger," he answered. "Coming this way and hearing the noise from the well, I was curious to know what it could mean." The bird answered: "It is the wedding-day of the son of

"What seek you here young man," asked the bird

the Peri-Padishah, and I am just going to fetch water for the guests." The Prince asked whether it were possible for him to see the wedding. The bird said: "I must go for the water, but if you will await my return I will take you down the well." So the Prince decided to wait. Presently the bird returned with the water, and said: "If I take you down and they see you, they will all run to you and cry that a mortal has no business there. In that event, turn to the Padishah and ask his aid and support in your misfortune. When he asks what troubles you, tell him whatsoever you will." On this the bird took the Prince by the hand and led him down the well.

At the bottom he found himself in a garden containing many trees and flowers, so magnificent and delightful that he imagined himself in Paradise. He saw also innumerable birds, which, as soon as they observed him, flew at him, crying: "O son of men, why have you come to us, and what do you want here?" Immediately the Shahzada turned to the Padishah and related his grief. "O youth, how was it possible for a son of earth to penetrate here?" demanded the King of the Peris. The Prince pointed to the bird that had carried the water, and the Padishah beckoned it to him, saying: "Take this youth wherever he wishes to go. Should misfortune befall you, exclaim but 'My shah!' and I will deliver you."

The bird took the Prince on its back and flew away with him direct to the place where the Dew lived. They delivered the Princess, and flew up with her to the seventh heaven. The Dew followed, but he could not find them, and so went back disappointed.

299

The danger now being over, the bird flew down with the youth and the maiden to the well, and conducted them before the Padishah, who addressed the Prince as follows: "If henceforth you will be known as Shah Meram and your wife as Sade Sultan, there is no cause for fear; but beware of using your former names by mistake." The youthful pair took careful note of their new names and departed on their homeward journey.

Arriving there by good fortune in safety, they celebrated their wedding a second time by forty days of feasting and revelry.

On the forty-first night the Dew penetrated to their sleeping-chamber, picked up the Princess, and was carrying her off again, when she woke up and shrieked: "Shah Meram!" "What ails you, Sade Sultan?" demanded the Prince. At these words the Dew was turned to stone, and in the morning he was carried out and set up for a statue by the pond in the garden of the Palace.

The Shahzada and his Princess took their daily walks in the garden, and often sat down by the pond. Sometimes they forgot the Peri-Padishah's warning, and called each other by their original names, when the stone Dew split and cracked. Seeing this, however, they quickly repaired their fault by addressing each other as Shah Meram and Sade Sultan, which caused the stone to close together again, so that the Dew was not delivered from the spell upon him.

One day, long after these events, it came to pass that in a dream the Princess saw a dervish, who addressed her as follows: "Should you again forget your new names and the Dew escape from the stone, take water from the pond and sprinkle the head of the stone form therewith. Gold and diamonds will fall from the stone into the pond, and you will be delivered from the Dew forever." Waking up, the Princess told her husband of the dream. The Shahzada asked: "What if, forgetting my new name, you should also forget to sprinkle the stone--what would then be the consequence?" But the Princess answered "Let us hope we may not forget it." With that the Prince had to be content.

One day when they were sitting by the pond the stone statue split asunder, and to their amazement they saw the Dew step forth. "Oh, woe is me, Shah Meram!" shrieked the Princess; and the Shahzada, instead of sprinkling the stone with water, drew his handschar and attacked the Dew. The latter grasped the youth round the waist and was about to carry him off when the Prince cried: "O Sade Sultan!" Immediately the Dew was changed again into stone and fell into the pond, the water of which was dyed with blood.

A few days afterwards they were again sitting by the pond and looking at the stone, when there appeared the dervish the Princess had seen in her dream. "If you had done exactly as I told you," he said, "gold and diamonds, and not blood, would have come from the stone. Beware of saying, 'Had we only done so,' lest the Dew even now appear again and carry you off in such wise that you may never meet any more."

301

When the dervish had disappeared the Shahzada said earnestly: "Let us henceforth shun this place, O my Sade

He drew his handschar
and attacked the Dew

Sultan, for if we should by chance forget again, there is no further prospect of deliverance." So they forsook the garden forever. Blood continues to flow from the stone and the pond is quite full, but beyond the garden the Prince and Princess pass their lives in happiness and peace.

The Wizard and his Pupil

There was once a woman who had a son. To whatever school she sent him, he always ran away. Perplexed, the mother asked the boy "Where shall I send you?" To which he answered: "Do not send me, but go with me; if I like the place I will not run away." So she took him with her to market, and there they watched a number of men working at various handicrafts, and among them was a wizard.

The boy was very much attracted by this last, and requested his mother to apprentice him to the wizard. She went to the man and told him her son's desire. The matter was soon arranged to their mutual satisfaction, and the boy was left with his master, as the wizard was henceforth to be.

In the course of time the youth had learnt all that the wizard was able to teach him, and one day his master said: "I will transform myself into a ram; take me to market and sell me, but be sure to keep the rope." The youth agreed, and the wizard accordingly changed himself into a ram. The youth took the animal to the auctioneer, who sold it in the marketplace. It was bought by a man for five hundred piastres, but the youth kept the rope as he was instructed. In the evening the master, having resumed his human form, escaped from the buyer of the ram and came home.

Next day the wizard said to his pupil: "I am now going to transform myself into a horse; take me and sell me, but guard the rope." "I understand," answered the youth, and led the horse to market, where it was sold by auction for a thousand piastres. The pupil kept the rope, however, and came home. An idea struck him: "Now let me see," said he to himself, "whether I cannot help myself," and he went to his mother. "Mother," said he when they met, "I have learnt all that was to be learnt. Many thanks for apprenticing me to that wizard; I shall now be able to make a great deal of money." The poor woman did not understand what he meant, and said: "My son, what will you do? I hope you are not going to run away again and give me further trouble." "No," he answered. "Tomorrow I shall change myself into a bathing establishment, which you will sell; but take care not to sell the key of the door with it, or I am lost."

While the youth was thus discoursing with his mother, the wizard escaped from the man who had bought him as a horse, and came home. Finding his apprentice not there, he became angry. "You good-for-nothing; you have sold me completely this time, it seems; but wait until you fall into my hands again!" That night he remained at home, and next morning went out in search of his truant pupil.

The youth transformed himself into a beautiful bathing establishment, which his mother put up for sale by auction. All the people of the town were astonished at its magnificence, and multitudes collected round the auctioneer. The wizard was among the crowd, and guessed at once that this stately building was in reality his rascally pupil. He said nothing of that, however, but when all the pashas, beys, and other people had bid their highest he bid higher still, and the building was knocked down to him. The woman was called, and when the wizard was about to hand her the money she explained that she could not give up the key. Then the wizard said he would not pay unless he received it. He showed her that he had plenty of money, and observed to the woman that that particular key was of no importance to her; she could easily buy another if she must have one. Many of the bystanders expressed their agreement with the purchaser, and as the woman knew not the true significance of keeping the key, she parted with it to the wizard in return for the price of the bathing establishment. When she gave up the key the youth felt that his time had come, so he changed himself into a bird and flew away. His master, however, changed himself into a falcon and pursued him. They both flew a long distance until they reached another town, where the Padishah was entertaining himself with his court in the palace garden.

As a last resource, the youth now changed himself into a beautiful rose and fell at the feet of the Padishah. The King expressed his surprise at seeing the rose, as that flower was not then in season. "It is a gift from Allah," he concluded. "It smells so sweetly that not even in the rose-flowering season could its equal be found."

He showed her that he had plenty of money

The wizard now resumed his human form and entered the garden, lute in hand, as a minnesinger. As he was striking his instrument he was observed by the Padishah, who, calling him, ordered him to play and sing his songs. In one of his impromptu ballads the singer requested the Padishah to give him the rose. Hearing this the King was angry, and said: "What say you, fellow? This rose was given me by Allah! How dare you, a mere wanderer, demand it?"

"O Shah," answered the singer, " my occupation is obvious; I have fallen in love with the rose you possess. I have been seeking it for many years, but till now have I been unable to find it. If you give it not to me I shall kill myself. Would not that be a pity? I have followed it over hill and fell, to find it now in the hands of the mild and gracious Padishah. Have you no pity for a poor man like me, who has lost love and light and happiness? Is it seemly to afflict me thus? I will not move from this spot until you give me the rose."

The Padishah was moved, and said to himself: "After all, of what consequence is the rose to me? Let the unfortunate man attain his object." Saying these words he stepped forward and handed the flower to the singer. But before the latter could grasp it, it fell to the ground and was changed into millet pulp. Quickly the wizard transformed himself into a cock and ate it up. One grain, however, fell under the Padishah's foot and so escaped the cock's attention. This grain suddenly changed into the youth, who picked up the cock and wrung its neck--in other words, he disposed of his master.

The Padishah was astonished at these strange proceedings, and commanded the young man to explain the riddle. He told the King everything from beginning to end, and the monarch was so delighted with his skill in magic that he appointed him Grand Vezir and gave him his daughter in marriage. The young man was now able to provide for his mother, and thus everybody lived happily ever after.

Ignace Kúnos

The Padishah of the Thirty Peris

VERY long time ago, when the fairies lived, while I was lounging about in forbidden gardens, I came across one in which I fared very badly. I painted my horse and thought its colour then looked quite natural; bought a donkey and thought it was my wife; when one day the donkey caught me a vicious kick, I thought my wife was caressing me. I went on and on, sleeping in ancient ruins inhabited by owls, until I fared very badly again. The great ball of Tophanes I put in my pocket for fruit; the

great minaret of Galata I stuck in my mouth for a trumpet; the fortress of Kyz Kulesi I hugged for a bear; I stuck myself in the midst of the sea for a rock: in short, I was the biggest fool among all the fools. My sin was the relation of these tales.

There was once a Padishah who had a daughter. Beautiful was she as the full moon, slender as a cypress; her eyes gleamed like live coals, her hair was as black as night, her eyebrows like bows and her eyelids like arrows.

There was a large garden in the palace, in the midst of which was a broad lake. By its side the Princess sat every day sewing and embroidering. Once, as the Princess's ring was lying on the table near her, a little dove flew down, took the ring in its beak, and flew off. The bird was so lovely that the Princess fell quite in love with it. Next day the maiden laid her bracelet on the table, and the bird carried that off likewise. The flame of her love had now reached such a pitch of intensity that she could neither eat nor drink, and scarce could wait until the following day.

On the third day she took the lace from the table and put it close beside her. The bird came as before and flew off with the lace. The maiden had now hardly strength enough to rise; she went in tears back to the palace and there broke down altogether. One of the court dames, perceiving her distress, asked: "O lady, why do you weep? Who has injured you?" "I am weary and sad at heart,"

The bald one took his mother on his back

answered the Sultan's daughter, weeping and sighing continually.

The Princess was the Padishah's only child, and the court dame feared to inform him of her illness. But seeing the maiden become paler day by day she overcame her fear and reported the Princess's condition to her father. The alarmed Padishah visited the maiden with a large train of physicians and hodjas, but no one could explain her malady. Next day the Vezir said to the King: "Physicians and hodjas are of no avail for your daughter; we must seek a remedy elsewhere." He advised the Padishah to have a large bath built, whose waters should cure all complaints; and everyone who came to use the bath should be obliged to relate his life-story. This was done, and a royal proclamation issued that by the use of that bath the bald should receive hair, the deaf should hear, the blind see, and the lame walk. The populace came in streams; each person had a free bath which cured his disease, and was allowed to go after relating his life-story.

One bald man had a lame mother; they also heard of the healing property of the bath. "Let us go," said the son; "peradventure we may be cured." "How can I go," mumbled the old woman, "when I cannot stand on my feet?" "That's easily managed," answered the bald one, taking his mother up on his back and setting out for the bath. As they went along the man grew tired, and reaching a field near a river, he put his mother down on the ground while he rested a little. A cock passed by with a jug of water on its back. Curious to know where it was going, the man followed it, until, coming to a great castle, the cock entered through a hole in the wall. The young man crept in after it, and found himself before a stately palace. Not a soul challenged him, and so he walked in.

Ascending the grand staircase, he entered the antechamber, and thence wandered from one richly decorated apartment to another until he was quite tired with walking. "Perhaps I shall see something alive shortly," he said to himself, and secreted himself in a chest, whence through a hole he could see all that went on outside. Presently he saw three doves fly in at the window; they shook themselves, and behold! they were trans formed into beautiful maidens, more lovely than any he had seen in his life before.

"We have been long away," observed one. "The Padishah

He received a terrible blow on his hand

will be here soon and nothing is ready." One took a broom and swept out the chamber, the other set the table, while the third brought in the dishes. Now they shook themselves once more and, as doves, flew out at the window. Meanwhile the bald one, feeling hungry, thought that, as there was no-one about, he might come forth from his hiding-place and help himself to food. As he stretched forth his hand to grasp the viands he received such a terrible blow on that member that it swelled up. He stretched out his other hand, with the same result. The bald man was terrified, and hastened back to his chest, and hardly had the lid closed upon him than a white dove flew into the room, shook its plumage, and appeared as a handsome youth.

Going to a small box he took therefrom a ring, a bracelet, and a lace table cover. "O ring," he soliloquized, "how happy you are, for her finger has worn you! O bracelet, how happy are you, for her arm has worn you!" As he wept, he wiped the tears from his eyes with the lace. Returning all the articles to the box, he ate the food prepared for him and then lay down. The hungry bald man hardly managed to live till next day, when the handsome youth arose, shook himself, and, as a bird, flew out at the window. The man now stole out of the chest, entered the courtyard, and through the hole in the wall escaped to freedom. There he rejoined his poor mother, who was weeping and moaning because she thought she had been forsaken by her son. He soon consoled her, and taking her on his back they wended their way to the bath. They bathed, and the old woman came forth without lameness and the bald man with hair. Then they related their story, and when the Sultan's daughter heard it she promised to give the man a rich reward if he would take her to the castle he described.

Next day, therefore, the Princess set off, with the formerly bald man for her guide, and in due time they arrived at their destination. He showed her the castle walls, assisted her through the hole, led her to the doves' room, and pointed out the chest wherein she might conceal herself. His duty done, the man went back, and with wealth and health he and his mother lived comfortably all their days.

Toward evening the three doves flew into the room. Transformed into maidens, they swept, put everything in order, set food on the table, and went off again. Soon in flew the white dove, and the Princess in the chest nearly swooned in ecstasy when she saw him transformed into a handsome youth. He went to the little box, drew forth the ring, the bracelet, and the lace which formerly had been in her possession. "O ring," he sighed, "how happy you are, for you have been worn on her dear finger! O bracelet, how happy you should be, for her arm has worn you!" His eyes were wet with tears, which he dried with the lace. The maiden's heart nearly burst with grief. She could not forbear knocking on the inside of the chest with her finger. The youth heard the sound, opened the chest, and behold! there stood before him his heart's love. They embraced each other, and for some minutes were unable to speak for very joy at this unexpected meeting.

Presently the youth inquired how she came there in the palace of the Peris, and she told him all. Then the youth told her that he was born of a mortal mother, but when he was only three days old the peris had stolen him, and now he had become their padishah. He was compelled to be with them the whole day except during two hours, when he was free. The maiden might stay there that day, and during the daytime she could go out and come in at pleasure; toward evening, however, she must hide, as then the thirty peris came home, and if they saw her they would put her to death. On the morrow he would show her his mother's konak, where she could dwell in peace and where he would daily pass his two free hours with her.

Next day the Peri-Padishah pointed out to the Princess his mother's konak. "Go," he said, "and greet her in the name of Bachtijar Bey, and she will take you in and be kind to you."

When the maiden knocked, there came to the door an old lady who, when she heard the name of her son, received her visitor most cordially. The Princess dwelt there a long time, and was visited every day by the little bird. In time it came to pass that a little son was born to the Princess, but the old lady did not know about the baby Prince, nor that her son visited the house.

Next day the little bird came as usual, flew in at the window and chirped: "How is my little boy?" "Nothing is the matter with him," answered the Princess, "but he awaits Bachtijar Bey." "If only my mother knew," sighed the youth, "she would furnish her best chamber for you." Then changing himself into a man, he caressed his wife and fondled the baby. When the two hours were expired he shook himself, was transformed into a bird, and flew away.

Meantime the mother had heard her son's voice and was beside herself with joy. She ran in to her daughter-in-law, kissed her again and again, then left and prepared her best room for the Princess. When all had been comfortably arranged the old lady inquired after her son. By this time she was aware that he had been stolen by the peris, and now she meant to devise some way to steal him back again. "When my son comes tomorrow," said she, "contrive to detain him later than usual; the rest is my affair."

Next day the bird flew to the window, and not seeing the Princess there, he flew to the best room and chirped: "How is my little boy?" The Princess answered: "Much is the matter with him, he awaits Bachtijar." The bird now changed himself into a man, and the happy husband and wife entertained each other so pleasantly that the flight of time was unnoticed.

What was the old lady doing meanwhile?

In front of the house grew a large cypress-tree, on whose branches the thirty peri-doves sometimes alighted. The old lady stuck poisoned pins all over the tree. Towards evening the peris came in search of their missing Padishah and sat on the tree: no sooner did they touch the poisoned pins than they fell dead.

When the youth saw that it was late he was terror-stricken. He ran to and fro, but chancing to look outside, he saw that the thirty peris were not on the tree. His joy was now as great as his anguish had been a moment before, and when his mother explained what had happened his delight knew no bounds. Mother and son, husband and wife, were restored one to another, and now with none to molest them they celebrated their union for forty days and forty nights.

The Deceiver
and the Thief

There was once a cunning woman who had two husbands, neither of whom knew of the other's existence. The one got his living by cheating, the other by stealing, each of which excellent industries they had learnt from the woman.

The thief went with his stolen goods to the merchant, sold them, and took the money to the woman. Then came the other to the merchant, gripped him by the collar, and said: "That is my property; that and more besides have been stolen from me--by thee I am certain. I will that thou takest it all back again to the place whence thou hast stolen it." But the other  protested: "Woe is me! I am no thief; I have bought these things from others; how sayest thou they are thine? Let me go, and seek the real thief." There was a great uproar. The thief perceived that they would soon be on his track, so he went home without loss of time. His wife informed him that his theft had been discovered, and advised him to go away for a few days to escape capture by the police.

The woman took a sheep's tail and cut it in two halves, one of which she made into a package with bread and gave to the thief, who soon shook the dust of the town from his feet.

In a short time the cheat came home and told the woman that his game was up; his deception could no longer be hidden. "Give me food," he said, "and I will withdraw myself from public notice until the storm has blown over." So the woman gave him the half loaf and the other half of the sheep's tail, and he quickly took himself off. The first, the thief, weary from long tramping, came to a river, where he sat down to rest. As he was unpacking his food the deceiver came up, sat down, and opening his packet

They sat down to eat

prepared to eat. The former said: "Friend, let us eat together." So they sat face to face. Presently the one called attention to the similarity of their respective pieces of bread, and putting them together they found the two formed a complete loaf. Presently the two pieces of sheep's tail attracted their notice; these were also put together, and a complete sheep's tail was the result.

Astounded, the deceiver said to the thief: "If I may ask, whence comest thou?" "From such and such a town," was the answer. "What street?" "In such and such a street lives a certain woman--she is my wife." The deceiver was almost choking with excitement. "Allah! Allah!" he cried; "that woman is my wife; she has been my wife for a year. Why dost thou lie?"

"Man, art thou out of thy senses, or joking?" returned the thief, "That woman has been my wife for a long time," Knowing not what to make of it, they both scratched their heads. At length the deceiver said: "This is a matter we cannot decide our- selves; let us go to the

The Deceiver abstracted the wallet from the man's bosom

woman and ask her. Thus shall we know which of us two is her husband." They got up and set forth together. When the woman saw them both coming together she suspected what was the matter. She greeted them, invited them to take seats, and sat herself opposite them. The deceiver opened the conversation. "Tell us," he said, "whose wife art thou?" "Hitherto," she replied, "I have been the wife of you both; henceforth I intend to be his who is the cleverer of you. I have taught you each a trade; he shall be my husband who plies it most to my satisfaction." Both men confessed them- selves content to abide by the lady's decision. Said the deceiver to the thief: "Today I will prove my skill, tomorrow thou canst prove thine." On this they left the house together and went to the marketplace.

Now the deceiver observed a man put a thousand gold-pieces into his wallet, which he then hid in his bosom. The former stole after him, and in the pressure of the crowd, abstracted the wallet from the man's bosom. Going to a secluded spot, he took out nine gold-pieces, slipped his seal-ring from his finger into the wallet, fastened it up, and went back and replaced it without observation in the bosom of its rightful owner.

We have said he did this "without observation"; there was one person, however, by whom the trick was observed-- this was the thief, The deceiver now went away, and returned some time after to the owner of the wallet, grasped him by the scruff of the neck, and shouted: "Ah, rascal! thou hast stolen my wallet with the ducats!" The man was embarrassed, not understanding the accusation, but answered: "My friend, go thy way and leave me in peace. I do not know thee." To this the deceiver replied: "It is not necessary for thee to know me; come with me to the judge." There was nothing for it but to go. The deceiver was the accuser. "How many gold-pieces are there here?"

demanded the judge of the accused. "A thousand," was the immediate answer. Then the judge turned to the accuser: "And how many have been stolen from thee?" "Nine hundred and ninety-one," readily replied he, "and my seal-ring will also be found in the wallet." The judge counted the ducats, and lo! there were exactly nine hundred and ninety-one and the seal-ring! The rightful owners was beaten severely, and the ducats handed to the deceiver, who went away.

The next evening the thief took a rope, and in company with the deceiver, went to the palace of the Padishah. The thief threw the rope over the wall, where it caught; he climbed up it and his friend followed. They entered the treasure chamber after trying various keys; and now the thief advised the deceiver to take away as many ducats as he could carry. He himself, dazzled by the sight of so much gold, got together as much as he could put on his back, and away they went. The thief went to the fowl-house, caught a goose, wrung its neck, put it on a spit, made a fire under it and set it to cook, ordering his companion to turn it to prevent its burning. This done he went back to the Padishah's sleeping-chamber. The deceiver called after him

The thief withdrew the raisin by means of the horse-hair

"Stop! Whither goest thou?" "I am going," he answered, "to tell the Padishah what a clever thing I've done, and to ask him whether he thinks the woman should belong to me or to thee." His companion called back: "For God's sake, let us go away from here. I'll give up the woman; thou canst have her." "Oh, yes," was the retort, "now thou sayst thus; tomorrow thou wilt alter thy mind. But if the Padishah decides the matter thou art bound to agree."

He slid stealthily into the Padishah's bed chamber. From where he hid he had a good view of the interior, and saw the Padishah lying in bed; a slave was chafing his feet and chewing a raisin. Taking a horsehair which lay on the floor, the thief stuck one end in the slave's mouth so that it adhered to the raisin. The slave being very sleepy he commenced to yawn, and no sooner had he opened his mouth than the thief withdrew the raisin by means of the horse hair and transferred it to his own mouth. The slave now opened his eyes very wide, looked all about the floor, but nowhere could he find his raisin. Shortly afterwards he fell asleep. The thief held a phial of strong spirits under his nose until he lost his senses and fell to the floor like a log. Lifting him gently, the thief put him in a basket, hung the basket from the balcony, and commenced himself to chafe the monarch's feet. (The deceiver, who had followed, saw all this from the door of the apartment.) Suddenly the Padishah stirred, and the thief said in a low tone: "O King, if thou permittest, I will tell thee a story." "It is well," murmured the sleepy Padishah; "let me hear."

On this the thief related all that had happened between him and his companion. (Turning to him at the door, he admonished him to go and turn the goose lest it should burn.) He told of his burglary of the treasure-chamber, of the theft of the slave's raisin from his mouth. (All this time his companion was trembling just outside the door and continually crying in his fear: "Come away; let us go." To which the thief, interrupting his story, would retort: "Go and mind the goose.") "Now, O Padishah," concluded the thief, "whose exploit is the greater, mine or my friend's? Which of us has won the woman?" The King answered that the thief's was certainly the greater, and therefore the woman was rightfully his.

The thief continued to chafe the Padishah's feet a little longer until the latter was fast asleep; he then stole noiselessly away and rejoined his companion. " Hast heard what the Padishah said--that the woman belongs to me?" "Yes, yes, I heard," answered the other. Then the thief pressed the point: "Whose is the woman?" "I have said it, she is thine," answered the other rather testily. "Now let us get away from here, lest we should be discovered. I am nearly dead; I shall soon lose my wits." The deceiver was certainly nearly out of his mind with fright. Then the thief began again: "Thou hast lied; I will go once more and ask the Padishah." Terror-stricken, the other shrieked: "Thou wilt be caught. For all the world, let us go away out of this. Not only shall the woman be thy wife, but I also will be thy bond-slave!" At length they went away and took the money with them. They went directly to the woman, who was so pleased with the thief's prowess that she married him without further delay.

Next morning the Padishah woke up and called for his slaves. Deep silence reigned everywhere. Seeing that no one came, the monarch waited a little, then called again. Still no slave came. Then, his anger rising, the Padishah sprang from his bed and saw the basket suspended from the balcony. "What's this?" he said, and taking down the basket, saw his attendant in a state of insensibility within. Then calling more loudly, a number of slaves ran in and brought back the stupefied man to consciousness. The King demanded to know what was the matter with the man. He was quite unable to say. Now it began to dawn upon the Padishah that he had during the night listened to some story told by a thief. He seated himself at once on his throne and sent for his vezirs. All the vezirs, beys, and mighty men came, and when they were assembled the King related his experience of the previous night. "This thief must be found," he concluded; "let heralds proclaim in all the city that he may come to me in confidence. I swear by Allah that no harm shall be done him; he may keep the gold he has stolen and he shall have a pension besides."

Thus the heralds proclaimed the will of their lord and master. The thief heard, and when he knew that the Padishah had sworn he went boldly into his presence and said: "O Shah, thou mayst kill me or reward me: I am the man!"

"Why hast thou done this thing?" demanded the monarch. The thief related all from beginning to end.

True to his oath, the Padishah allowed the thief to keep the stolen treasure, and settled a pension on him for life. But the latter, out of gratitude for the Padishah's clemency, vowed on his heart and soul that he would never steal again; and both he and his wife prayed constantly for the health and happiness of the Padishah as long as they lived.

The Snake-Peri

and the

Majic Mirror

There was once a poor woodcutter who said to his son: "When I am dead you must continue my work. Go daily to the forest. Every tree you may fell, except that on the edge of the forest, that you must spare." Some days afterwards he died, and was buried.

The young man took up his father's work and felled trees for his livelihood. Being one day in the neighbourhood of the forbidden tree, he found himself wondering what could be the reason for it being spared while all the rest were to come down. Presently, scarcely knowing why, he took his hatchet and began to cut down the tree. But behold! as though the tree had feet it began to retreat from him, and his blows cut only the

327

air. The wood-cutter bestrode his ass and trotted after the tree, but night fell and he had not caught it. Tying up his animal to another tree, he climbed into its leafy branches and settled himself to wait till morning.

Next day he descended to find that nothing was left of his ass but its bones. "No matter, I must go on foot," said the woodcutter, and ran after the tree. He followed it all day, but could not overtake it. On the third day he was preparing to follow it again, when suddenly he came upon a snake and an elephant fighting. He stood and watched the combat until it ended in the snake swallowing the elephant. The snake got it down, but the tusks stuck in its throat. Both beast and reptile saw the young man, and both appealed to him for assistance. The elephant promised him everything possible if only he would kill the snake. On the other hand, the snake said: "Break off his tusks; that task is easier and the reward will be greater." Thinking that was the most sensible thing to do, the youth struck off the tusks with his hatchet. The snake was extremely grateful for the service rendered, and told the young man to come with him and receive the promised reward.

Stopping at a spring on the way, the snake said to his companion: "Remain here while I take a bath; and whatever happens, fear not."

Hardly had the snake glided into the water when a fearful hurricane arose; lightning flashed and thunder rolled, as though the end of the world had come. Soon, however, all became calm again; the snake emerged from the water in the form of a man, and they pursued their journey.

The youth struck off the tusks with his hatchet

They travelled merrily along, drinking coffee, smoking their chibouques, and sowing violets, until, when they were nearly at home, the Snake-peri said to the young man: "Soon we shall arrive at the house of my mother. When she opens the door I shall address you as 'Brother,' and call you into the house. You will be offered coffee, but accept it not; food will be set before you, but do not touch it. By the gate you will find a small piece of mirror; request my mother to give it to you."

They reached the house, and as the peri knocked at the door, his mother herself opened it. "Come in, brother," he said to the young man. "Who is your brother?" inquired his mother. "One who has saved my life," replied the peri, and told his mother what had happened. They entered the house, and the woman offered coffee and a chibouque to the young man, but he did not accept them. "I am in a hurry," said he in excuse; "I cannot remain here." "At least rest awhile," suggested the woman; "we cannot allow a guest to go without taking something." "I need nothing," answered he. "But by the gate is a small piece of mirror; if you will offer me that, I will accept it." The woman was not disposed to give it, but her son was angry that she should refuse such a trifling thing to the preserver of his life; therefore she gave it--but unwillingly.

The young man departed with the piece of mirror, and on the road he looked at it, turning it over on all sides, wondering of what use it could be to him. While he was thus fingering it an Arab appeared, one of whose lips touched the sky and the other swept the ground. The young man would have died of fright if the apparition had not reassured him, and asked: "your command, my Sultan?" It was all he could do to find courage enough to ask for something to eat. In a trice the most delicious food was set before him, such as he had never seen before. This done, the Arab disappeared.

An Arab appeared

The youth's curiosity was now aroused about the piece of mirror; he took it out again and looked at it. Immediately the Arab was before him, saying: "your command, my Sultan!"

In his confusion the young man stammered out something about a palace, and behold! there rose up before him an edifice much more magnificent than the Padishah inhabited. "Take it away," said the youth, and the palace instantly disappeared. He was now very proud of his wonderful possession, and thought of nothing but what he should wish for next. He remembered that the Padishah had a lovely daughter, and at once he looked in the mirror. "Your command, my Sultan!" exclaimed the thick-lipped Arab; and the youth ordered a magnificent palace with the Padishah's daughter herself in it. Hardly had he uttered the wish, when he found himself in the palace and the Princess sitting by his side. They embraced, and kissed each other, and were as happy as the days were long.

Out jumped the old Woman

In the meantime the Padishah was informed of the mysterious disappearance of his daughter. He commanded search to be made for her throughout the land, but all in vain; it was impossible to find her. Then came an old woman who advised the Padishah to have a box made, lined with tin. Into this he must put the old woman and cast her into the sea. She promised to find the Princess, either on this side of the ocean or on the other.

The box was accordingly made, and well supplied with food, then the old woman was enclosed and thrown into the sea. Borne on the crest of the billows, the box at length was cast up on the shore of the city where was the palace of the young man and the Sultan' s daughter. Some fishermen who were standing on the beach saw the box, and throwing out hooks and ropes, they dragged it ashore. As soon as they opened it, out jumped the old woman, and in answer to the inquiry whence she came, she said: "May my enemy be struck blind!--I have not deserved such treatment." As she wept, every one believed that she was a cruelly used old woman. "Where is the Bey of this city?" she asked; "perchance he will pity me and give me shelter in his house." The onlookers showed her the way to the palace and encouraged her to believe that there she would meet with aid.

Arrived at the palace she knocked at the door, and the Princess called from above asking what she wanted. The old woman recognised the voice, but as though she were a stranger she begged to be taken in as a domestic servant. "My husband will be home this evening," answered the Princess; "till then remain in the corner." When the master came he gave orders that the old woman should be taken into his service.

Though the old woman had been several weeks in the palace she had never once seen a cook or a servant of any sort, yet the richest and costliest foods were served up and the most scrupulous cleanliness prevailed everywhere. One day she ventured to ask the Princess whether she did not feel lonely, and suggested: "With your permission, I would spend some of the time in your company; that were surely better." "I will speak with my husband on the matter," answered the Princess. The youth offering no objection, the old woman now daily spent a considerable time in the Princess's private apartment. One day the former made bold to ask whence came the food and where were the servants. As the Princess was unaware of the existence of the mirror she could not say. "Ask your husband," suggested the old woman, and when he came home the Princess was so amiable with him that he showed her his treasure.

This was not sufficient, however, for two or three days later the old woman advised her mistress to ask her husband to give her the mirror, to amuse herself with during his absence. He could refuse her nothing, and so he gave it to her.

Now was the old woman's opportunity. Discovering the place where the Princess kept the mirror, she stole it, and looked in it. When the thick-lipped Arab appeared and asked, "What is your command?" she ordered: "Take me and the Princess to her father." She further commanded him to burn down the palace, and when the woodcutter's son came in the evening he found nothing but his cat warming itself at the smoking ashes of his beautiful home. He happened to find the remains of

333

some food which the Princess had thrown away, and putting this into his knapsack he set forth to seek his wife, even though he should have to go to the world's end to find her.

He wandered so long and so far that at length he reached the town where dwelt the Padishah, his father-in-law. He went to the palace kitchen and begged the cook to employ him; this was done out of pity for his destitute condition. After a few days he learnt from his fellow-servants that the Sultan's daughter had returned home after a mysterious absence.

One day the cook was taken ill, and the young woodcutter offered to take his place. The cook gratefully accepted the offer and explained his duties. Everything was done satisfactorily, only, when sending in the dishes, the temporary cook laid the broken food he had picked up at his ruined home on the Princess's plate. When she saw it she

The Mouse Padishah begged him to save his kingdom

realised that her husband was somewhere close at hand. She sent for the cook and asked who was with him in the kitchen. At first he denied but finally admitted that a

334

young man was assisting him. The Princess now hastened to her father and told him that in the kitchen was a young servant who made such delicious coffee that she desired to have him for her own coffeemaker. Henceforth he made the coffee and took it up personally to the Princess. Thus they came together again, and the Princess told her husband who was the cause of their misfortunes. They deliberated constantly on the best means to recover the mirror.

The young man visited the Princess so often and remained with her so long at a time that the old woman's suspicions were aroused. To be brief, she looked into the mirror and had him carried off to the ashes of his former palace. He found his cat still there, she having kept herself alive by catching and eating mice.

She had devoured such an army of mice, however, that the Mouse Padishah had not enough soldiers left to defend his realm. The King of the Mice was much concerned about it, but none of them dared approach the cat on the subject.

One day he saw the young man and begged his aid to save his kingdom from ruin. "I would gladly help you," returned the youth, "but I myself am bowed down with grief." "What troubles you?" asked the Mouse-Padishah. The woodcutter's son now told him the story of the mirror that had been stolen from him by the old woman. "That matter can be rectified without difficulty," the Mouse-Padishah assured him, Calling all his mice together, he asked which of them inhabited the palace and whether they knew where the mirror was hidden. An old lame

335

mouse limped up, bowed low, and kissing the earth before the Padishah, said he had seen the mirror, which the old woman placed under the pillow every night.

The Padishah ordered him to obtain possession of it without delay. Two of his companions offered to accompany him, and as he was so old and infirm they carried him on their backs to the palace. It was night when they arrived, and the old woman had just eaten a good supper. "We are in nice time for a feed," said the lame mouse, as they entered the room. They ate their fill, and awaited an opportunity to accomplish their object. When the old woman had gone to bed they waited patiently until she was fast asleep. Then the lame mouse climbed upon the bed and tickled the old woman's nose with his tail until she sneezed so violently that her head nearly fell from her body. While this was happening the other mice dislodged the mirror from under the pillow; after which they took the lame mouse on their backs again and scurried away.

The youth, delighted to have recovered his cherished mirror, took up his cat, that she might not harm his friends the mice, and withdrew. Now he took out the mirror and glanced at it. Instantly the Arab stood before him. "Your command, my Sultan?" he asked. The youth requested a suit of cloth-of-gold and a mighty army. Turning round next moment he saw the raiment ready to hand, and he put it on. A prancing steed stood before him, and when he had mounted it an immense army followed him. Thus he entered his native town in triumph.

He drew up before the palace gates and his soldiers formed a cordon round the building. When the Padishah saw the invading host he trembled for his life and throne.

The youth approached the monarch and assured him that there was no cause for fear if he would give him his daughter in marriage. Overwhelmed with joyful surprise the Padishah was willing to give the young man, not only his daughter, but even his kingdom as well. The old woman was dragged off by the thick-lipped Arab; and the lovers lived happily ever after--never parting with the piece of mirror, which proved to be their help in every need.

Little Hyacinth's Kiosk

There was once a Padishah who had a son of incomparable beauty. Whoever saw him was struck with the handsome young Prince, and his father could hardly endure to be away from his son for a single half-hour.

Unhappily, however, the Padishah was taken ill and died, in spite of the attention of the most skilful physicians and learned hodjas of the kingdom. Bitter lamentations ascended from the whole serai, but they availed nothing. A stately mausoleum was built and the remains of the late ruler laid to rest within; then the Shahzada, who was in his twenty-fifth year, ascended the throne.

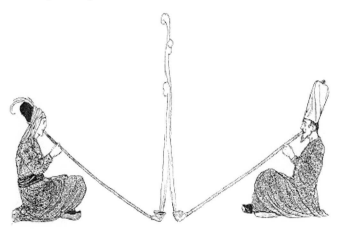

Years passed away, and being one day somewhat indisposed he resolved to seek change of air by making a tour with his lala. Not overburdening themselves with luggage, they mounted their horses, halting not until they had accomplished a day's journey. They continued their onward course until they reached a spring in the midst of a wide plain. The bubbling water was partly hidden by trees; the meadows around them were covered by sweet-smelling flowers. It was like a smiling garden, and the ice-cold water of the spring was refreshing and reviving. When the Padishah, who since his father's death had grieved continually, saw this, he said to his lala: "I am charmed with this place; let us sit down that I may leave my feet in this cooling stream and afterwards rest." The lala was encouraged to hope that the loveliness of this spot would assuage his master's grief. They sat down, drank coffee, and lighted their chibouques. Throughout the evening they heard the songs of nightingales, and so agreeable was the spot that they found it hard to leave it. "I must stop here some days longer," said the young Padishah, "for surely this delightful place is without compare in all the world." The lala agreed that it was indeed delightful, yet as it was in the desert they could not well remain there at night. "Then for the present we will remain tonight only," said the Padishah; "but in a few days we will come here again."

After they had been sitting some time, the Shah arose and walked to and fro. "Inshallah," he said, "I will have a kiosk built here, where I may pass my summers." While speaking, they saw in the distance an old man approaching with a jug in his hand. Presently he came up

340

and filled his jug at the spring. The Padishah's curiosity being excited he exclaimed: "O father, who are you and whence do you come?" The old man answered: "At half an hour's distance is a kiosk belonging to a maiden called 'Little Hyacinth.' This spring also is hers. She comes here every year to spend three days. Forty Dews guard her. How did you dare to come here? I advise you to depart quickly before you are observed, or you will be put to death."

Though alarmed, the Padishah was also curious, and asked the old man who this maiden was to live in such a place, guarded by forty Dews. The old man smiled, and repeated his warning. "I am sorry for you," he said, "but you must hasten away from this neighbourhood." The Shah, however, would not give in. The old man observed the remarkable beauty of the youth. Surely there could not be a handsomer man in the world? He was as beautiful as their Hyacinth as like as one half. apple is to its corresponding half. Therefore he now said: "young man, at one hour's distance, behind a high mountain, dwells the mother of the Dews that guard the maiden. Go there and seek her protection, and ask her how you may see Hyacinth."

The Shah determined to follow the advice of the old man, and set off with his lala. In due time they crossed the mountain, and there saw a sight that might cause the stoutest heart to quail. A Dew woman, tall as a minaret, sat in the valley, one leg upon the mountain and the other stretched out before her. She chewed a piece of resin as large as a house, and the sound made thereby could be heard two miles off. When she breathed she caused a whirlwind which blew up sand and earth; and her arms were eight yards long. The two men were so frightened and bewildered that they were hardly able to greet her as

"O Father who art thou?" asked the Padishah

"Mother," and embrace her as they had been instructed. They managed the feat, however, and the old woman answered: "I should have crushed you like flies if you had not embraced me and called me Mother. Who sent you here?" Trembling from head to foot the Prince replied: "O Mother, at a well we met an old man, one of the servants of Little Hyacinth, who warned us to come to you if we would escape death. O Mother, how looks Little Hyacinth? Since first I heard her name I have had no peace, and I must see her."

"Little Hyacinth is of wonderful beauty," answered the woman. "Her equal does not exist on earth. Many have

342

attempted to see her, but none have succeeded, though nearly all of them have died for her. I have forty sons who guard her kiosk by day and by night. They never allow so much as a bird to approach her. Put the idea out of your mind; otherwise you will die, and that would be a pity."

Nevertheless the Shah implored: "Deign to help us, Mother, and I will repay you." He begged so long and so humbly that the Dew-woman softened at length, and changing the lala into a broom and the Padishah into a tobacco-box, which she put in her belt, she set forth and in three strides was at the kiosk. She now took from her pocket a handful of sand, strewed it about the floor, and said to the transformed Shah: "Fear nothing. At present the Dews are all asleep. Go straight to the chamber wherein the maiden lies sleeping. Do nothing more, however, than take the ring from her finger and bring it to me." The Padishah took courage and entered the chamber where the maiden was sleeping. What a sight met his gaze! The choicest words could not accurately describe the maiden. Her arms glistened like turquoises, and as she lay in bed she looked truly like a houri from Paradise. His eyes were dazzled by the sight of her, and he almost lost his presence of mind. However, remembering the words of the Dew-mother, he drew the ring from her finger and hastened back to the giantess. She picked him up, and in three strides they were back at her house, where she changed him into a jug and set him beside her. Waking from sleep next morning the maiden observed that her ring was missing from her finger. "Where can I have put it? she mused. "Perhaps it has fallen down somewhere." She searched the kiosk, but in vain she sought it in the

343

garden, equally in vain. Then she called the Dews and questioned them, but they did not know. The maiden was angry and scolded them; so they went in forty different directions to seek the missing ring, but failed to find it. After, wards they went to their mother and asked her whether she knew anything about it; but their mother answered them: "Have you lost your wits? Can anyone enter the kiosk so long as we are here? Who knows? Probably the frivolous girl has dropped it somewhere." And she sent her sons away.

In three strides she was back to her house

Next evening the Shah begged the Dew-mother to let him see the maiden once more. The woman took him again to the kiosk, strewed sand as before, and said: "Now go to the maiden, but beware of doing anything save what I tell you. Take one of her earrings and come back quickly." The Shah, going straight to the maiden's chamber, took one of the rings out of her ear, and, though he found it hard to leave her, he ran quickly back to the Dew-woman. Changing him again into a jug, the woman went home and set it on the floor.

When she awoke next morning, Hyacinth observed that now one of her earrings was missing, Very angry at this second outrage, she sent for the old man, who, though he well knew what had happened, answered: "My daughter, no bird flies over here, no caravan passes, no snake crawls here. That you have been robbed is impossible; perchance the rings fell in the grass when you were walking. I will seek, and if I find either or both I will bring them to you."

With such words he attempted to calm the maiden. She was not so easily satisfied, however, and said: "Those are mere words. It is certain that someone has entered my chamber and stolen my jewellery." She then made the Dews understand that if anything further happened to her she would know what to do. Throughout the day she was exceedingly angry.

At the Shah's earnest supplication the Dew-mother took him again to the kiosk, but forbade him to do more than kiss both cheeks of the maiden and return quickly to her. Full of joy, the youth entered the chamber. But the maiden, owing to her excitement, could not sleep and was gazing round her. As soon as her eyes lit on the handsome youth she was overcome with rapture. He, however, thinking she slept, kissed her cheeks, and was about to depart when she clasped him in her arms, saying: "Darling of my heart, how came you here? Fear not; I am yours. I have now found that which I have long sought." The Shah could hardly believe his good fortune, and overcome by the maiden's loveliness, he swooned away. She brought him to consciousness with rose-water, and they talked with one another until daybreak.

Then said the maiden: "Henceforth I am yours and you are mine. I will never part from you although I cannot leave this place. If you love me, remain here." The Padishah replied: "O my Sultana, I am a king. When travelling one day I saw a spring in this neighbourhood and resolved to build a summer residence near it." Then he told her all his adventures. "If that is the case," said the maiden, "let us go to your capital city for our marriage and afterwards divide our time between your country and mine." Calling the Dews, they all went together to the Dew-mother, and the maiden said: "O Mother, we have found each other, and we go hence. May Allah bless and protect you"

The Dew-woman replied: "Go safe and sound; but send me forty sheep daily or you will not prosper." "We owe you so much," said the Padishah, " that I will gladly send the forty sheep daily, and your sons shall continue to guard this place."

Thus they departed, and in due time arrived in the Padishah's capital. The whole serai turned out to welcome them home. The Grand Vezir was summoned, and the betrothal took place. Then followed forty days and forty nights of revelry and rejoicing, and on the forty-first their union was solemnized.

He kissed her cheeks.

They lived together in perfect harmony and bliss to the end of their long lives, partly in the Padishah's realm and partly in Hyacinth's kiosk; and never once did they forget the daily toll of forty sheep to the Dew-mother.

Prince Ahmed

There was once a Padishah who had a
son. One day the Padishah, being angry with his son,
commanded that he should be beheaded. The Vezir
endeavoured to dissuade the King from his cruel purpose,
saying: "O, Padishah, forty years are as one day and you
have but one son; kill him not or you will surely repent of
it." The monarch therefore contented himself with sending
the Prince into exile. "If my only child is to be sent from
me," said his mother, " I will not remain here." So they left
the palace together.

After considerable wandering
they reached a lake, where
they sojourned for some time.
While strolling along the
waterside one day Prince
Ahmed kicked his foot against
a stone, and on taking it up
he was quite dazzled by its
splendour.

The Prince put the stone in his
pocket, after which mother and
son resumed their journey, and
presently came to a town,
where they hired a house and
commenced house-keeping.

349

The Padishah who dwelt here had issued a decree forbidding the lighting of candles, lamps, or any illumination at night; but the stone which the youth had found, when laid on a table in the room, illuminated not only the house but the whole city. The woman advised her son to hide the stone, as when its brightness was perceived it would be taken from them, and moreover they might get into trouble on account of it. But the Prince would not listen to her, arguing that as they had lighted neither candle nor lamp they had not transgressed the royal command.

One night the Padishah, looking out of his window, saw the bright light which emanated from the glistening stone. He called his Vezir and inquired what this illumination could mean. All the lala could tell him was that the light issued from a certain house. Immediately servants were sent to investigate. They knocked at the door and informed the youth that he was summoned to the Padishah's presence. The youth accordingly went to the palace, and the King asked him how he dared to set at naught the royal command. Prince Ahmed excused himself. by saying that he had done nothing contrary to the King's decree; the light came neither from candle nor lamp, but from a stone which he had picked up. "Bring me the stone," ordered the Padishah. So the youth returned home for the stone, took it to the palace and delivered it to the King, glad that the danger was past.

The Padishah showed the stone to his Vezir, who said: "My Shah, that is a diamond; demand from the man who brought it a sackful, for where this one was there must be many more." Immediately the Padishah again summoned the youth and ordered him to bring a sackful of diamonds. "Whence shall I obtain them?" asked the youth. "That is your affair," replied the Padishah; "and if in forty days you fail to procure them, I will have your head."

Very crestfallen, the young Prince went home to his mother and told her of the task imposed upon him. " Did I not tell you the stone would bring us much ill-luck?" ejaculated his mother; "where can we get so many diamonds?" and she burst into tears. They both continued in a state of despair for several days, and then the mother with sudden resolution said: "Weeping will not avail; something must be done Go where you found the stone and see if you can find others."

The youth mounted his horse and rode quickly to the spot. While he was searching for stones he saw a large mountain in the distance, Curiosity led him to cross it, and on the other side he saw a serai. He approached it and found the edifice was guarded by a seven-headed dragon. "What was I seeking, and what have I found!" exclaimed the youth, and in his rage he drew his handschar and struck off six of the dragon's heads at one blow. "Strike once more if you are a man," challenged the dragon. "Not I," replied the youth, and left the dragon to his fate.

Suddenly he heard a great noise issuing from the serai, and caught the words: "you have killed my enemy, and are now forsaking me!" He returned to the spot and, entering the palace, saw a maiden of radiant beauty, who said: "O youth, it is ten years since I was taken captive by the dragon; now I am yours; take me whithersoever you will." The youth told her that at present he had other grave matters to attend to; but the maiden implored him not to forsake her, so eventually he set her before him on horseback and they returned together to the Prince's mother.

He struck off six of the Dragon's heads at one blow

The youth's grief and sorrow were observed by the maiden, and one day she ventured to inquire what trouble oppressed his heart. "Ask me not," replied the youth; "Allah alone can aid me." But she gave him no peace until he told her, whereupon she said: "It were a pity to grieve over such a trifling matter; I will help you. At present, however, I am very thirsty; bring me a jug of water from the spring and let me take a good draught." The youth thought within himself that he had brought her home only to be a vexation, She was his guest, however, and, though somewhat cross, he brought water from the spring and gave it to her. Instead of drinking it, however, the maiden told the youth to sprinkle her with the water from head to foot. He did so, and lo! the water fell from her in the form of resplendent diamonds. "Now gather them up, put them in a sack, and take them to the Padishah," said the maiden joyfully; and this he did accordingly.

After Prince Ahmed had taken his departure, the Padishah called his Vezir and showed him the diamonds. "Now you see," replied the Vezir triumphantly, "I was right. Demand from him next a sackful of pearls," "Where can he get them?" asked the Padishah, "From the same place as the diamonds," answered the Vezir; "do as I advise you." So the Padishah sent for the youth once more, and ordered him to bring a sackful of pearls. "Whence can I get so many pearls?" asked the youth,

"I give you forty days," replied the King; "if by then they are not here your life shall pay for it."

With downcast head and sorrowful countenance the youth went home. "What is the matter?" was the maiden's greeting, and he told her his new trouble. "Go," she answered, "and behind the serai where you first met me you will find another serai containing what you seek."

The youth mounted his horse and set forth. In due time he arrived at the serai, where he slew another dragon. Entering the palace and looking round, he saw another maiden more beautiful than the first. Her also he took home with him. There she requested him to sprinkle her body with water, which fell from her in the form of

353

lustrous pearls. The youth collected them all in a sack and delivered them to the Padishah.

The avaricious Vezir, seeing the pearls, was still unsatisfied, and advised the Padishah to demand a sackful of rubies. The sorely tried Prince told the maiden of his third task. "Now," said she, "beyond the second serai is a third. There you will find what you need." Obediently the youth mounted his horse and rode off.

Again fortune favoured him, he found the third serai, slew the guardian dragon, and entering discovered a maiden lovelier than either of the others, He mounted her before him on his horse, and took her home to his mother's house. He sprinkled her with water, which fell from her body transformed into rubies. These he gathered into a sack and took to the Padishah.

When the Vezir saw them he said to the King: "Now you see! Demand this time a kiosk of diamonds, pearls, and rubies, erected in the midst of the sea." The Padishah doubted whether the youth could really perform such a difficult task, but he made known to him the royal will, and gave him forty days' grace in which to fulfil it. The youth deeply repented ever coming to that city, and went home with a countenance clouded by sadness.

As the maidens welcomed him and perceived his sorrowful mien, they demanded to know the cause, which the youth told.

He delivered them to the Padishah

Then said the eldest: "Go to such and such a place, where there is a mountain; ascend that mountain, and from its summit shout with all your might: 'Hadji Baba!' and when you hear a voice reply, say: 'Your eldest daughter desires her smallest serai.' If no reply be vouchsafed, beware not to shout again or you are lost."

Mounting his horse, the youth proceeded direct to the place indicated. He arrived at the mountaintop, and shouted as loud as he could: "Hadji Baba!" The earth seemed to shake beneath him, and a voice demanded: "What do you seek here?" "Your eldest daughter desires her smallest serai," answered the youth. Then came again a rumbling of the earth, and a sepulchral voice said: "Her wish is granted even before she asked it." Waiting for nothing else the youth hastened homeward.

355

Next morning when the Padishah rose from his bed and looked through the window, his eyes were so dazzled by what he saw that he had to shut them. "What can it be?" he wondered, and rubbing his eyes, he clapped his hands to summon his Vezir. "What has happened to my eyes?" he asked; "I cannot look outside without blinking." "It is the kiosk of precious stones in the midst of the sea that dazzles your eyes, O Padishah," answered the Vezir. On hearing this the King was impatient to go with all his vezirs, pashas, and beys to inspect his latest possession.

While the whole court was thus engaged in inspecting the kiosk the maiden advised the youth to go to the mountain and ask for the kiosk to be taken back. So the youth hastened forth, galloped up the mountain and shouted, "Take back the kiosk!" The ground trembled beneath him, and the same sepulchral voice answered: "We have taken it back!" On his return home the youth saw that the kiosk was no longer where it had been, and he was informed that the Padishah and his whole court had been drowned in the sea. Then said the maidens: "This city is no longer the place for us; let us go, my Shahzada." So Prince Ahmed with the three maidens and his mother set out on the journey to their native land.

On the road they encountered a lame Dew. The youth would have slain him instantly, but the Dew implored him to spare his life, hinting that the youth might find him useful. As the maidens supported the Dew's petition, he was spared and joined the party.

The lame Dew

When they arrived within sight of the capital they sat down to rest, and the eldest maiden by her magic art created on the spot a palace more magnificent than anyone had ever seen before.

It chanced that the Padishah, the young Prince's father, looking out of the window, saw this fine palace, and summoning his Vezir, asked the meaning of it. Servants were dispatched to inquire, and they returned with the intelligence that this wonderful palace was the residence of Prince Ahmed, who was the Padishah's own son. On hearing this the Padishah went himself to the palace. His son received him with every mark of respect and great joy, and presented the three maidens, whose beauty so fascinated the monarch that he wished to have them in his own palace.

When he returned to his own palace he said to his Vezir: "Let Prince Ahmed be put to death." The Vezir attempted to dissuade him, reminding him how once before he had banished his son in anger. "Who knows," he continued, "what sufferings he endured!" Notwithstanding all the Vezir s pleading the Padishah insisted that his son must be put to death. "Then if it must be so," said the Vezir, sighing, "invite him to the palace and poison his food."

357

Next day the Prince received an invitation to dine at his father's palace, and as he was departing the maiden took a ring from her finger and gave it to him, saying: "When you are in the palace, touch with this ring whatever food is set before you." Putting the ring on his finger, the youth went his way. He conversed with his father for some time, after which food was brought in. All the dishes intended for the Prince were poisoned, but unobserved he touched them with the ring before eating them, and they did him no harm. The table was cleared and he took his leave. Seeing his son did not die from eating the poisoned food, the Padishah summoned his Vezir and asked what must be done now. The latter advised the King to invite his son to play a game of tawla with him, the loser to agree to be bound with cords. "If the Prince loses," said the Vezir, "you will bind him and put him to death." Thus once more the youth was invited to his father's palace. After a repast the Padishah said: "Come, my son, let us play at tawla, the loser to be bound by the winner." They played and the Padishah lost. The Prince, however, waived the forfeit, not suspecting any evil intention on his father's part, and they resumed the game. A second time the Padishah lost. Again the youth waived the forfeit, with deep respect requesting his father to continue the game, and intentionally allowed the King to win. Then said the Padishah to his son: "I shall now bind you in accordance with our agreement." The Prince offering no objection, his father bound him with strong cords, and afterwards sent for the executioner. Meanwhile the Prince gave his bonds a strong pull and freed himself.

When the Padishah saw this, he pretended that the whole thing was only a joke, as he wished to find out whether his son possessed manly strength. "In that case," said the Prince, "bind me with iron chains." Accordingly this was done, but the Prince broke the chains also at a single pull. Secretly angry, the Padishah endeavoured to devise some means of destroying his son. Outwardly smiling, he said to the Prince: "I see, my son, that you are a valiant fellow; but perhaps you will tell me wherein lies the secret of your strength." Suspecting no evil, the Prince answered that if three hairs were taken from his head and bound round his finger, he would be rendered quite helpless. The Padishah said he would like to test it, and the Prince being willing to submit, he himself pulled out three of his hairs and handed them to his father. The Padishah bound them round the finger of his son, who became as helpless as a babe.

Now the Padishah called in the executioner and ordered him to cut off the Prince's head. The executioner, however, refused and ran away. The Padishah knew not what to do next. After a while he himself put out his son's eyes, placed them in his pocket, and had the Prince taken to a distant dry well and cast therein. The Prince's little dog followed his master to the well, jumped in after him, and remained his faithful companion in misfortune.

A brief period elapsed, and the Padishah made known his intention of taking the three maidens to his palace. They stipulated, however, that he should send for them forty carriages, each occupied by a maid, and forty empty carriages besides for their belongings.

This was done accordingly, but the three maidens cut off the heads of the forty maids and sent them back in the empty carriages. This aroused the Padishah's wrath and caused him to proclaim war on the maidens; but the maidens, aided by the lame Dew, completely destroyed the army sent against them.

Meanwhile a caravan stopped in the neighbourhood of the well into which Prince Ahmed had been cast. His little dog made friendly overtures to the people, who gave him bread. This he took direct to the well and let it fall down, returning to the caravan again, and yet a third time. The leader of the caravan seeing this, said: "This dog either has young ones or some one is in hiding." He followed the creature and saw it cast the bread into the well; he then went to the well and shouted down, hearing in answer the words: "Deliver me from this well."

Without delay a rope was let down, and the person at the bottom directed to seize it; but the cry was returned that the unfortunate prisoner's hands were so bound that he could not grasp anything. The Prince related how his enemy had dealt with him. Then said the leader of the caravan: "If we take you with us it may be thought that we have so treated you, and thus our caravan would be subjected to many annoyances. It were best that you remain here and pray to Allah for aid." On this they gave him food and drink and abandoned him. Prince Ahmed was grateful for this small mercy; and as he sat lamenting next night a pir appeared before him. He took two eyes from his pocket and adjusted them in the empty sockets of Prince Ahmed, who instantly received his sight. The pir to whom he owed this good fortune, however, had disappeared before the Prince could look at him.

The youth now returned direct to his native town. He went to his father's serai, and finding that the Padishah was at war with the maidens he said: "My Shah and father, in three days I will capture the Dew and deliver him into your hands." His father rejoiced at this, and promised, if he did so, to grant all his wishes. Hitherto the Dew had slain all who had been sent against him. Prince Ahmed requested his father to allow him to choose a horse and sword for himself. His own horse and sword had remained in the palace since the fateful day when his eyes had been put out, and he chose these. Girding on his sword and mounting his steed he sallied forth to meet the Dew.

When the maidens saw this youth coming alone against them, they concluded the Padishah had no more men to send. As the Prince approached, the Dew, instead of attacking him, suddenly desisted, and the two opponents faced each other with drawn swords. Renewing their friendship, the two returned together to the palace of the Padishah. At sight of the Dew the King was seized with terror. "Bring him not hither," cried the King trembling; but the Prince scornfully replied: "Our arrangement was that I should capture the Dew; now you shall kill him."

The Dew threw him down from his throne

Upon this the Dew set upon the Padishah, threw him down from his throne, and killed him. Then turning to the Vezirs, the Dew said: "Behold! His son Ahmed it was who brought me here." The Vezirs, who had never approved of the Padishah's cruel behaviour toward the Shahzada, now set the Prince on the throne amid great rejoicing.

His first act as Padishah was to send for his mother and the three maidens, who all shared in the happiness of his glorious reign.

Ignacz Kúnos

The Liver

AN old woman once fancied some liver to eat, so she gave her daughter a few paras with which to buy a portion. "Wash it in the pond and bring it straight home," she said. The girl went accordingly to the tscharschi, and having bought the liver, carried it to the pond and washed it. As she withdrew it from the water, however, a stork swooped down upon the liver and flew off with it. The girl exclaimed: "Give me back the liver, O stork, that I may take it to my mother, or she will beat me."

"If thou wilt give me barley, I will give thee back the liver," replied the stork.

The girl accordingly went to the farmer and said: "Farmer, give me barley, that I may give it to the stork, who will give me back the liver, that I may take it to my mother." Said the farmer: "If thou wilt pray to Allah for rain, I will give thee barley."

This seemed very simple, but while she was praying: "Send rain, O Allah, to the farmer, who will give me barley, that I may give it to the stork, who will give me back the liver, that I may take it to my mother," there came a man who said that without incense prayer could not avail.

"Merchant, give me incense", said the girl

So the girl went to the merchant and said: "Merchant, give me incense, that I may burn it before Allah, who will send rain to the farmer, who will give me barley, that I may give it to the stork, who will give me back the liver, that I may take it to my mother."

"I will give thee some," answered the merchant, "if thou wilt bring me shoes from the shoemaker."

Off the girl went to the shoemaker and said: "Shoemaker, give me shoes, that I may give them to the merchant, who will give me incense, that I may burn it before Allah, who will send rain to the farmer, who will give me barley, that I may give it to the stork, who will give me back the liver, that I may take it to my mother."

But the shoemaker replied: "First bring me ox-leather, then will I give thee shoes."

So the girl went to the tanner, and said: "Tanner, give me leather, that I may give it to the shoemaker, who will give me shoes, that I may give them to the merchant, who will give me incense, that I may burn it before Allah, who will send rain to the farmer, who will give me barley, that I may give it to the stork, who will give me back the liver, that I may take it to
my mother."

"Bring me a hide from an ox and I will give thee leather," answered the tanner. So the girl went to the ox and said: "Ox, give me a hide, that I may take it to the tanner, who will give me leather, that I may give it to the shoemaker, who will give me shoes, that I may give them to the

"Bring me a hide from an ox" answered the Tanner

merchant, who will give me incense, that I may burn it before Allah, who will send rain to the farmer, who will give me barley, that I may give it to the stork, who will give me back the liver, that I may take it to my mother."

The ox made answer: "If thou wilt bring me straw I will give thee a hide."

366

The girl now went to a peasant and said: "Peasant, give me straw, that I may give it to the ox, who will give me a hide, that I may take it to the tanner, who will give me leather, that I may give it to the shoemaker, who will give me shoes, that I may give them to the merchant, who will give me incense, that I may burn it before Allah, who will send rain to the farmer, who will give me barley, that I may give it to the stork, who will give me back the liver, that I may take it to my mother."

How could the peasant refuse? "I will give thee straw if thou wilt kiss me," said he.

The girl concluded that she must kiss the peasant if she would attain her object. So she kissed him and received the price. She took the straw to the ox, who gave her a hide, which she took to the tanner, who gave her leather, which she took to the shoemaker, who gave her shoes, which she took to the merchant, who gave her incense, which she burnt before Allah, praying: "Give rain, O Allah!" Allah gave her rain, which she took to the farmer, who gave her barley, which she took to the stork, who now gave her back the liver, which she took to her mother, who cooked it, and they ate it up.

Ignacz Kúnos

The Fortune Teller

THERE *was once a widow* who had three daughters. One spun cotton, the others sewed, and thus they earned their daily bread.

Once these girls saw a gipsy passing along the street, and said to each other: "Let us have our fortunes told." All agreeing, they called the old woman, who, having had her hand crossed with silver, said to the eldest of the sisters: "Thy kismet is at the bottom of a well." To the middle sister she said: "Thy kismet is in the cemetery"; and to the youngest she said: "Thy kismet is in shame." Having uttered these ominous words, the gipsy disappeared.

One day while the eldest girl was spinning, her thread broke, the spindle flew up ward, then fell and rolled over and over until it suddenly disappeared down the well. "Oh dear!" she exclaimed, "my spindle is in the well; help

368

me to recover it." Her sisters bound a rope round her body and let her down the well.

Now when the girl reached the bottom she saw an iron gate. She opened it, and entering saw a youth and a maiden lying asleep, a baby in a cradle by their side. She took off her shawl and covered the youth and the maiden with it;

and her eyes lighting on a knife, she picked it up and stuck it in her girdle. This accomplished, she re. turned to the mouth of the well and gave the signal to her sisters to pull her to the surface. Arrived at the top, she was asked why she had been so long down the well. "I sought my spindle until I found it," was the answer, and with that they had to be content.

He cried them for sale in the streets

The youth was the son of a rich man, the maiden was a peri, and as she had fallen in love with him, they met every day at the bottom of the well. When she woke up and saw the shawl around her she was greatly distressed. "Oh dear!" she cried, "a mortal has discovered us," and instantly she disappeared, taking the baby with her. When the youth missed his knife and failed to find it he observed: "Now I am delivered from the peri I will discover, if possible, who has taken my knife." He climbed

369

out of the well, purchased a collection of odds and ends, and cried them for sale in the streets. Whoever wished to buy from him was informed that he was not selling for money, but that he would gladly trade with anyone who had a knife of any kind.

Going up and down the streets, he came at length to the house wherein dwelt the three sisters. They called him in and chose distaffs, needles, and silks; and when they asked the price the merchant told them he could not accept money for the articles, but would take an old knife. Upon this the eldest sister produced the knife she had brought up out of the well.

This he accepted in exchange for the goods, then went home and told his mother she must go to the maiden who had delivered him from the peri and ask her in marriage for him. The lady went on her son's behalf; the maiden consented to become his wife, and in due time the wedding took place.

LEAVING this happy couple, let us follow the fortunes of the remaining sisters. One day they went together to the bath. They washed, and were on their homeward journey, when suddenly the middle sister discovered that the youngest was no longer by her side--she had disappeared entirely. The disquieted sister searched the district for the lost one, but she had gone without leaving the slightest trace behind. Being completely exhausted with her efforts, the middle sister sat down to rest in a cemetery, and there, overcome by fatigue, she fell asleep. Suddenly she was awakened from sleep by the neighing of a horse, and looking round she saw a man alight from a steed. He went to a certain tomb, which he opened, brought forth a youth, gave him something to smell, and thus restored him to consciousness. He then gave him food and drink and demanded to know whether the youth would obey him. "I would rather die," answered the youth, whereon the man shut him up again in the tomb and went away.

The youth was a shahzada who had once been very ill, and the man was a physician on whom the sick Prince's beauty had made such an impression that he could not endure the thought of being parted from him. "I will cure you," said the physician one day, "but only if you promise to obey me ever after." The Prince would not agree, and the physician in revenge administered to the Prince a stupefying draught, on which he fell into a deathlike trance. His parents, believing him dead, buried him in the vault, and there every night went the physician to torment the poor youth until he should yield to his wishes.

Having witnessed this dramatic scene, the maiden waited till day dawned, then went home, purchasing a plateful of lokma on the way, as she was very hungry, While eating it she observed that all the people in the shop were weeping, and she inquired the cause. "The Shahzada died forty days ago," they said, "and his lokma remains on our hands." On this she requested to be taken before the Sultana, for whom she had an important message.

She was accordingly conducted to the palace, and when the Sultana appeared the maiden informed her that her son was not dead as she supposed, but alive. "Give him to me for my husband and I will restore him to you," said the maiden to the Sultana. "My dear, you are surely mad," answered the Sultana. "He died forty days ago; today his bones must be all that is left of him."

The maiden, however, swore that the Shahzada was still alive. "If you do not believe, come with me this night and I will show you your son." The Sultana

The wicked Physician had his head struck off

consulted the Padishah on the matter, and at night they went to the cemetery. Here they concealed themselves and watched. At midnight the physician appeared, opened the tomb, and having restored the Shahzada to consciousness, put his question, and received the same answer as before. Hearing their son's voice the royal parents hastened to the tomb and, weeping, pressed him to their hearts. Later the wicked physician had his head struck off, and the maiden

"I would rather die," answered the youth.

who had been the means of restoring the Prince was united with him in marriage.

Meanwhile the youngest girl, having found her way home, was waiting and waiting for her sister to return. As she did not come she put on a worn-out feredje and set out in search of her, begging her bread from house to house as she went.

One day she called at a house where the tenant had a son who did nothing from morn till eve but lie on his back with his head between a couple of pillows. His parents had often wished to get him married, but he would not look at a prospective bride, and so all the girls had refused to have anything to do with him.

The youth kept his head stuck between two pillows

When the youngest sister knocked at the door her speech and pretty face gave great pleasure to the old parents. They received her kindly, and after a little reflection asked: "My child, we have a son, would you like to become his wife?" "yes, indeed," replied the maiden. "But," said the mother, "our son will not speak a word to any-one." "Never mind," answered the maiden, "I will soon make him speak when he becomes my husband."

374

So they were married, and the girl was left alone with the young man to make his acquaintance. The girl now saw that he was actually as he had been described.

He kept his head stuck between two pillows, and never opened his mouth to anyone. The maiden closed the door of the room, went towards the young man, and as though speaking to him said: "My darling, let me go; do not hold me so tight!" The old people were listening outside, and hearing the words, concluded that the maiden had succeeded in awakening their son's interest.

In the evening food was set before the young pair, but the young man never deigned to raise his head from his cushions. So the maiden ate both portions, after which she lay down and pretended to sleep, keeping an eye on the young man over the top of the bedcover. When he thought she was asleep he got up quietly, opened the door, and went upstairs. The girl followed him stealthily and saw his meeting with a lovely creature, beautiful as the full moon, who greeted him with these words: "O my boy, why have you been so long? I was tired of waiting; if you had delayed longer I should have left you." The youth explained what had happened, and how he had been obliged to wait until the girl was asleep.

The lovely maiden was the daughter of the Padishah of the Peris, whom the youth had first seen in a dream and fallen in love with. "If you will look at no other woman but me," the peri-maiden had said, "I will visit you every night." Thus it was that the youth stuck his head between the pillows and refused to glance at any other woman. When the peri maiden heard of the youngest sister she said: "If you look at her but once, you will never see me again."

As soon as the eavesdropper heard these words she returned to the room and locked the door. When the youth returned to his own room, he found the door locked against him. There was no alternative but to beg the maiden within to open the door for him. She answered that she would let him in only on his solemn promise to converse with her awhile. As there was no avoiding it, he promised. The maiden, opening the door, let him in, and as his glance fell on her a wall rose up by magic between the stairs and the door--a sign that the peri-maiden would never more return.

The youth's parents blessed Allah for the change in their son's disposition, and were so pleased with their strangely found daughter-in-law that they celebrated the marriage with festivities lasting forty days and forty nights.

Ignácz Kúnos

Sister and Brother

THERE once lived a man named Ahmed Aga. He was very rich, and beside his wife had no one belonging to him. The only thing that disturbed his happiness was the fact that he had no child. "Allah," said he, "has endowed me with much property and wealth; I have also an honourable name; would that He might vouchsafe me a child! Then were my happiness complete. After my death he would inherit my whole fortune, and my fame would be enhanced."

One night he was brooding as usual over this matter and said to his wife: "Would it not have been better if Allah had given us poverty with a child?" These words pained his wife very deeply, and before she went to bed she prayed to Allah for consolation, In the night she dreamt that she was  sitting by the sea-shore. A mermaid came to the surface of the water with a pot in her hand and said to the woman

378

"Tell your husband Allah has given him this kismet; let him come and fetch it." She hastened home to tell her husband and in her excitement woke Ahmed Aga as well as herself. "What is the matter?" asked the man. "Nothing," answered the woman; "but you have waked me."

"No," returned the man, "it was you who roused me." Then his wife recounted what she had seen and heard in her dream. "Then that was why you woke me," muttered her husband, and turning over went to sleep again. To his wife, however, the dream was a thing of good omen.

Rising next morning, the woman advised her husband to go down to the seashore. "It might be no vain dream after all," she mused. "Do not be foolish," retorted her husband, "our kismet is not in dreams; if Allah has any gift to bestow on us He will do it by other means." His wife, how-ever, gave him no peace. "Nevertheless go," she insisted; "the sea will not engulf you, and maybe Allah will bless us in this wise." The man could not further withstand his wife, so when he went out for a stroll, he took the direction of the seashore.

While pacing up and down he noticed that some dark object was being washed ashore on the crest of the billows. As it came nearer he could see that it was a pot, the mouth of which was securely bound. Alternating betwixt hope and fear, he seized the pot and with a bismillah opened it. Imagine his joy to find therein two newborn babes.

When Ahmed Aga saw them he was like a child himself; in his delight he knew not what to do first. Taking off his cloak, he wrapped the babes carefully in it and ran all the way home. He arrived out of breath, and dropped the bundle in his wife's lap. When she opened it and saw what

He found in the pot two new-born babes

it contained she too was frantic with joy, kissing the children and pressing them to her heart. The babes being hungry soon began to cry lustily. This brought the worthy couple to their senses, and soon Ahmed was on the road in search of a nurse for their unexpected family. Before long he found a suitable woman, and engaged her at a very generous wage. As soon as she arrived the cries of the infants were stilled immediately. On the following day two more nurses were engaged, and thus cared for the children, a boy and a girl, grew fat and strong.

IN another town there was likewise a man who had no children, although, like Ahmed Aga, he greatly desired a son. So he and his wife prayed earnestly to Allah that he would give them a child, and when they learned that their prayers were to be answered, their rejoicing was unbounded. The good news came to the ears of a servant who at one time had been in that household, but having been dismissed by the wife for neglecting her duties, she was desperately jealous at the happiness which was coming to her former mistress. Determined to take her revenge, she presented herself as a nurse, and was engaged. In due time twin babies, a boy and a girl, were born; but while their mother was sleeping, and before ever their father had seen them, the false nurse put the children into a pot, and having sealed it carefully, cast it into the sea. While the husband was sleeping, the false woman sat by him and whispered in his ear so that he thought it was a dream sent by Allah. She told him that he had been deceived and had, after all, no child. As the mother had been asleep, she could not tell what had become of her children, and certainly they were nowhere to be found. So the husband, believing his dream, was very angry at what he thought was his wife's attempt to deceive him, and he drove her out of his house. The poor creature had not a friend in the world, and went forth weeping bitterly.

She wandered on from one hill to another, until one day, although it was dark, it seemed as though each hill was a different colour from the others. Fear seized upon her heart and tears started from her eyes. Hunger and fatigue overcame her, and she knew not what to do. Seeing a tree, she climbed up to spend the night in it and await Allah's pleasure toward her. Having settled herself among the leafy branches, she wept herself to sleep. When morning dawned she descended in the hope of meeting with a passerby or coming to a village where she might obtain a little bread. But, alas! no aid was nigh, and after wandering for many hours she sank down from sheer exhaustion.

Presently, however, she saw in the distance a shepherd, and, summoning the remainder of her little strength, she accosted him. Offering her bread, the shepherd asked her trouble. When he had heard it he took pity upon her and led her home to his wife, his son, and his daughter.

The Shepherd asked

As time went on the poor woman had almost forgotten her sorrow, excepting her grief for the loss of her children, over whom she often sighed and wept. How fared they in the meantime?

With the good Ahmed Aga and his wife they grew up to their fourteenth year and went together to school. One day the boy was playing with a companion, who, jealous of his superiority over him, said: "Be off, you fatherless and motherless brat, found by Ahmed Aga on the seashore." At these words the boy's brow became clouded, and he ran away angrily to his foster-mother, telling her what had been said to him. She endeavoured to calm him, but that same night the boy dreamt of the shepherd's hut and of his mother, who in the dream related all her sufferings.

382

The false woman sat by him and whispered in his ear.

The boy flung a large stone at the ugly beast

When he repeated the dream to his sister, lo! she also had had a similar dream. Then the boy knew that what his playfellows had taunted him with was no untruth, but the fact. They went together to their kind foster-father and told him what they had both dreamt. The good man was troubled, but confessed that he had indeed found them in a pot washed up by the waves; of their mother he knew nothing. The brother and sister were in despair at the thought of their poor mother living in a shepherd's cottage. It was impossible to comfort them, and finally the boy declared his intention of setting out to find his mother. His sister was left behind in the kind hands of her foster-parents.

Spurred on by his heroic courage and anxiety for his mother, the boy made all haste, and as he lay down to rest

384

under the stars one night the place of his mother's sojourn was revealed to him in a dream. To cut our story shorter, we will only say that in one day he covered a five-days, journey without experiencing either hunger or fear. As he followed the course indicated in his dream he found his further progress barred by a hideous dragon. The boy had no weapon, but picking up a large stone he flung it at the ugly beast with such tremendous force that the creature reeled backward and fell to the earth. "If you are a man throw another stone at me," shouted the dragon; but the youth went his way, leaving the dragon to perish.

Indefatigably the boy travelled, and in due time reached the valley where his mother had once spent the night in a tree. Here he stopped, and at the foot of the tree sought the rest that had long been denied him. While he slept, the brother of the dead dragon, having heard what had happened, came in search of the boy. The monster's heavy strides caused the earth to tremble and awoke the youth. "I am certain you are the youth who has killed my brother," began the dragon. "Now it is my turn." Saying this, with jaws foaming and fire issuing from his nostrils, he sprang upon the lad. In self-defence the youth grasped the dragon's foreleg, using such strength that he tore it from the body and flung it away. Then the dragon sank down weakening from loss of blood, saying: "To him who has taken my life belongs my treasure." The unwieldy beast rolled over and over and finally disappeared into a cavern at the foot of a mountain.

Prompted by curiosity, the youth glanced into the mouth of the cavern and saw a staircase leading downward. Descending, he found a palace, which he entered and

explored in all directions. In one apartment was a maiden sitting on a throne--a maiden so lovely that his heart was a thou sand times filled with love of her. On her part the maiden was enraptured with the youth's comeliness; but, not knowing of the dragon's destruction, she cried: "Woe unto us! If the dragon sees this youth he will kill us both." Then addressing the youth she asked: "How came you into this palace of the Breathless Dragon? Whomsoever he looks upon is slain by his mere glance."

A lovely maiden was sitting on a throne

Now the youth related to the maiden how he had slain both dragons, and he besought her to come away with him. As she appeared not to comprehend, he repeated his words and urged her to hasten, as he had other business to fulfil. "That being so," said the maiden at last, "there is much here that we might take away with us." The maiden leading the way and the youth following, they entered the forty rooms of the palace, each of which was filled with gold, diamonds, and precious stones. However, the youth said: "My dear, I have first an important duty to perform;

when that is done, we will return and take away as much of this treasure as we please."

Thus they departed, and at some distance saw the shepherd's hut which sheltered the youth's mother. At once he recognised it as the building seen in his dream. Hurrying up, he knocked at the door, and it was opened by his mother herself. Each recognised the other from their dreams, and they fell into each other's arms.

Next morning they all set off together for the dragon's palace. On the backs of the horse and donkey they brought with them, they packed as many sacks of gold and diamonds as the animals could possibly carry. Then they hastened, with brief pauses for rest, to the home of Ahmed Aga, where the youth rejoined his sister and the mother saw her daughter. Now the joyful woman was repaid for all her past sufferings, and they all lived happily together for many years.

The worthy shepherd's son was betrothed to the youth's sister, while the youth himself was betrothed to the maiden of the dragon's palace. A suitable husband was found for the shepherd's daughter, and they were all married on the same day, the festivities lasting forty days and forty nights, and their happiness forever.

Shah Jussuf

IN a certain country lived a man who had three daughters. So poor were they that one day there was not even a crust of bread in the house; and not knowing what else to do, the girls spun some thread. This they gave to their father, saying: "Take this to the tscharschi, sell it for a few paras, and bring home something to eat." The old man took the thread, but no one in the tscharschi would look at him.

While pacing to and fro in deep dejection, an Arab appeared before him and asked: "What hast thou to sell, father?" The old man showed him the thread, and remarked that he must sell it in order to obtain food. The Arab asked who had spun it. "My daughters at home," was the reply. The Arab bought the thread and paid generously for it. He then asked the man to give him one of his daughters. "I will speak to my daughters on the subject," said the man, "and if I can persuade one of them,

389

thou shalt have her." So the Arab accompanied him home. Arriving there, the father said to his eldest daughter: "If I offered thee an Arab for husband, wouldst go to him?" She replied: "What could I do with an Arab? Marry me to some one more useful." He then put the same question to his middle daughter, whose answer was the same as that of her elder sister. His youngest daughter, however, said she was prepared to marry the Arab in order to lighten in some measure their burden of poverty.

The Arab accordingly took the maiden under his care, and, giving the old man much gold, he departed with her.

AFTER they had gone some distance the Arab said to the maiden: "Shut your eyes--open your eyes!" Immediately she found herself in a magnificent palace with slaves supporting her arms as she ascended the grand staircase. She imagined herself in Paradise, it was all so wonderful. At the top of the stairs other slaves escorted her into a chamber glistening with diamonds and pearls, for the walls and floor were inlaid with these gems, while the ceiling was ornamented with gold and silver stars. When she had taken a seat, these slaves remained at hand with bowed heads and folded arms, while other slaves appeared with a sable robe and a dress ornamented with gold and silver sequins in which they clothed her.

In the evening delicious food was served to her in golden dishes, the repast concluding with a glass of sherbet, after drinking which she fell into a deep sleep. Immediately the slaves lifted her up and carried her to bed. While she slept the bey of the palace entered, and gazed at her in admiration, but departed before she awaked. When the maiden rose next morning, slaves appeared to bathe and clothe her and obey her slightest behest. Such was her daily life for three whole months, until homesickness seized her and she longed for a sight of her father and sisters.

One day she spoke of the matter to the Arab who had brought her thither. "Lala," said she, "may I not be allowed to spend a few days with my father and sisters?" The Arab replied: "Call me not lala: my name is Laklak Aga. I am the guard of the palace." Next day she addressed him again as lala, and repeated her request; but the Arab simply corrected her as before. On the third day, however, when she addressed him as "Laklak, my Aga," he listened to her request: "I am longing to spend one or two days with my father and sisters." "Very well," promised the Aga, "tomorrow we will go."

The Arab spoke to his master, the bey, on the subject. The latter had no objection, but impressed upon the Arab that he must not allow the maiden to remain long out of his sight. Thus, on the following morning the maiden prepared for her journey home with Laklak Aga, who supplied himself well with gold. "Shut your eyes--open your eyes! commanded Laklak Aga, and behold! they were at their destination, and in a few moments the maiden was receiving the caresses of her now happy father and sisters. There was great joy in the house that day.

Ignace Kúnos

With the money he had first received the old man had opened a shop, and now the Arab gave him more gold with which to extend his business.

Meanwhile the other girls asked their sister how it fared with her, "Not very well," she replied; "every night I have to drink a glass of sherbet and I fall asleep directly." They next asked her whether she had ever seen the bey. She answered that the Arab was the only man she had ever seen. On this they gave her a sponge, saying: "When sherbet is next brought to you, pretend to drink it, but instead let the sponge absorb it; then lie down and seem to be asleep. You will thus see what happens to you."

When the few days had expired she took leave of her father and sisters and left her home under the Arab's escort. With " Shut your eyes--open your eyes! " she found herself back again in the serai.

In the evening sherbet was brought as usual; but the maiden very cleverly, while pretending to drink it, allowed it to fall into the sponge she held. This done, she lay down and appeared to go to sleep. Slaves carried her to bed, and, as usual, the bey came and stood looking at her. Hearing footsteps, she could not help opening her eyes to see who had entered, and the bey, seeing that she was awake, knew she must have deceived them all about the sherbet. "So thou hast thought by cheating us to satisfy your curiosity?" he exclaimed angrily.

"As a punishment thou shalt be shod with iron shoes, and with an iron staff in thy hand thou shalt seek me for seven years till thou findest me." With these words he disappeared.

The maiden was accordingly shod with iron shoes, and taking an iron staff in her hand she set out on her pilgrimage. She wandered over mountains, through valleys, and across plains, though on looking back she found the distance she had travelled was but the length of a barley-corn. Pursuing her way, ere long she met a Dew-woman who had a horn on her head and tremendous feet. She greeted the Dew-woman with "Salaam!" whereupon the creature answered: "If thou hadst not greeted me I should have pulled thee to pieces and devoured thee." "And if thou hadst not returned my greeting," retorted the maiden, "I should have knocked thee down with my staff."

She met a Dew-Woman

The Dew-woman now asked whence she came and whither she went, and the maiden told her all. Then the Dew-woman informed her that Shah Jussuf the bey had just passed that place, if she would go farther she would meet another Dew-woman who would tell her more.

The maiden wended her way onward until she met the second Dew, woman, who informed her that Shah Jussuf

394

had passed not long ago. Farther and farther she went, until she met a third Dew-woman, who was cleaning a warm oven. The maiden asked her whether she had seen anything of Shah Jussuf. "Why dost thou ask?" inquired the woman, who was in fact the bey's aunt. After the maiden had told her story the Dew-woman observed: "If thou wilt, thou shalt remain with me. Shah Jussuf visits me every seven years; thus thou canst meet him here."

Kissing the woman's hand, the maiden consented to stay. But the woman proceeded: "Thou canst not remain with me in thy present form, however, for I have forty sons, and if they saw thee they would eat thee up." Saying this the Dew-woman gave the maiden a knock, changing her into an apple, which the woman set on a shelf.

At night the Dew-sons came home and said to their mother: "We smell human flesh!"

"What should a human being be doing here?" was the rejoinder. Nevertheless, when they had finished their supper the mother asked: "If anyone should stray hither, and, kissing my hand, beg me to receive him as my child, what would ye do in my place?" "Accept him as our brother and do him no harm," answered the Dew-sons. At these words the Dew-woman took down the apple from the shelf, and giving it a slap, transformed it again into a maiden. "Go and kiss your brothers' hands," she commanded. The maiden did so, and the Dew-sons accepted her as their sister. Shortly after her arrival among them a little son was born to the girl, and him also the Dews accepted as a relative, and treated with kindness.

SEVEN years the maiden passed in their company, and when the seventh year had nearly run out, the Dew-woman observed one day to the maiden: "Shah Jussuf will be here soon. If he requests a glass of water, bring it, and when he returns the empty glass, let it fall from thy hand and break. I shall then pretend to be angry with thee, and by that we shall see whether he loves thee. If so, he will not permit me to beat thee."

Some days later Jussuf appeared, looking very sad and careworn. After greetings had been exchanged, his aunt asked him why he was so downcast, instead of in his usual merry mood. "I am suffering the pangs of grief," answered the youth; "wherefore am I sad." The woman professed not to understand. Food was brought in, and while eating Shah Jussuf asked for a glass of water. It was brought by the maiden, and in drinking Jussuf kept his eyes continually upon her; he could not help seeing in her a vivid resemblance to the wife he was seeking. Having emptied the glass, he handed it back to the maiden, who, as though from carelessness, let it fall to the floor, where it broke in pieces. Now the Dew-woman sprang up from her seat, overwhelmed the girl with reproaches, and would have beaten her soundly had not the Shah interceded on her behalf, placing the blame on himself instead of the maiden. The Dew-woman immediately calmed down, and dismissed the girl with the words: "Get out of my sight."

Shah Jussuf could not help thinking of the maiden, and he questioned his aunt as to whence she procured her, and whether she would not sell her to him. The Dew-woman, however, would not agree to part with her, saying that the girl was indispensable in the house.

Shah Jussuf remained a few days longer and then departed. Yet not. withstanding, that it was his custom to visit his aunt but once in every seven years, in three months he was back again. " Thou rascal!" exclaimed the woman playfully on seeing him again so soon. But to the maiden she said: "On thy account is he come; when thou bringest in the food, upset the dish."

They sat down to supper, and the maiden on entering with the food stumbled, and the dish overturned and fell. In a great rage the woman mercilessly scolded her for her clumsiness in the presence of their guest, and would have beaten the girl had not the Shah forcibly held her back, entreating her once more to pardon the poor girl. Gradually the Dew. woman became calm, but seemingly with great difficulty.

Again the Shah took his departure. When he was gone the woman said to the maiden: "He cannot endure it much longer; he will surely come again very soon, and when he does, open the door to him and tell him who thou art. Moreover, wear the dress thou didst wear when with him, and have the child by thy side."

Looking out of the window one morning she saw Shah Jussuf approaching in the distance. She hastened to dress, and, with her son, ran out to meet him. Seeing her in the dress she wore while at his palace, the Shah knew the woman was surely his wife and the boy by her side his son. Shyly and shamefacedly he glanced first at the maiden and then at the child. Leaving the boy the wife fell on her husband's breast, and with tears of joy at their reunion, told him all that had befallen her during their long separation.

Shah Jussuf now sought his aunt and, kissing her hand, begged her permission to take his wife and child away. "Take her and be happy--she has suffered enough," said the Dew-woman.

Now with hearts overflowing with joy they set out for the palace of Shah Jussuf. On their arrival home they were received with every demonstration of gladness, for during seven long years the Shah in his grief had not inhabited his palace but had wandered over the face of the earth. Their return was celebrated with forty days and forty nights of festivity and merrymaking. Shah Jussuf invited his wife's father and sisters to take up their residence at his palace, and they all lived together in happiness to the end of a long life.

The Black Dragon and the Red Dragon

THERE was once a Padishah who had the misfortune to have all his children stolen as soon as they reached their seventh year. Grief at this terrible affliction caused him almost to lose his reason, "Forty children have been born to me," said he, "each seeming more beautiful than the one which preceded it, so that I never tired of regarding them. O that one at least had been spared to me! Better that I should have had none than that each should have caused me so much grief." He brooded continually over the loss of his children, and at length, unable to endure it longer, he left his palace at night and wandered no one knew whither. When morning broke he was already a good distance from his capital. Presently he reached a spring, and was about to take an abdest to say the prayer namaz, when he observed what appeared like a black cloud in the sky, moving towards him.

When it came quite near he saw that it was a flight of forty birds, which, twittering and cooing, alighted at the spring.

Alarmed, the Padishah hid himself. As they drank at the spring one of the birds said: "Mother's-milk was never our kismet. We must perforce drink mountain water. Neither father nor mother care for us." Then said another: "Even if they think about us, they cannot know where we are." At these words they flew away. The Padishah murmured to himself: "Poor things! Even such small creatures, it seems, grieve over the absence of their parents."

When he had taken his abdest and said his prayers the day had fully dawned and the nightingales filled the air with their delightful songs Having travelled all night, he could not keep his eyes open longer from fatigue, and he fell into a slumber while his mind was still occupied with thoughts of his lost children. In a dream he saw a dervish

400

approaching him. The Padishah offered him a place at his side and made the newcomer the confidant of his sorrow.

The Padishah offered him a place at his side

Now the dervish knew what had befallen the Padishah's children, and said: "My Shah, grieve not; though thou seest not thy children, thy children see thee. The birds that came to the spring while thou wast praying were thy children. They were stolen by the peris, and their abode is at a year's distance from here. They can, if they will, fly not only here but even into thy palace, but they fear the peris. When thou departest from here, drink like the doves from the spring, and Allah will restore to thee thy children."

The Padishah woke up from his sleep and, reflecting a little, he remembered the words of the dervish in his dream, and he decided to bend his steps towards the spring. What a sight his eyes beheld there! Blood was flowing from the spring. Alarmed, he wondered whether he were sleeping or waking. Presently the sun appeared above the horizon and he was convinced it was no dream. Closing his eyes and repressing his aversion, he drank from the bloody spring as though it were pure water; then, turning to the right, he hastened on his way.

All at once he saw in the distance what seemed like a great army drawn up in battle array. Not knowing whether they were enemies or friends, he hesitated about proceeding, but at length resolved to go forward and take his chance. On approaching the army he was surprised to find it was composed of dragons of all sizes, the smallest, however, being as large as a camel. "Woe is me!" he groaned; "who knows but what I thought a dream was sorcery! What shall I do now? If I go forward I shall certainly be cut to pieces, and I cannot go back without being seen." He prayed to Allah for deliverance from this danger which threatened him.

It happened, however, that these were only newly-born dragons, the oldest being but a few days old. None of them had their eyes open, Thus they were wandering about blindly, unable to find their home, though keeping together by instinct.

This discovery was very reassuring for the Padishah, who gave the dragons a wide berth and so continued his way without molestation.

NIGHT came on, and as he wended his way among the mountains the sound of a terrible howling smote his ears. It was the dragon-mother calling her lost children. The Padishah was seized with fear as the dragon, seeing him, exclaimed: "At last I have thee; my young ones have fared ill at thy hands; thou shalt not escape--thou who hast slain a thousand of my offspring."

The Padishah answered tremblingly that he had indeed seen the young dragons, but had done them no harm; not being a hunter, he had no thought of harming anyone. "If thou speakest the truth," returned the dragon-mother, "tell me in what direction my children have gone." The Padishah accordingly explained where he had seen them, whereupon the old dragon changed him into a tobacco-box, which she stuck in her girdle. Thus she carried him with her on her search for the missing young ones, and after a while she found them quite safe and sound.

The Dragon-mother drove her children home before her, the Padishah still as a tobacco-box in her girdle. By and by they came across the four walls of a fortress standing in the midst of the desert. Taking a whip from her girdle the dragon struck the walls a mighty blow, on which they fell down and a larger dragon came forth from the ruins. The walls now destroyed had enclosed a fine serai, which they entered. The female Dragon, having changed the Padishah again to his original form, took him into one of the apartments of the palace and thus addressed him: "Child of men, why camest thou hither? I see thou hadst no evil intention."

403

404

When the Padishah had related his story, the Dragon observed: "The matter can easily be rectified. All thy children are in the Hyacinth Kiosk. The place is a good distance away, and if thou goest alone thou wilt hardly succeed in reaching it. After crossing the mountain thou wilt come to a desert where my brother lives; his children are bigger than mine and know the place well. Go to him, present my compliments, and ask him to escort thee to the Hyacinth Kiosk." The dragon now took leave of the Padishah, who set off on his journey.

It was a long time ere he had crossed the mountain and come in sight of the desert. After traversing the latter for some time he saw a serai much larger than the one he had left. At the gate stood a dragon twice as large as the other, at a thousand paces distant its eyes seemed to be closed, but from the narrow opening between the upper and lower lids came a ray of flame sufficient to scorch any human being that might come within reach of it. When the Padishah saw this he thought to himself: "My last hour is surely come." At the top of his voice he shouted to the dragon his sister's greeting. Hearing the words the great beast opened his eyes and as he did so, it seemed as though the whole region was enveloped in flames. The Padishah, unable to endure the sight, ran back. To the dragon he seemed no larger than a flea, and consequently not worth troubling about.

The Padishah returned to the dragon-mother and related his terrifying experience. Said she: "I forgot to tell you that I am called the Black Dragon, my brother, the Red Dragon. Go back and say that the Black

405

Dragon sends greeting. As my name is known to no one, my brother will recognise that I have sent you. Then he will turn his back towards you, and you can approach him without danger; but beware of getting in front of him, or you will become a victim of the fiery glances of his eyes."

Now the Padishah set out to return to the Red Dragon, and when he had reached the spot he cried with a loud voice: "Thy sister, the Black Dragon, sends thee greeting! " On this the beast turned his back towards him. Approaching the dragon, the Padishah made known his wish to go to the Hyacinth Kiosk. The dragon took a whip from his girdle and smote the earth with it so mightily that the mountain seemed rent in twain. In a little while the Padishah saw approaching a rather large dragon, and as he came near he felt the heat that glowed from his great eyes. This dragon also turned his back toward the Padishah. "My son, if thou wouldst enter the Hyacinth Kiosk," said the Red Dragon, "cry before thou enterest, 'The Red Dragon has sent me!' On this an Arab will appear: this is the very peri that has robbed thee of thy children. When he asks what thou wilt, tell him that the great dragon demands possession of the largest of the stolen children. If he refuses, ask for the smallest. If again he refuses, tell him the Red Dragon demands himself. Say no more, but return here in peace."

The Padishah now mounted the back of the dragon which the Red Dragon had summoned and set off. Seeing the Hyacinth Kiosk in the distance the Padishah shouted: "Greeting from the Red Dragon!"

The Arab

So mighty was the shout that earth and sky seemed to be shaken. Immediately a swarthy Arab with fan shaped lips appeared, grasping an enormous club in his hand. Stepping out into the open air, he inquired what was the matter. "The Red Dragon," said the Padishah, "demands the largest of the stolen children." "The largest is ill," answered the peri. "Then send the

smallest to him," rejoined the Padishah. "He has gone to fetch water," replied the Arab. "If that is so," continued the Padishah, "the Red Dragon demands thyself." "I am going into the kiosk," said the Arab, and disappeared. The Padishah returned to the Red Dragon, to whom he related how he had fulfilled his mission.

Meanwhile the Arab came forth, in each hand a great club, wooden shoes three yards long on his feet, and on his head a cap as high as a minaret. Seeing him, the Red Dragon said: "So-ho! my dear Hyacinther; thou hast the children of this Padishah; be good enough to deliver them up." "I have a request to make," replied the Arab, "and if the Padishah will grant it I will gladly give him his children back again. Ten years ago I stole the son of a certain Padishah, and when he was twelve years old he was stolen away from me by a Dew-woman named Porsuk. Every day she sends the boy to the spring for water, gives him an ashcake to eat, and compels him to drink a glass of human blood. If I can but regain possession of this youth, I desire nothing more, for never in the whole world have I seen such a handsome lad. This Porsuk has a son who loves me, and evil has been done me because I will not adopt him in place of the stolen boy. I am aware that the children of this Padishah are brave and handsome, and I stole them to mitigate my sufferings. Let him but fulfil my wish, and I will fulfil thine."

Having uttered this speech the Arab went away.

The Red Dragon reflected a little, then spoke as follows: "My son, fear not. This Porsuk is not particularly valiant, though skilled in sorcery. She cannot be vanquished by magic; but it is her custom on one day in the year to work no magic, therefore on that day she may be overcome. One month must thou wait, during which I will discover the exact day and inform thee thereof,"

The Padishah agreeing to this, the Red Dragon dispatched his sons to discover the precise day on which the Dew worked no magic. As soon as they returned with the desired information it was duly imparted to the Padishah, with the additional fact that on that day the Dew always slept. "When thou arrivest," the Red Dragon counselled the Padishah, "the youth she retains will come to fetch water from the spring. Take his cap off his head and set it on thine own: thus he will be unable to stir from the spot, and thou canst do what thou wilt with him."

The Red Dragon then sent for his sons, instructing them to escort the Padishah to the Porsuk-Dew's spring, wait there until he had accomplished his object, and then accompany both back in safety.

The Padishah whisked off the youth's cap

Arrived at the spring, all hid themselves until the youth came for water. While he was filling his bottle the Padishah sprang forth suddenly, whisked off the youth's cap, set it on his own head, and instantly disappeared into his hiding-place. The youth looked around, and seeing no one, could not think what had happened. Then the young dragons swooped down upon him, captured him, and with the Padishah led him a prisoner to the Red Dragon.

Striking the earth with his whip, the Red Dragon brought the Hyacinth Arab on the scene, and as soon as he caught sight of the boy he sprang towards him, embraced and kissed him, expressing his deep gratitude to the friends who had restored him.

Now he in his turn clapped his hands and stamped his feet on the ground and immediately forty birds flew up twittering merrily. Taking a flask from his girdle, the Arab sprinkled them with the liquid it contained, and lo! the birds were transformed into forty lovely maidens and handsome youths, who drew up in line and stood at attention. " Now, my Shah," said the Arab, "behold thy children! Take them and be happy, and pardon me the suffering I have caused thee."

Had anyone begged the Padishah's costliest treasure at that moment it would have been given him, so overwhelmed with joy was the monarch at recovering his children. He freely pardoned the Hyacinth Arab, and would even have rewarded him had there been anything he desired.

The Padishah now bade goodbye to the Red Dragon. At the moment of parting the Red Dragon pulled out a hair from behind his ear and, giving it to the Padishah, said:

"Take this, and when in trouble of any sort break it in two and I will hasten to thy aid."

Thus the Padishah and his children set out, and in due course arrived at the abode of the Black Dragon. She also took a hair from behind her ear and presented it to the Padishah with the following advice: "Marry thy children at once, and if on their wedding day thou wilt fumigate

410

them with this hair, they will be forever delivered from the power of the Porsuk-Dew."

The Padishah expressed his thanks, bade the Black Dragon a hearty good. bye, and all proceeded on their way.

During the journey the Padishah entertained his children by relating his adventures, and then he listened to those of his sons and daughters. Suddenly a fearful storm arose. None of the party knew what their fate would be, yet all waited in trembling expectancy. At length one of the maidens exclaimed: "Dear father and Shah, I have heard the Arab say that whenever the Porsuk-Dew passes she is accompanied by a storm such as this. I believe it is she who is now passing, and no other." Collecting his courage, the Padishah drew forth the hair of the Red Dragon and broke it in two. The Porsuk Dew at once fell down from the sky with a crash, and at the same moment the Red Dragon came up swinging and cracking his whip. The Dew was found to have broken her arm s and smashed her nose, so that she was quite incapable of inflicting further mischief.

The Padishah was exceedingly afraid lest he should lose one of his children again, but the Red Dragon reassured him. "Fear not, my Shah," said he; "take this whip." The Padishah accepted it, and as he cracked it he felt the sensation o f being lifted into the air.

The Dew smashed her rose

Descending to earth again, he found himself just outside the gates of his own capital city. "Now thou art quite safe," said the Red Dragon as he disappeared. At sight of the domes and minarets and familiar walls of their birthplace they all cast themselves on their knees and wept for joy. Since the Padishah had left his palace continual lamentation and gloom had reigned supreme, and now all the pashas and beys came out joyfully to meet their returning master and his children. The Sultana went down the whole line embracing and kissing her beautiful sons and daughters, and the delighted Padishah ordered seven days and seven nights of merrymaking in honour of the glad event.

These festivities were scarcely over when wives for the Padishah's sons and husbands for his daughters were sought and found, and then commenced forty days and forty nights of revelry in celebration of the grand wedding.

Unfortunately, on the wedding day the Padishah forgot to fumigate them all with the Black Dragon's hair, with the result that as soon as the ceremony was over rain began to

412

fall in a deluging torrent, and the wind blew so fiercely that nothing could withstand it. At first the Padishah thought it was merely a great storm, but later he remembered the Porsuk-Dew, and cried out in his fear. Hearing the clamour, the inmates of the serai, including the newly-wedded princes and princesses, came in to see what was the matter. The frightened Padishah gave the Black Dragon's hair to the Vezir and commanded him to burn it immediately. No one understood the order, and all thought the Padishah must have lost his wits; nevertheless his wish was obeyed and the hair burnt. Immediately a fearful howling was heard in the garden outside, and the Porsuk-Dew cried with a loud voice: "Thou hast burnt me, O Padishah! Henceforth in thy garden shall no blade of grass grow." Next morning it was seen that every tree and flower in the garden was scorched, as though a conflagration had raged over the scene.

The Padishah, however, did not allow this loss to trouble him; he had his children again with him, and that joy eclipsed any ordinary misfortunes that might befall him. He explained everything to his suite, who could hardly believe what they heard, it was all so astonishing. No further danger was to be feared, and thus the Padishah and his family, with their husbands and wives, lived happily together until their lives' end.

Madjūn

THERE was once a bald-headed young man whose mother was very old. The woman wished her son to learn a trade, but no matter where she put him for that purpose he always ran away. One day he caught a glimpse of the Sultan's daughter, and from that moment he could think of nothing but the Princess. He went home and said to his mother: "Go to the Padishah and ask him to give me his daughter." His mother was astonished and answered: "Why, lad, thou dost not possess five paras and knowest no trade!

Thinkest thou the Padishah would give his daughter to such a numskull?" Nevertheless as the young man insisted, the woman saw that he could be satisfied only by her going to the King on his behalf.

When she found herself in the presence of the Padishah she said: "O my lord! I have a son who has tormented me every day with the request that I should come to thee and ask thee to give him thy daughter in marriage. I could bear his importunities no longer, wherefore am I come. Slay me or hang me, or otherwise do unto me what seemeth good in thy sight."

414

The monarch answered: "Send thy son to me," and dismissed her.

She went home and informed her son that he was summoned to the presence of the Padishah. When the youth arrived at the palace the Padishah saw with disapproval that he was bald, and with a view to getting rid of him said: "I will give thee my daughter if thou canst gather together on this spot all the birds in the world." The young man, discomfited, departed from the serai, absorbed in gloomy reflection, and fearing lest the Padishah might order him to be put to death he resolved to travel. Many days after this,

The Dervish listened patiently

wandering in the wilderness, he met a dervish, to whom he related his difficulty. The dervish listened patiently and then said: "Go to a certain place where there is a tall cypress tree; sit down beneath it. All the birds in the world will come and alight thereon, and thou hast only to utter the word 'Madjun!' to cause them to stick fast to the tree.

415

Then collect them all and take them to the Padishah..

Thanking the dervish for his useful advice, the young man went his way until he arrived at the place indicated, where he sat down to rest under the tall cypress tree. He waited until all the birds in the world had alighted thereon, then said "Madjun!" and no bird was able to fly away. Collecting them, he returned home and

All of them were unable to move head or foot

next morning carried his captives into the presence of the Padishah. The monarch, not at all pleased that the apparently impossible task he imposed had been accomplished, said: "Now go and get a covering of hair on thy bald pate and I will then give thee my daughter."

The young man, very disappointed, took himself off and spent several days in deep thought. Meanwhile the Padishah betrothed the Princess to a son of his Vezir, and preparations for the wedding were hurried forward.

The young man, hearing of this, went on the bridal night to the serai and hid himself on the roof, above the chamber in which the Vezir's son and his bride were to sleep. As soon as he saw them both enter he pronounced the word "Madjun!" and they were unable to move so much as an eyelid.

Night passed and the day broke. As the day wore on and the newly, wedded couple failed to appear, a slave went, and peeping through a chink in the door of their room, endeavoured to discover if anything was the matter.

"O merciful Allah, what is this?" cried the Padishah!

417

He waited until all the birds in the world had alighted.

The bald headed one above, seeing this, cried "Madjun!" and the slave found himself unable to stir from the spot.

In short, as one after the other came to the door, until everyone in the palace was gathered there, the word "Madjun!" was uttered and all became transfixed, unable to move hand or foot.

The Padishah was at a loss to know the meaning of it all, and sent for a certain hodja, who would surely help him in this strange matter.

The young man came down from his elevated position on the roof and stole after the Padishah's messengers. On the way they entered a butcher's shop to buy some meat, and as they laid their hands on a carcass to indicate what they wanted, the bald man, having overtaken them, cried "Madjun!" and they all found themselves stuck fast to the meat.

Meanwhile the Padishah was impatiently awaiting the return of his messengers and be. coming angry at their delay. At length, unable to endure it longer, he himself went after them. Passing the butcher's shop, imagine his surprise to see all his servants stuck by their hands to a piece of meat "O merciful Allah! what is this?" cried the Padishah, and ran immediately to fetch the hodja. When the latter arrived he said: "My lord, thou hast promised thy daughter to a certain bald-headed young man, and as thou hast not fulfilled thy word, he it is that is doing these things."

"What is to be done?" asked the King. The hodja answered: "Nothing can be done except to give him thy daughter."

The Padishah returned to his palace and summoned the youth to his presence. When the latter heard that the King's servants were seeking him he hastened home and instructed his mother as follows: "If I am asked for, say I am not at home and have not been seen for a long time. If they ask where I may be found, answer that for so many gold-pieces thou wilt undertake to find me."

Hardly had he said this than there came a loud knocking at the door. When the old woman opened it she was asked whether the bald young man was at home. She answered as her son had advised her. "But where must we look for him?" demanded the messengers. "The Padishah requests him to present himself, and receive the Princess in marriage." At these words the old woman's interest appeared to increase. "I know not whither he is gone," she answered, "but give me a thousand gold pieces and I engage to find him." The stipulated amount was paid over. "Go, then," said the King's servants, "bring him hither and thou shalt receive even more." A few days later the bald-headed one appeared at the palace and was led into the presence of the Padishah. As soon as the King saw him he greeted him cordially. "My dear son," he exclaimed, "I have waited long for thee. Where hast thou been all this time?"

To this the youth answered: "O Padishah! I asked thee for thy daughter, but thou gayest her not to me; therefore have I wandered in the world."

420

Without further delay the Vezirs were summoned, the Princess sent for, and the pair were betrothed with the customary ceremonies. Then the bald-headed young man, having accomplished his purpose, went to all those who were under the spell and unable to move. "Be released from Madjun!" he exclaimed; and immediately they were free and skipped about for joy. As for the son of the Vezir, who had been married to the Princess, he was no sooner released than he ran away and has never been seen since. The Princess was now married to the bald youth, and they lived happily ever after.

The Forlorn Princess

THERE was once a Padishah who had a daughter. This being his only child, the monarch lavished all his affection upon her and was never happy unless she were at his side. One day, when the Princess was about fifteen years old, the Padishah said: "My child, is there anything thou desirest of me?" "Yes, father," she answered. "Let my mother hold the basin when I wash my hands and face every morning, and do thou hold the towels in readiness." Such a request was so unexpected that the Padishah became very angry, and ordered the Princess to be executed instantly. The executioners, however, took pity upon her, and instead of cutting off her head they took her to the top of a mountain and left her there.

Thus abandoned, the maiden looked about everywhere, and finally set out in a certain direction. She wandered long up hill and down dale and across plains until she reached another mountain, whence she saw a palace. When she came up to it she opened the gate, and entering, could see no one about. Going into the kitchen, she noticed the carcass of a sheep hanging from the wall. "Now,"thought the maiden: "There must certainly be someone living here, as the sheep is intended for food."

She then cut up the sheep and put it into the oven to cook; when cooked she set it in dishes and put it in the cupboard. That done, she turned her  attention to the room and set everything in order; filling the mangal, preparing the coffee, and laying the table.

Towards nightfall she heard approaching footsteps, and had just time to hide herself before the door of the serai was opened and a being, half-man, half-dew, entered. The maiden trembled with fright at sight of the creature, and could not take her eyes off him. He went straight to the kitchen and observed that the sheep had been cooked and put into the cupboard. He then looked in his own room and saw the mangal filled with fire, and his chibouque and coffee awaiting him. Everything was in its place; the most admirable order prevailed. When the Dew, who was very old, saw all this, he was most grateful and pronounced a blessing on the one who had done it, whoever it might be.

Sitting down comfortably he lit his chibouque, drank his coffee, and thinking aloud, said: "Whoever it is that has been here, if a male person shall be my son, and if a female my daughter. Let him or her come forward, they shall suffer no harm."

At these words the maiden came from her hiding-place and timidly approached the Dew, who seeing her, smiled and said: "My blessings on thee, child! Who art thou? Whence comest and whither goest thou?" She answered "I am alone in the

A half-man half-dew entered

world. Wandering about in the mountains I chanced to find this place." Then said the Dew: "My child, thou shalt be my daughter for ever; I am lonely and old. This serai shall be thine. Have no fear, but go about thy daily work and spend the afternoon in amusing thyself." They sat with each other for a while, and afterwards retired to rest.

Next morning the maiden rose betimes, and when the Dew had drunk his coffee, smoked his chibouque, and eaten his meal, he said to her: "My child, I am now going out. Here is a key; unlock the door of that room. An Arab is in there; tell him thy clothing is dirty and he will give thee clean linen. Put it on and be at peace." At these words he was gone.

The Arab returned with a bundle of clean linen

Opening the door of the room indicated she called "Dady!" and an Arab instantly presented himself. Her wishes were hardly expressed when the Arab disappeared and quickly returned with a bundle of clean linen, which the maiden took and presently put on. Before leaving her the Arab said: "When thou art weary, take a walk in the garden." So when all her work was finished, the maiden went into the garden. Here, floating on a pond, she saw a duck whose wings and head were of diamonds. No sooner did the duck espy the maiden than it shrieked aloud: "O thou shameless one! Art thou come to take away my Shahzada?" Its wings flapped so furiously that one of them broke off. Alarmed, the maiden cried: "O woe is me! Why did I come here? When the Dew-father sees what has happened he will surely kill me!" and ran back into the palace.

In the evening the Dew returned, and they both ate and drank together. It was evident that the Dew was not aware of what had happened in .the garden, so when bedtime came they retired to their respective apartments without reference being made to the incident.

Next morning the Dew requested the maiden to go and obtain fresh linen from the dady. This she did after the Dew's departure, and the Arab, as before, advised her to go into the garden. As soon as the duck caught sight of her it exclaimed angrily: "Hast thou decked thyself out with thy finery to take away my Shahzada?" It quacked at such an astonishing rate that its other wing broke off. Fearing the Dew-father's wrath, the maiden ran back into the palace as fast as she could.

Night fell and the Dew came home as usual. They ate and drank together, and as the Dew made no reference to the affair of the duck the maiden retired peacefully to her chamber and slept well. Next day the Dew went out again, while the maiden changed her clothing and repaired as usual to the garden. This time, at seeing her, the duck set up a loud shriek and its head fell off; thus it died.

Now this duck was the Dew's daughter, with whom a certain Padishah's son had fallen violently in love. This Prince used to visit a kiosk, the garden of which adjoined that of the Dew, and thus he first saw the lady, who, for reasons of her own, not wishing to be seen again by the Prince, changed herself into a duck and swam about on the pond. The youth had been a witness of all that had happened and heard the words spoken by the duck. When he saw that the maiden was more beautiful than the Dew's daughter had been, he loved her with all his heart. The maiden, on her part, knew not who the duck was; she thought merely that it was the Dew's duck, and feared he would be so angry, when he knew what had happened, that he would kill her without mercy. When she saw,

427

however, that the Dew made no reference whatever to the matter she gathered courage. Yet every morning when the Dew went away the old fear returned lest he should discover it and wreak his vengeance upon her.

Meanwhile the Shahzada went to his father, saying: "Dear father and Shah! A certain Dew has a lovely daughter with whom I am deeply in love. Obtain her for my wife, or I cannot continue to live." Accordingly the Padishah wrote a letter to the Dew and sent it by the hands of one of his servants.

Having read the missive the Dew replied verbally: "Tell the Padishah that my daughter is at his disposal; but I am very poor, so that more than my daughter he must not expect. If he agrees, the betrothal may take place next week. Tell him further, however, that as I am a very poor man he must not bring a retinue exceeding a thousand persons, as that number is all I could entertain." The King's servant departed and delivered the Dew's message to his master.

On the morning of the appointed day the Dew gave the maiden a bunch of keys, saying: "My child, take these keys; open such and such rooms, clap your hands and many slaves will appear. Do not be afraid of them." She did exactly as she was told, and in a short time had gathered around her a host of slaves of all sorts, white and black, male and female, who kissed the hem of her garment and made reverential salaams. She led them all before the Dew, who apportioned to all their duties.

428

The gates of the palace were thrown open and the Padishah and his thousand followers entered for the solemnization of the betrothal. The ceremony concluded, a rich banquet was served, after which the royal guest and his gorgeous retinue took their departure. At leave-taking the Dew observed to the Padishah: "When sending for the bride, O King, send only five hundred carriages for her trousseau, for I am too poor to give more." Then as a farewell gift he presented a magnificent garment to each of the thousand men.

A week later five hundred carriages were sent to the Dew's palace for the bride's trousseau, and with them came the Padishah's own state coach for the accommodation of the bride herself. The vehicle, however, failed to please the Dew, who ordered his slaves to bring out the least splendid of his equipages for his adopted daughter's use. Such a superb coach had never been seen before at the palace of the Padishah, where in due course the maiden arrived. The wedding took place with great ceremony, and was accompanied by forty days and forty nights of feasting and revelry.

Time passed away quickly with the happy couple, who lived together in unalloyed bliss. One day the Shahzada went on a long journey. During his absence his wife was taken ill; slaves were dispatched in all haste for the physicians. None of them, however, seemed able to do her any good, and for three days and nights she suffered such pain that it was thought advisable to send for the Dew-father.

Hastening to the maiden's side, the old man said: "Grasp my arm, child!" As she did so, lo! the arm broke off as though it were made of some-brittle substance, and the sufferer moaned: "Woe is me! my dear father's arm is broken!" The Dew, however, consoled her, saying: "It matters not, my child." Turning to one of the slaves he said: "Take it, and set it in the corner." No sooner was this done than the arm blossomed forth into a diamond-tree. As he turned his other arm to his daughter she grasped it, with similar result--this arm likewise broke off, fell to the floor, and was transformed immediately into another diamond-tree.

"Take hold of this foot", said the Dew

Now said the Dew, "Take hold of this foot." His daughter did so and it broke off. It was put into a corner, where it became a golden stool. The same fate befell the other foot, which became another golden stool. Armless and footless the Dew now said: "Hold my head, my daughter," and just as she grasped it, the Dew's head fell off. "dear father!" exclaimed the young Princess, "thy head has fallen off!" "Never mind," said the old man, "throw it into the middle of the room." This was accordingly done, and behold! in place of the severed head was a magnificent bed whose like had never been seen before. Now the Dew's body fell to the floor and became a carpet. The Princess was laid in the bed, and news of the wonderful circumstances quickly spread. All the people for miles around came to feast their eyes on the miraculous scene.

Among them were the parents of the young woman, though they were unaware that it was their own daughter. Just as they arrived the Princess and the Shahzada were at dinner in their room. The Princess recognized her parents immediately, though they did not know her. As for the old Padishah, his eyes were constantly on his daughter, whose appearance he could not help admiring. Numerous slaves were standing round.

The old Padishah picked up a towel and a can of water. "Sultana," he said to his wife, "let us get nearer to these slaves." "I will take this towel and you pour the water; while doing so, we can get a closer view of the Princess." The meal finished, the old couple approached the Shahzada and the Princess and did the office of slaves in washing and wiping the latter's hands. In the midst of this performance the Princess exclaimed: "My dear father, when thou didst ask my desire, and I answered that my mother should hold the basin and thou shouldst hold the towel for me, thou wert angry and didst drive me from home. Now behold what a great journey thou hast made with my mother to do those same things. Thus it is clear that the wish I then expressed did not originate from myself; consequently thou wast wrong in driving me away."

431

To this the Padishah replied: "I was wrong, my daughter. May Allah pardon me my sin, and do thou also pardon me. Thy wish has now been fulfilled." Thus parents and child became reconciled, and forty days and forty nights of festivities celebrated the happy event.

The Beautiful
Helwa Maiden

HERE once lived a poor combmaker who said to his wife one day: "Give me a few paras, and I will take my stock of combs into a coffee-house. Perchance I may sell five or six of them and bring home the proceeds."

Going into the coffee-house he sat down, and while he was drinking his coffee and thinking over the problem of his precarious existence, several merchants came in and began to inquire for a combmaker. At this the combmaker got up and produced his combs for the merchants' inspection. His wares evidently gave satisfaction, for besides disposing of all he had with him he secured an order for a thousand more. Delighted with his luck the

433

combmaker went home, and in the course of a couple of months the thousand combs were ready for delivery. He took them to the merchants, and received the price agreed upon, with a handsome present into the bargain.

The combmaker was now no longer poor indeed he was a rich man, and he proposed to his wife that they should make a pilgrimage to the Prophet's Tomb at Hedjaz. "By all means let us go," answered his wife; "but we cannot take our daughter with us." "We will leave her in the care of the hodja," said the combmaker; "he is a very well-disposed person." Thus the matter was settled, and they prepared for their long journey, taking only their young son with them and leaving their daughter in the good hands (as they believed) of the hodja.

It happened that the hodja, in whose house the combmaker and his wife had placed their daughter, was envious of the combmaker's success, and secretly had long wished to injure him. Now he determined to kill the girl left in his charge, but he wished her death to appear an accident. It being the custom of that land for everyone to visit daily the great bath houses of the city, he thought it would be easy to get the girl to one of these baths and quietly drown her.

Going to the bathhouse, he pressed a couple of gold-pieces into the palm of the bath-woman, and induced her to persuade the girl to bathe there. Accordingly on the following day the bath-woman appeared at the hodja's house and said to the girl: "Why dost thou not go sometimes to the bath?"

434

"Because I have no one to accompany me," replied the girl.

"Come with me, then," rejoined the woman, "and I will assist thee." Thus they went together to the bath. The woman took her to the hot-air bath and--called in the hodja.

When the poor girl caught sight of the hodja she began to comprehend that she had fallen into a trap, but, determined not to betray any embarrassment, she greeted the hodja: "I am glad thou art come; I will help thee to wash thy head." And she soaped him to such purpose that, when she had done with him, his head could not be seen for lather. Then taking off her heavy wooden clogs and tying them together with a bath-towel, the girl thrashed the hodja so mercilessly therewith that he could not afterward stir for bruises. The girl hurriedly escaped and ran all the way back to the house of her parents.

By and by the hodja recovered consciousness, wiped the soap from his head, dressed himself, and also went home. For more than a week after he still felt the effects of his punishment. Then in revenge he wrote a letter to the girl's parents, in which he stated that she had run away from his care after stealing money from him.

When in due time the parents received the letter they were naturally very shocked and angry. They charged their son to return home with all speed, take the dishonoured girl to the top of a hill and kill her, bringing back her bloodstained clothes in token that he had fulfilled his mission.

435

The young man appeared and, seizing his sister, took her to the hilltop. However, he had not the heart to put her to death, but set her free to go whither she would; while, to save appearances, he cut his foot slightly and dyed his sister's garments with the blood that flowed from the wound. These he took back to his parents.

His head could not be seen for lather

After her brother had left her the maiden set off in an opposite direction, wandering over mountains, across plains, and through valleys until she came to a spring. While resting she saw the Padishah of that country hunting with his Vezir; and, fearing them, she climbed a tree, hiding herself amidst the foliage.

The two huntsmen came to the spot, and the Padishah said to the other: "Vezir, I will undertake an abdest here and say many prayers. While praying the Padishah lifted up his head and saw the maiden in the tree; she seemed to him as beautiful as the noonday sun. His devotions finished, he turned to his Vezir and exclaimed: "I have already unearthed my quarry!" Casting his eyes up to the girl, he asked: "Art thou an in or a jin?"

"Neither in nor jin, but a child of the dust like thyself," was the answer.

The Padishah begged her to descend, which she did, and they returned to the palace together, where, with three days and nights of merrymaking, they became husband and wife.

One day she related to the Padishah the story of her life, and at the same time told him how she longed to see her parents and her brother once more. The Padishah sympathized with her, and ordered preparations to be made for her journey. He sent her in charge of his Vezir, instructing him to bring the Sultana's parents back with him if they were willing to come. On the day fixed the Sultana set out, accompanied-by the Vezir and a strong escort of soldiers.

After travelling many days they arrived at the foot of a hill, where they decided to pitch their tents for the night. At midnight the Vezir entered the Sultana's tent and said: "Thou belongest to me as well as to the Padishah, for we both found thee. Since thou hast married the Padishah rather than me, I will kill thee."

The poor Sultana begged him, before he put her to death, to allow her to retire for a few moments' prayer. He gave

437

the required permission, but to provide against her escape fastened a rope round her waist. Bound as she was she retired into another compartment of the tent, where, favoured by Providence, she was able to release herself and flee.

Meanwhile the Vezir became tired of waiting and went to seek the woman. What was his surprise to find the rope bound round a stone, but of the Sultana no trace! He roused his soldiers from their sleep and made up for them an ingenious account of how the Sultana had endeavoured to murder him, and then escaped. It was resolved to strike tents and return to their own country.

The fugitive Sultana hastened on in the direction of her parents' home. Meeting a shepherd, she begged him to lend her a suit of men's clothing in exchange for her own rich attire. The shepherd raised no objections to making such a good bargain. Disguised now as a young man, the Sultana entered a shop where helwa was made and sold, and applied for the post of assistant. She was taken

The Vezir found the rope bound round a stone

438

on, and the report soon spread that the helwa-shop had a handsome new assistant who was very clever in making that favourite sweetmeat. The Sultana's father had by this time retired from business as a comb maker and opened a coffeehouse. He was among those who came often to the helwa-shop to see the famous new assistant. The disguised helwa-maker knew her father in a moment, but it was no surprising matter that he did not recognize his daughter.

We will now return to the Padishah. Since the false Vezir had returned with his lying report the Padishah had known no peace. He was continually brooding over the loss of his wife, sighing and groaning and weeping. "I want my wife, Vezir," he said one day. "I must seek her, or I die." The Vezir protested in vain. The Padishah, taking the Vezir with him, quitted the palace and set out in search of the Sultana.

After long wandering they reached the place where she was actually sojourning; and being tired and hungry, inquired for an inn. They were informed there was no inn in the place, there was, how. ever, a shop where a young man sold the most excellent helwa ever eaten.

The Padishah and the Vezir resolved to try this much-praised establishment, and wended their way thither. As soon as they entered the shop the Sultana knew them both, but they failed to recognize her in the handsome young shopman. "Here, young man, let me taste thy helwa," said the Padishah, putting down several paras. "If, my lord," said the assistant, "thou wilt remain here all night, I will make helwa especially for thee, and besides

439

will relate to thee a strange story." Drawn unaccountably to the handsome young shopman, the Padishah willingly consented to remain and listen to what the youth had to say.

A "helwa evening" had been planned to take place in the town, and the clever young helwa-maker was asked to come and prepare the cakes for the occasion. "I would gladly do so, but I have guests," was the helwa-maker's reply to the invitation. Not to be denied, the deputation returned. "Bring thy guests with thee," they said; " we shall be happy to welcome them and accord them places of honour."

Thus it was arranged, and in the evening all three repaired to the helwa feast. Places were chosen, and for the present the helwa-maker disappeared into the kitchen to prepare the cakes.

When all was ready she appeared again with plates and a mangal in her hands and went among the guests, recognizing in the gathering, besides the Padishah and the Vezir, her father, her brother, and the hodja.

While distributing the helwa she spoke as follows: "As we are here for entertainment, let each of us tell a little story out of his own life." Conversation began, and many interesting personal reminiscences were related. Then it

"Forty bridles for our enemies,
for ourselves forty mules,"
they answered

came to the turn of the helwa-maker, who before beginning her narration imposed the condition that no one should leave the room during the recital. "If anyone must go," said she, "let him do so now." "Begin," said the audience; "no one shall quit his place."

Taking her seat before the closed door she commenced her story. She began with her visit to the bath--at which the hodja declared he felt rather unwell and must go out into the fresh air. "Sit down," commanded the storyteller with a flash of scorn. Then continuing, she described the atrocious conduct of the Vezir.

As the Padishah listened spellbound, his eyes filled with tears, for he as well as the Vezir, the hodja, her father and her brother, all understood the story. Concluding the narration of the great wrongs she had suffered, she exclaimed: "Know thou, O my hearers, that this Vezir and the hodja were my enemies; they are in this company tonight, as are also my father and my brother and my husband, the Padishah." At these words she ran towards her husband, who clasped her in his arms, weeping tears of joy.

Next day the Padishah summoned the Vezir and the hodja to his presence and asked whether they preferred forty mules or forty knives. They answered: "Forty knives for our enemies; for ourselves, forty mules." Whereupon they were bound fast to forty mules, which rent them asunder, and so there was an end of them.

After a happy sojourn at her old home with her parents and brother, the Sultana and her husband returned to their palace to begin life anew after the long period of affliction and cruel separation from each other.

"Sit down" commanded the story-teller.

Astrology

THERE was once a shepherd who had a wife and two sons. Every day the shepherd gathered together all the sheep of the neighbourhood and led them to graze in a meadow lying between the mountains. When evening came he led them back again to their owners, from whom he received five to ten paras for his services, and on this income he had to support himself and his family.

One day the shepherd died, and his occupation was taken up by the elder son. This first bereavement was soon followed by the death of the mother, and this double loss so affected the younger son that he could not rest at home, but was obliged to go away.

For many weeks he wandered on, up hill and down dale, until the minarets of the city of Bagdad came in sight. Strolling about the streets one day he met a man who accosted him with "Whence comest thou, my son? What art thou doing here? and what is thy name?" The young man answered; "I am come from a foreign land; I want employment; and my name is Mahomet."

The former offered to take Mahomet into his service, and the youth agreeing, they set out together for the stranger's house. Every day Mahomet set the house in order and did all in his power to please his master and win his confidence. One day the master called him and said: "Mahomet, my son, take this rope and this sack and let us be off." They travelled a long time until the foot of a hill was reached. Here they found

a well, and after they had removed the large slabs of stone that covered it the master said: "Now, Mahomet, listen to me. I shall let thee down the well by means of the rope; fill the sack with whatever thou findest at the bottom, then attach it to the rope and I will pull it up; afterwards I shall let down the rope again for thine own ascent."

Mahomet assented, fastening the rope round his waist and taking the sack in his hand, ready to descend.

Arrived at the bottom of the well, a dazzling sight met his astonished eyes. There were piles of gold, silver, diamonds, and pearls. He soon filled his sack, and attached it to the rope, when it disappeared upwards. Then, sad to relate, the stone slabs were replaced over the

445

mouth of the well, and poor Mahomet was abandoned to his fate.

As he paced to and fro on the bottom of the well, wondering whatever would become of him, he espied a narrow passage. He at once made in that direction, and after walking until he was quite tired he reached the border of a valley. Here he sat down to rest awhile and to devise, if possible, some means of requiting the rascality of the man whom he had served to the best of his ability. Feeling somewhat refreshed he got up, and, changing his clothes on the way, ere long found himself once more in the city.

Loitering about, whom should he see but the very man who had served him such a sorry trick at the well. Mahomet being differently clothed, his former master did not recognize him and inquired: "Whence comest thou, my son?" Mahomet replied that he was formerly a merchant in such and such a town, but having been robbed of all his property he was in search of any employment he could get. "Wouldst enter my service?" asked the man. "With pleasure," answered the young man, who now gave the name of Hassan; and they accordingly went home together.

Some ten days elapsed and the master called his servant. "Hassan," said he, "take this rope and the sack and we will be off." Their destination proved to be the same as before-- the well. Then said the master: "I am going to let thee down; fill the sack with what thou findest at the bottom, and--." He proceeded no further, for Mahomet (otherwise

Hassan) turned upon him angrily: "Thou wretch!" he exclaimed, "Thou hast deceived me once, and now thou thinkest to leave me in the well a second time, eh?" Springing upon him with a knife, Mahomet cut off the man's head and cast it down the well. Replacing the slabs he returned to the city.

He now took a house and having furnished it luxuriously, lived very happily. Helping himself freely, through the secret way he had discovered, to the treasures at the bottom of the well, he soon became known as the richest man in the whole kingdom.

Mahomet turned upon him angrily

It happened about this time that the Padishah had declared war upon his neighbour; but, as he had little money, gold was being collected on all sides to meet the expenses of the campaign. Mahomet, having such wealth, gave on a most liberal scale, and by this means the Padishah was able to

447

conquer his enemy. But peace had hardly been signed when the Padishah died. Now the great men of the land met in council, and as Mahomet was so enormously rich, they decided to elect him to the rank and dignity of Padishah, which was accordingly done.

After much discussion it was further resolved that, as the new Padishah could neither read nor write, a hodja must be appointed to teach him. A suitable hodja was forthcoming and the instruction began. One night the hodja said to his master, who was also his pupil:

"O Padishah, I must instruct thee in the science of astrology." "What is that, and of what use is it?" asked the Padishah. "Let us learn something else." Then said the hodja: "Near the staircase outside is a book; fetch it, and I will explain to thee what astrology is." Taking a candle the Padishah went out of the room and saw that at the foot of the stairs a book really was lying. He set the candle on the floor and picked up the book, and was just on the point of

He picked up the book

returning to the room when a great bird seized him and flew off with him. It flew with him a considerable distance, and eventually set him down in an unknown spot and left him there. As it was quite dark, the Padishah remained where he was until morning broke, when, looking round him, he found he was close to a cemetery.

He walked to the nearest town, and strolling about the streets, inquired of the passersby how far it was to Bagdad. No one was able to enlighten him, for it appeared that no one had ever heard of a city of that name. As he proceeded farther, however, and pursued his inquiries, a very old man answered: "I do not know where Bagdad is, but my grandfather's father was there about two hundred years ago. I have heard my father say so, but how far it is from here I know not." At this the Padishah heaved a deep sigh, for he thought he should never reach Bagdad again. By degrees, however, he grew more resigned to his fate, and entering a coffeehouse he sat down to the enjoyment of a cup of coffee and a chibouque.

When he got up to pay for his coffee he discovered, to his dismay, that his purse was gone. He told the coffeehouse keeper of his difficulty, and then, returning to the cemetery, looked about in the hope of finding his missing property. The search was in vain, and he went back disconsolately to the coffeehouse keeper, who advised him that a certain man in the marketplace could find his money for him.

Accordingly the Padishah sought the person indicated, and related his misfortune. The man asked what kind of a purse it was, and the Padishah replied: "Partly red and partly blue." The man then opened a cupboard, and taking out the identical purse, asked "Is this it?" "Indeed it is!"

449

answered the Padishah, wondering by what extraordinary means this man had come to possess his purse. He was glad to recover his money, and as he liked the town he resolved to stay there for the present.

Some days later he went again to the coffeehouse, and telling the coffeehouse keeper he intended to marry, asked whether he could recommend to him a suitable bride.

"Maiden or widow?" queried the Kavedji.

"It makes no difference to me, so long as she is honest and respectable," replied the Padishah. On this the Kavedji advised him to go again to the marketplace, where he would find a man who could procure him a suitable wife.

Mahomet sought out the man and acquainted him with his requirement. The latter promptly informed his client that at such and such an address there was the very person he needed--a widow in every way suitable. He then wrote a note and gave it to Mahomet, telling him to take it to the imam, who would introduce the woman.

The imam read the note and then addressed Mahomet as follows: "This matter can be easily arranged, only if thou marriest this woman thou must beware of meddling in the things of Allah; otherwise thou art a lost man." Mahomet bowed his head in assent; the woman was introduced and the pair were married, after which they went to the woman's house.

She handed a hundred gold pieces to her husband

Next day the woman handed a hundred gold pieces to her husband, saying: "Take this money and open a shop, but be sure to sell all the goods at cost price." In accordance with his wife's advice Mahomet set up a shop in the marketplace, selling everything at the exact price he gave for it. He conducted his business in this fashion from day to day, year in and year out, until one fine day his stock was sold out and there was no money left to buy in again.

"What shall we do now?" he asked his wife sadly. The woman opened a

cupboard, took therefrom a bag, and counting out a hundred gold-pieces, said: "Here are another hundred gold-pieces; buy in a stock of goods and sell them again as before." "But, my dear," objected Mahomet, " what is the meaning of this? With thy first hundred gold-pieces I traded without profit until the whole sum was exhausted;

451

now thou givest me another hundred and tellest me to do again likewise! How can it be possible?" The woman answered: "That is Allah's affair, in which we may not meddle." But Mahomet was inquisitive to get at the bottom of the matter, and as he would give his wife no peace she opened the window and cried: "Dear neighbours, help! My husband is meddling in the things of Allah. Help!"

Instantly there was an uproar: neighbours ran in, armed with sticks, with which they set upon Mahomet, so that he took to flight and ran for his life out of the town.

While in this predicament the great bird swooped down upon him again, seized him, and carried him back to the foot of the stairs whence he had been taken so many years before. He observed that the candle was still where he had put it, and that everything else was undisturbed. He picked up the book, which he had dropped when the bird seized him the first time, and took it to the hodja.

"What a long while thou hast tarried," observed the hodja; on which the Padishah related his adventures.

"Now thou knowest " returned the hodja, "what is the science of astrology."

The Padishah paid heed to the words of his teacher, kissed his hand, and applied himself diligently to the study of reading and writing.

Kŭnterbŭnt

WE were three brothers; two of us were silly, and neither of us had a bit of sense. We went to the bow-maker's and bought three bows, two of which were broken, and the third had no string.

In a stream without a drop of water swam three ducks, two of which were dead, while the third hadn't a spark of life. We shot one with an arrow, and taking it in our hand, set off up hill and down dale, drinking coffee and smoking tobacco,

gathering tulips and hyacinths, until we had travelled the length of a barleycorn.

On and on we went, until we came to three houses, two of which were in ruins, while the third had no foundation. There lay three men, two dead and one without life. We asked the dead men to give us a vessel to cook our duck in. They showed us three cupboards, two of which were broken and the third had no sides. In them we found three plates, two full of holes and the third without bottom. In the plate without bottom we cooked the duck. One of us said, "I have eaten sufficient;" the other, "I've no appetite," and I said, "No more, thank you." He who said he had eaten sufficient ate up the whole duck, he who said he had

no appetite ate up the bones; at which I became angry and ran away to a melon-field.

Taking my knife from my girdle I cut a melon. Where my knife was, there was I. Meeting a caravan, I asked where my knife was. They answered me: "For forty years we have been looking for twelve camels we have lost. As we have not been able to find them, how do you think we could find your knife?"

At this I went away in anger and came to a tree. Close by was a basket in which someone had put a murdered man. As I looked at him I saw forty thieves approaching; so I took to my heels, they after me. Running till I was out of breath I reached an old tumbledown djami, in the court of which I sat down to rest. The thieves followed and chased me round and round the court, until in my despair I sought to escape them by climbing to the pinnacle of the minaret. One of the thieves drew his knife and came at me, when with a loud shriek I loosed my hold and fell to earth.

In mortal terror I suddenly opened my eyes--to discover that I had been dreaming!

The Meaning of Turkish Words used in the Text

A

Abdest	Religious ablution
Aga	Officer, chief
Anka	Mythical bird
"Amin!"	"Amen!"

B

Bey	Nobleman
"Bismillah"	"In the name of God"

C

Cadi	Judge
Chibouque	Pipe with long stem

D

Dady	Nurse
Dervish	Mendicant monk
Dew	Evil spirit
Djami	Oratory

E

"Essalaam alejkum"	"Peace be upon you"

F

Feredje	Overcoat
Fez	The characteristic Turkish red cap (formerly made in Fez, Morocco)

H

Han	Inn
Handschar	Large knife, or dagger, with curved blade
Helwa	Turkish delight
Hodja	Teacher, letter-writer
Houri	Large-eyed girl figuring in Paradise

I

Ifrid	Apparition
Imam	Head of a religious community
In	Good spirit
"Inshallah"	"If it please God"

J

Jin	Evil spirit

K

Kaftan	Long outer coat of thin material
Kavedji	Coffee-maker
Kiosk	Palace or villa in a garden
Kismet	Fate
Kuliba	Hut
Kunterbunt	This may be freely rendered "Higgledy-piggledy"

L

Lala	Court chamberlain
Leblebi	Roasted peas
Lira	Gold piece, value about 18s. 6d.
Lokma	Turkish sweetmeat

M

Madjun	Spell-food
Mangal	Chafing-dish

N

Namaz	Prayer
Nargile	Pipe with long tube and bowl
containing	
	scented water through which the smoke passes before entering the smoker's mouth

P

Padishah	Sultan
Peri	Fairy
Piaster	Silver piece, value about 21d.
Pilaf	Mutton with rice
Pir	An old man

R

Romak	A word used in exorcism

S

"Salaam"	"Peace"
Schalwar	Trousers (for men or women)
Selamlik	That part of dwelling where men live
Serai	Palace

Shahzada	Crown Prince
Sheikh	Chief of Dervishes, master
Softa	Student of religious law
"Selámin alejkum"	"Peace be upon you" (salutation); "Ve alejkum selám," And upon you be peace" (response)

T

Tandir	An Oriental warming apparatus, in appearance like a round table. A quilt is suspended from the top, and Turkish women sitting round the tandir on their low divans pull this over their feet
Tawla	A game; backgammon board
Tellal	Auction agent
Tespih	Rosary
Turbe	Tomb
Tscharschi	Marketplace

V

Vali	Governor of province
Vezir	Prime minister

W

"Wallahi!"	"By God!"

republishing

YESTERDAY'S BOOKS

for

TOMORROW'S EDUCATIONS

www.AbelaPublishing.com

Ignácz Kúnos

CPSIA information can be obtained at www.ICGtesting.com
Printed in the USA
BVOW012238110312

284954BV00001B/3/P